PRAISE FOR
# The Case of the Roasted Onion

"A savvy sleuth with a kind heart . . . An intriguing blend of violence and veterinary medicine, this novel will appeal to animal lovers as well as fans of the genre."
—*Richmond Times-Dispatch*

"A cleverly constructed who-done-it with so many layers to peel that the protagonists have to stay alert for any clue because the killer left almost no evidence behind. The love between Austin and Madeline permeates the whole story line and uplifts the audience to see two passionate seniors care about one another and life in general."
—*Midwest Book Review*

"A swift gallop through the interconnecting worlds of both high-society horse events and veterinary practice . . . Fascinating . . . There is quite a lot to enjoy in here as well as some interesting characters." —*MyShelf.com*

"A solid cast of characters . . . A very satisfying mystery."
—*GumshoeReview.com*

"[A] diverting mystery . . . From protagonist Austin McKenzie and his wife, Madeline, to their collie, Lincoln, each of these well-developed characters leaps off the page." —*Romantic Times*

# The Case of the
# TOUGH-TALKING TURKEY

# CLAUDIA BISHOP

**BERKLEY PRIME CRIME, NEW YORK**

**THE BERKLEY PUBLISHING GROUP**
**Published by the Penguin Group**
**Penguin Group (USA) Inc.**
**375 Hudson Street, New York, New York 10014, USA**
Penguin Group (Canada), 90 Eglinton Avenue East, Suite 700, Toronto, Ontario M4P 2Y3, Canada
(a division of Pearson Penguin Canada Inc.)
Penguin Books Ltd., 80 Strand, London WC2R 0RL, England
Penguin Group Ireland, 25 St. Stephen's Green, Dublin 2, Ireland (a division of Penguin Books Ltd.)
Penguin Group (Australia), 250 Camberwell Road, Camberwell, Victoria 3124, Australia
(a division of Pearson Australia Group Pty. Ltd.)
Penguin Books India Pvt. Ltd., 11 Community Centre, Panchsheel Park, New Delhi—110 017, India
Penguin Group (NZ), 67 Apollo Drive, Rosedale, North Shore 0745, Auckland, New Zealand
(a division of Pearson New Zealand Ltd.)
Penguin Books (South Africa) (Pty.) Ltd., 24 Sturdee Avenue, Rosebank, Johannesburg 2196, South Africa

Penguin Books Ltd., Registered Offices: 80 Strand, London WC2R 0RL, England

This is a work of fiction. Names, characters, places, and incidents either are the product of the author's imagination or are used fictitiously, and any resemblance to actual persons, living or dead, business establishments, events, or locales is entirely coincidental. The publisher does not have any control over and does not assume any responsibility for author or third-party websites or their content.

THE CASE OF THE TOUGH-TALKING TURKEY

A Berkley Prime Crime Book / published by arrangement with the author

PRINTING HISTORY
Berkley Prime Crime mass-market edition / August 2007

Copyright © 2007 by Mary Stanton.
Cover art by Mary Ann Lasher.
Cover design by Annette Fiore.
Interior text design by Kristin del Rosario.

ISBN: 978-0-425-21669-9

BERKLEY® PRIME CRIME
Berkley Prime Crime Books are published by The Berkley Publishing Group,
a division of Penguin Group (USA) Inc.,
375 Hudson Street, New York, New York 10014.
The name BERKLEY PRIME CRIME and the BERKLEY PRIME CRIME design are trademarks of Penguin Group (USA) Inc.

PRINTED IN THE UNITED STATES OF AMERICA

10  9  8  7  6  5  4  3  2  1

*For the Spice Girls:*
*Lavender, Biscuit, Tarragon,*
*Basil, Parsley, Paprika,*
*and Dill*

# Cast of Characters

〰〰

**At McKenzie Veterinary Practice, Inc.**

**Austin McKenzie,**  DVM
**Madeline McKenzie,**  his wife
**Allegra Fulbright,**  an assistant
**Joe Turnblad,**  an assistant


**At O'Leary's Poultry Farms**

**Lewis O'Leary,**  owner
**Angela O'Leary,**  his wife
**Ronald O'Leary,**  Lewis's oldest son
**Linda O'Leary,**  Ron's wife
**Jensen O'Leary,**  Lewis's middle son
**Maired O'Leary,**  Jensen's wife
**Cordwainer "Cordy" O'Leary,**  Lewis's youngest son


**Citizens of Summersville**

**Victor Bergland,**  DVM, chair of bovine sciences
**Thelma Bergland,**  his wife

**Lila Gernsback,** a horsewoman
**Rita Santelli,** editor/publisher of the *Summersville Sentinel*
**Nigel Fish,** a reporter
**Simon Provost,** Lieutenant, Summerville Police Department
**Rudy Schwartz,** owner, the Monrovian Embassy
**Deirdre Montoya,** a waitress
**Gilbert "Gil" Finnegan,** salesman, Green Seal Farm Feeds
**Karen Crown,** district manager, Green Seal Farm Feeds
**Lucinda Whitby,** a graduate student
**Alan Krippendorf,** a postdoc in poultry sciences

And Friends

**Lincoln,** a collie
**Odie,** a house cat
**Juno,** a puppy
**Hacker,** a Swedish Warmblood
**Andrew,** a Quarterhorse
**Pony,** a Shetland pony

# Prologue

〰〰

## I

MAYBE global warming wasn't a scam cooked up by loser politicians after all.

The rain had started slow and quiet, just as Jensen O'Leary eased the tractor-trailer onto Route 15. He was loaded with two and a half tons of fresh carcasses, bound for cold storage, and traction was lousy even on dry and sunny days. Now the rain came down with a dull and steady thrum, an inexorable cascade of water that came too fast to drain from the macadam. Water rose calf-high in the dips in the highway and flooded the ditches on either side. Jensen imagined a giant spigot in the heavens, the handle cranked wide, the spout aimed directly at him and the truck.

Hadn't he read somewhere that the glaciers were melting? Jensen had wakened to a misty sky pregnant with moisture. He needed an early start to avoid the downpours forecast for the afternoon, so he'd gotten on the road by six. It'd been the hottest, wettest June as far back as he could remember, which was forty years and some. Even further back than that, if you believed the old man. Which they did. Nobody in Jensen's family questioned his father's word. At sixty-eight, Lewis O'Leary might still take the skin off your backside with his leather belt, given half a chance.

The trailer fishtailed slightly as he bent around a curve, and he downshifted, his hands slick with sweat on the steering wheel, his shirt sticky under his arms. The air-conditioning in the cab had died last year and the cab was hot. He couldn't crack the window; on his one attempt the rain had boiled in like a tidal wave, drenching his coveralls. He felt the truck straighten and breathed out, his mouth slightly open in concentration. In the rearview mirror, a lone Ford Taurus dogged his bumper. He downshifted twice more and slowed to forty.

The truck cell phone sang at him, some half-cocked classical piece Maired had programmed into it, and he tapped the remote.

"Yeah?"

"That you, Jensen?"

"It's me, Pa."

"Crider's just called. Where the hell are you? That load should have been there a good hour ago." His father's voice was loud, and always had been, an assaulting bass roar that you could hear half a mile away. It was raspy now, from years of cheap cigars and cheaper whiskey. It sent a throb of pain through Jensen's left temple. All he needed in the middle of this flippin' storm was one of his headaches.

"About twenty minutes away. Half hour at the outside," he lied.

"Ron should have taken this load." You could cut the contempt in Lewis O'Leary's voice with a knife. If Jensen'd had a knife he would have tried cutting something else. Like his father's mottled, wattled throat.

"You get a look at this rain?" Jensen said.

"You get a look at this rain?" Lewis mocked. "Coupla inches. So what? You step on it, son. We lose this account, I swear I'll cut your pay another twenty percent."

Twenty percent of nothing's still nothing, Jensen thought, but he said, "I'm on it."

"He's on it," his father mimicked. Then, his voice distant

as he turned from the speaker, "You hear that, Cordy? He's on it. Ain't that a relief."

His older brother's voice came on the phone, unperturbed. "You got a real-time estimate for the delivery, little brother? Crider's got that Valu-Mart truck headed their way at two. And time and Valu-Mart wait for no man."

Was there a faint echo of their father's mockery in Cordy's voice? A familiar swell of resentment rose in Jensen's throat. "No problem."

Lewis grunted, "Better not be. You get a move on," and cut the connection. Silence filled the cab. Jensen downshifted once again, to the fury of the Taurus in his wake. He ignored the blasts from the driver's horn, and rolled down the rain-drenched highway at a steady thirty miles an hour.

## II

Maired O'Leary stood at the main entrance of the Carousel Mall in Syracuse and watched the rain come down like Niagara Falls. She hated this. She hated all of it. The rain, the mall, O'Leary's Interstate Poultry Farms, her hometown of Summersville—all of upstate New York, if anybody cared to ask. She wanted to get *out*. She shoved open the heavy glass door to a warm, dense rain that was like a shower with a million showerheads, all aimed directly at her. She backed up in a rage as futile as it was familiar and let the door whoosh close.

She'd booked a room at the nearby Hilton, which was a five-minute walk from where she stood. She'd planned it just right. If it hadn't been for this . . . this torrent, she'd be walking across the parking lot. The rain meant she'd have to take the car and park it right at the hotel, as close to the entrance as she could get. And Cordy'd have a fit. As if anyone they knew from Summersville-Hicksville-Dullsville would be checking out the parking lot of the Hilton for her car in the middle of a storm like this. And even if they did, so what? She'd just tell everyone she'd switched the place where she got her facials. That the only place you could get a halfway decent facial this far away from civilization was a lousy hotel chain. And nobody'd notice Cordy's car no matter what. That pickup Cordy drove was interchangeable with fifty others of the exact same kind in Summersville.

The opening bars to Mozart's Minuet in G tinkled from her purse. She scrabbled for her cell phone and flipped it open.

"Sorry," Cordy said. "Mission aborted. The county Mounties closed off 15 north of us. The road's flooded."

"Don't be ridiculous." Maired wanted to shriek right here in the middle of the mall. If Cordy really meant that he wasn't coming, maybe she would shriek. "I haven't seen you all week."

"You saw me last night at supper." Cordy sounded amused.

A shriek wasn't loud enough. She'd scream her throat bloody. Sunday dinners at Pa's were the usual nightmare end to her usual nightmare week. The old man bellowed, drank, and bellowed some more. Which didn't mean that his spiteful eye wasn't on everybody and everything every single minute. Sunday dinner meant she never even looked at Cordy, much less tightened her fingers in his thick, black hair.

"How many times do I have to tell you not to use that hick word *supper*? Anyhow, you know Sunday *dinner* doesn't count." She sounded petulant even to herself. But she hated that farmy talk.

"Can't do much about the rain, kiddo."

"You could get here if you tried." She glanced around the mall. Only a few shoppers had dared the downpour, and they were concentrating on the sheets of rain outside, not on her. She lowered her voice; "I paid cash for the room. No credit cards, you said. What if they don't give it back?"

"It's getting a little expensive, meeting like this," he said. "But you've always managed to dig up what you need when you need it from Jensen, Maired. Unless my little brother's finally cut you off?"

That cheap little Cheryl from the bank? Was the tart getting to him after all? They both knew it had to look like he had a real girlfriend. Which is why Cheryl was such a clever choice. His parents hated her like poison. So it wasn't Cheryl. It couldn't be Cheryl. This dancing around, this backing off, this was just nerves. Or something. "So how am I supposed to get home in this weather, if everything's supposedly cut off?" she hissed. "You can tell them I got stranded. That you had to come and get me."

"Resourceful Maired," Cordy said with more than a hint of unpleasant humor. "You'll find a way. But I'm not coming out. I can't. Sorry about the cash."

His coolness panicked her. "It's not the money," she said. "You know it's not about the money. I need to see you, Cordy, I need to hold you."

"Look, Maired. I've been thinking that maybe we should back off this thing. Pa's been asking some pretty pointed questions . . ."

"Don't you say another word." Despite herself, her voice rose. A woman in a cheap tank top and a skintight pair of jeans had been bent over a grubby baby in a stroller. She raised her head, shot a startled glance at Maired, and then pushed the stroller nearer. Maired turned her back and walked away from the foyer toward the Saks Fifth Avenue store. "That awful old man. He's got you all on a leash like a bunch of sorry dogs."

"Temper, temper," he chided. And clicked off.

Maired snapped the phone shut, shoved it back into her purse, and stared into Saks's huge plateglass window. A trio of mannequins posed gracefully around a formal dining table. A blonde in a red cocktail dress held a wineglass to her lips.

Lewis drank Amaretto in a wineglass after each of those interminable Sunday dinners. Wasn't there some quick acting poison that tasted like Amaretto? She'd love to watch Lewis raise a wineglass full of almond-tasting poison, swill it down in that sloppy, belching way he had, and fall over and die.

There had to be a way to get some.

## III

Lucinda Whitby squelched deeper into the massive roots of the weeping willow and tried to make herself one with the rain. The river water had slopped into her rubber boots and the scrape of the boot lining against her bare ankle was horrible, a squeaky chafing that reminded her of fingernails on a blackboard. The rivulet of water down the back of her neck, past her shoulder blades, and down to her underpants was horrible, too. Her jeans were leaden with wet mud. Her T-shirt sucked against the inside of her anorak.

She closed her eyes and made a conscious effort to relax. "Kaaaaaaaaaaaa." She exhaled her mantra just as her teacher at the meditation center had said, in one long, unbroken breath. "Oh, kaaaaaaaaaaa."

Lucinda slumped back against the comforting strength of the huge old tree. Despite her best efforts at becoming one with the rain, she was wet, cold, and miserable. She must have a stain on her soul. Or something. She'd dozed off during that part of the lecture on Mahayana Buddhism that talked about the stages of purity.

The earth shook beneath her, and she struggled upright, the rain forgotten, her attention all on the soggy swamp in front of her. There he was—or one of them, anyhow—driving that monstrous green tractor. Behind the tractor was a huge green manure spreader, filled with the bodies of dead birds. Heaps of soft, white feathers and broken necks.

Lucinda exhaled a long, satisfied sigh. She had been right.

The tractor came to a chugging halt. The driver threw a switch. The track began to roll, and the mass of corpses rolled off the spreader into the swampy ditch, an avian landslide.

*Krick!* squalled a birdy voice. *Krick!*

Lucinda stifled a shriek. Was one of the damn things still alive? She scrambled upright, not caring if the O'Leary driving the tractor saw her or not. Poultry farmers could yammer all they wanted to about how the poor little birds just up and died without any real cause at all and that this kind of disposal was just as green as any other kind of recycling, but she'd known better and hadn't she been right after all. Dead bird bodies dumped in the dirt. And maybe live birds, too. Disgusting. And illegal.

She fumbled in the pocket of her jacket for her camera, then froze as the bird called to her again for help: *Krick!*

"Stop!" she screamed. "Murderer! Stop!"

The roar of the motor and the clang of the spreader deafened the driver. Even if he did hear her, she knew he didn't care. The cascade of feathered bodies went on and on.

*Krick!*

Lucinda stopped screaming and bit her lower lip. That caw hadn't come from the mass grave. She was too far away, And even if she'd been closer, with all the machinery noise, she couldn't have heard a blast from three sticks of TNT, much less the call of a desperate bird caught in the shredder. No. That call had come from the bracken beyond the willow, not three feet from where she was standing now.

She sloshed through the puddles toward the brush and shaded her eyes with one hand, as if that would help draw aside the curtain of rain.

And there they were, racing through the brush like a fleet of rural taxicabs. *Meleagris gallopavo*. Wild turkeys. Turkeys living as they were meant to live. Free, gloriously free. She clasped her hands and breathed her mantra after them like a blessing. "Kaaaaaaaaaaa."

Then she turned and got thirty-six color photos of an O'Leary violating every biohazard rule in the state. She'd get that Lewis O'Leary if it was the last thing she did in this life.


## IV

Alan Krippendorf's office at the Cornell Ag School's poultry wing was about the size of a hospital broom closet and just as cluttered. The floor was a litter of books, manuscripts, student papers, and unopened mail sprawled over large glass jars of embalmed turkey parts. One wall groaned against the weight of an overloaded floor-to-ceiling bookshelf. The opposite wall was a confusion of posters that featured anatomical drawings of turkey innards, handwritten lists of things to do, and a couple of photographs of two birdy-looking children and a stout young woman with a wild corona of frizzy brown hair. All three scowled into the camera.

Krippendorf himself bore a striking resemblance to a Narragansett Bronze—one of the nobler breeds of turkey, but a turkey nonetheless. His reddish hair stuck up in a comblike way. His nonexistent chin disappeared into his neck in folds of pale, wattlelike flesh. He had a habit of reading while standing on one long, thin leg with the opposite foot tucked against the back of his knee. It was an unsteady pose and he fell forward onto his untidy desk when his department chair pulled open Alan's office door and walked in, unannounced.

"Get a grip, there, Alan," John Wu said, not unkindly.

Krippendorf righted himself, sending a cascade of papers to the floor. "Dr. Wu?"

John Wu nodded gravely, as if he hadn't met Krippendorf once a week for the past three years. "The very same."

"Did we have an appointment?"

Wu looked at his watch. "For three o'clock. That'd be twenty minutes ago. In my office. When you didn't show up, I came looking for you."

Krippendorf ran one hand through his hair, and then scrabbled in his shirt pocket for his diary. "Are you absolutely sure?" he said fussily. "It's not like me to forget something as important as that . . ."

"It's very like you to forget something like that." John Wu sighed, looked around for a place to sit, gave it up as a bad job, then folded his arms and rocked back on his heels. "Just dropped in to see how things were going, Alan."

Krippendorf nodded vigorously, with a curious pecking motion. "Just fine, Dr. Wu. Just fine."

"Not things in general, Alan. With the study out at O'Leary's."

"Yes?" Alan said brightly.

"The grant committee's meeting tomorrow. We'd hoped to have some good news about the results of the feed additive in O'Leary's brooder flock." Wu spoke loudly and patiently.

"Yes. Well. The incidence of coccidiosis has dropped dramatically, of course."

A smile creased Wu's face. "That's *very* good news. There have been no deaths at all?"

"Well, one or two." Krippendorf ran his forefinger around the collar of his shirt, as if to loosen it.

"One or two?" Wu said with a frown. "That doesn't make a lot of sense."

"No, sir," Krippendorf said.

"We need to take a look at this. You know that the potential value to the department is immeasurable. I've been counting on moving from patent-pending status to patent awarded. And it's not just the cash we're going to realize from the sale of this product that's good for the department, Alan. It's the fact that we've developed a cheap, foolproof method of inoculation against one of the most insidious poultry killers in the industry."

He gave Krippendorf's shoulder a hearty clap, pitching the grad student forward against the desk once again. "I want you to get to work, kiddo. I'd like all the paperwork ready for me to review by next week."

"Uh," Krippendorf said.

Wu's gaze sharpened. "You've got all your ducks in a row, right? The lab results, the field results, O'Leary's sign-off verifying your data?"

"Sure," Krippendorf said feebly.

"We'll want the whole megillah on Friday." The warning in Wu's voice was as clear as the Cornell carillon at noon. He rapped Krippendorf's left bicep and went out. The door closed behind him with a thud.

" 'Exit'," Krippendorf said hollowly, " 'pursued by a bear.' "

Except Wu was the bear pursuing him. And he, Alan Krippendorf, was the one who was going to exit his postdoc if he didn't get that bastard O'Leary to sign off on the study data.

He'd pinned the photos of Robin and their two kids between the schedule for his summer lab and a newspaper clipping about the return of wild turkeys to the suburbs of Summersville. He wasn't in those pictures. Not literally. Not figuratively. The successful conclusion of his postdoc was part of his campaign to bring her back to him. Not to mention the fact that the successful conclusion of his postdoc was part of his campaign to have enough money to pay the rent on his studio off West Seneca Avenue. And pay the loan on his eight-year-old Ford Fiesta. And eat.

Lewis O'Leary stood in the way of it. All of it.

## V

"Who were you talking to, son?" Angela O'Leary pushed her worn and stocky body into Cordy's office, as if she were an overloaded cart. She had a plastic-sheeted shirt over one arm and carried an umbrella. Her gray hair was scraped back in its usual severe bun, but she wore a dash of lipstick and the dress she wore to Mass.

Cordy glanced nervously at the phone, as if Maired's rage

had left tangible smoke pouring from the earpiece. "Just letting Crider's know Jensen's going to be a little later than he thought. Rain's slowing him down some."

Angela sniffed. "Thought your Pa took that call some while ago. Crider's not a customer we want to fool with. We send them . . ."

". . . half a million carcasses a year," Cordy finished for her. "You don't have to tell me again, Ma."

". . . and with times as tight as they are . . ."

"They aren't going to cancel on us, Ma. Where else are they going to get fifty thousand carcasses on a minute's notice? They're antsy, that's all. Although god knows, with all this rain, that Valu-Mart semi's not going to make it, either." He rose from his desk chair, stretched, and wrapped one long arm around his mother's shoulder. "You're all dressed up? Got a date in town?"

Angela stepped away from his embrace, frowning. "We're going to that feed seminar over to the high school. I thought you meant to go with us."

"Too much to take care of here. This rain keeps up, someone's got to keep an eye on the barns. I don't know that the culverts can handle it, especially the hatchery."

"I thought you were going to go with us to see if we can switch our business over to Whole Farms," Angela repeated. "Pa's bound and determined to switch suppliers. Him from Green Seal . . ."

"Gil Finnegan?"

"The one who's selling feed," Angela said.

"Gil Finnegan," Cordy said, in rising irritation.

"Him. Pa says he's shorting us on the tonnage."

"Gil's not shorting us on anything," Cordy snapped. His mother stared at him reproachfully. "Sorry. But Pa's going to pull this once too often. He did the same thing to Agway, remember? Got a couple of thousand dollars knocked off the bill and the salesman fired, and nobody believed a word of it. If he keeps this up, there's not a supplier in Tompkins County that's going to want to deal with us."

Both of them knew this wasn't true. O'Leary's Poultry Farms was huge. Eight hundred thousand carcasses a year. The feed and equipment salesmen were all over them like a thick, warm blanket. Cordy couldn't think of a crime his father could commit that would keep the sales guys away.

He sat down at his desk and made a show of riffling through the current bills. His mother's forehead wrinkled with worry. "We short again this month?"

"A bit to the good, as a matter of fact. Hadn't you better see if the seminar's still on? The weather's going to keep a lot of people from showing up."

His mother jutted her chin. "Any trouble on the roads is trouble north of here. The high school's in the other direction. There's a pretty good supper the feed company sets out. And they bought our turkeys to cook up, so we have to be there. Besides, since I thought you were going to go with us, I didn't fix a thing for you."

"I'll be fine," Cordy said. "I'll catch something at the Embassy after I talk to Walt about the culverts."

"If you had a wife," Angela went on inexorably, "she'd be fixing supper for you instead of me and you wouldn't be spending all your time down to the Embassy drinking beer. I'd even put up with that cheap little bank clerk Cheryl if I had to." She looked out the small window that was the sole source of daylight in his office. "Rain's stopped, anyway. If we were going to flood, we would have flooded by now."

Cordy stared past her into the farmyard. His office was at the west end of the largest hatchery barn, and it faced the old farmhouse. Beyond the house, down the quarter-mile driveway to Route 335, the water streamed in the drainage ditches. The sun shouldered its way through the last remnants of cloud. Water puddled everywhere. But there wasn't any flood. The hatchery barns were on lower ground than the breeder farm, which lay a mile to the east, and the poult barns lay a mile beyond that, upwind, and if the hatchery hadn't flooded, nothing else would.

His mother tapped him on the arm. "Listen up. So. You can come with us. Ron and Linda are going to meet us there. Jensen's not back yet from the run to Crider's, but he and Maired are supposed to be there, too. And Pa'll want you in a farm shirt," she warned. "I got a fresh ironed one right here." She hung the shirt on the coatrack, next to the rain slickers. "Pa said five o'clock. It's quarter to, now."

The O'Leary Poultry Farms logo stared out at him through the plastic, a fanned-out turkey tail with his name underneath in bright green stitching. Chain stitching, his mother said. His brother Ron had one just like it. His brother Jensen had one, too. He and his brothers were chain-stitched into the fabric of this place. "You going to change, or do I have to get your father after you?"

Cordy's hands tightened around the heavy brass paperweight that his mother had picked up at a garage sale some years ago. It was a male turkey with tiny eyes of bright red stone. "Right. I'll be with you in a minute."

Angela turned and plodded out the door. He watched her cross the yard to the back steps of the farmhouse. She kept a kitchen garden and the rain had flattened the parsley and the dill. Tomatoes gleamed bloodred among the wire cones that held them upright. Angela stumped onto the porch and settled into the battered wicker rocker where she shelled the peas and shucked corn in the summertime. She put her black plastic purse on her lap, held it firmly with both hands and began to rock, waiting.

Cordy flipped open the ledger and stared at the running balance. His father made all the deposits. Cordy paid all the bills. The balance showed a ten-thousand-dollar profit for the month—but the electric bill hadn't come in yet and the utility cost for running three houses, seventeen barns, and a ton of equipment was huge.

He looked out the window at his mother, waiting for the rattletrap Ford his father drove to come and pick her up. Pick both of them up and then bring them both back again.

He was going to be trapped here until he died.

Or his father died first.

# One

〰〰

"IT's like this, Dr. McKenzie." Gil Finnegan poked an earnest forefinger into my sternum. "You've got the perfect face to sell turkeys."

I was not amused. But a short, hilarity-ridden silence prevailed among the others standing in my office. The unexpectedly heavy rains had trapped us in my clinic with the Green Seal Farm Feeds salesman. I quelled my wife and assistants with a stern lowering of my brow, directed a suitably ironic expression at Finnegan, and said merely, "No."

"Thing is," Finnegan said with an explanatory wriggle of his fat shoulders, "my customers would trust a guy with your looks right off the bat. No offense, Doc, but old white guys inspire confidence in a lot of people."

"Like Colonel Sanders?" I asked icily.

Finnegan's round face creased with the effort of thinking hard. "Yeah. I guess. Except he's dead."

Madeline's sapphire eyes met mine. A faint blush suffused her creamy complexion. It was not the flush of shyness. I have been married to Madeline for well over twenty years and she is not of a retiring disposition. She, like our two clinic assistants Joe Turnblad and Allegra Fulbright, was biting back a chortle. She said, "Well now, Austin, maybe we shouldn't be so quick to turn Mr. Finnegan down."

I gestured at the four walls of our clinic. "These are the offices of the McKenzie Veterinary Practice, Inc. The practice—and take note, please, of the emphasis I am placing on the next phrase—is limited to large animals."

My large and amiable collie, Lincoln, uttered an approving bark. Juno, Allegra's Lab-Akita pup, bit Lincoln's ear in excitement.

"But to most people a vet's a vet," Allegra said. She had been a pretty child when she joined us as an assistant several months ago, and she had gotten even prettier. Her hair is the color of Hershey bars. Her eyes are green. Her disposition is generally sunny—although she had been somewhat melancholy of late. She is a first-year vet student at my former sinecure, Cornell University. "Most people haven't a clue what the words 'large animal' really mean. Most of them probably think it's like, Great Danes or whatever. And you do have a trustworthy face, Dr. Mac. *I* think you'd be terrific as a turkey feed spokesperson."

I directed a speaking glance at the fifth human occupant of my office, Joe Turnblad. Joe slouched against the wall, arms folded across his chest. He will enter his third year as a veterinary student this fall. Like Allegra, his clinical assistance at Sunny Skies is of great value to Madeline and me. His hair is the color of Hershey bars, too. Joe grinned at me and shrugged. "Whatever."

"Maybe this'll do a little convincing, Doc. Here's what corporate thinks is a darn fair offer." Finnegan scribbled numbers on a small slip of paper and held it out to me. Madeline seized it with the purposefulness of a cat after an errant kitten. She read it. Her eyes brightened. Holding the paper between thumb and forefinger, she made a gesture to me so small it went unnoticed by the others.

The amount did not need to be large to bring that flush of approbation to Madeline's cheeks. We were, to be frank, somewhat low in funds. That tiny plea struck me to the heart.

I see I must digress.

After forty years as the chair of bovine sciences at the Cornell School of Agriculture, I retired to our small farm and a happy life with Madeline. And then—many months ago, I took out a loan against our comfortable income and invested the lot in Enblad, Inc. The same Enblad whose CFO now resides on a tropical island with no extradition treaty with the United States of America. He reputedly has enough company cash to buy a small African country.

Hence the creation of McKenzie Veterinary Services, Inc. (Practice Limited to Large Animals).

My marriage twenty-odd years ago made me the most fortunate of men, and I remain as fortunate to this day. Not one word of blame over the ruin of our hopes for a peaceful retirement has ever passed Madeline's lips. But her tiny gesture with the folded note reminded me that the consulting fee would be more than welcome. Our assistants needed that small salary we provided. Our resident animals required that same Green Seal Farm Feed that Finnegan sold not just to us, but all over Tompkins County. In short, we had bills to pay.

And yet, I hesitated. How seemly was this offer?

Madeline's gaze lingered on my face for a long moment. She addressed Finnegan with a flutter of her long eyelashes. "I suppose if Austin turns you down, you'll have to find someone else?"

Finnegan thrust his hands in the pocket of his Green Seal coveralls and rocked back on his heels. "Yup. Yup. That we will. We got to have a spokesperson to give talks around the area. And we need a expert to talk to the newspapers. That kind of stuff. So, yeah, we'll have to find somebody other than the doc, here. Which is a shame. He's kind of a legend around Summersville, what with the way he talks on and on, you know."

"You'd need to find someone like Victor Bergland, I suppose?" Madeline raised her eyebrows in mild inquiry.

"Who?" Finnegan puckered his brow with a puzzled air.

"Bergland!" I said. "That old so-and-so."

Victor Bergland supplanted me upon my retirement as chair of bovine studies. He is a goat. And a booby.

Madeline shook her head. "You wouldn't believe it. But it looks like Victor is doing a bunch of this public-sector stuff, Austin. I ran into Thelma at Wegman's yesterday. She was full of herself, I have to say. Victor's been interviewed for a *Front-line* special on mad cow disease. The feature's supposed to run Sunday. I totally forgot to tell you, Austin. Until now." She turned and directed a big sunny smile at Finnegan. "But I suppose Dr. Bergland'd be a logical choice for you Green Seal people, Gil."

Gil nodded eager agreement, and then said, "Who's this again?"

"Just what does this consulting jointure require?" I intervened. Victor Bergland! The man is admittedly sound in some areas of veterinary medicine. But his on-screen persona leaves much to be desired. And what did he know about poultry feed anyway?

"It wouldn't be on the bags of feed or anything," Finnegan said. "Your puss, I mean. We'd just like you to write a article for the newsletter . . ."

"An article," I said testily.

Finnegan frowned. The effort it took this man to think was noticeable. "Yeah. A article."

"It is not *a* article, it is *an* article. The article *an* modifies nouns beginning with vowels."

"Right," Finnegan said in total befuddlement.

I smoothed my mustache. "And of course, news articles are something of a forte of mine."

"Hah?"

"I refer of course, to 'Ask Dr. McKenzie!' "

"The advice column Austin writes for the *Summersville Sentinel*," Madeline said. Her dimples were more prominent when she suppressed a smile, as she was doing now. "Surely you must have seen it, Gil. I imagine that's what brought Austin to your attention in the first place."

"Sure. Yeah. 'Course." Finnegan scratched his armpit unself-consciously. "And we'd be asking you to do more of the talks like you're giving tonight at the feed seminar."

" 'The Efficacy of the Feed Additive NoCos in the Prophylactic Treatment of Coccidiosis.' " I said. "Yes, indeed."

"Prophylactic?" Finnegan said with a look of alarm. "This NoCos is a crumbly mineral thing, Doc. Cuts poultry deaths way down." He sent an alarmed look Allegra's way and whispered, "I'm not all that sure what you mean by prophylactic."

"It means prevention," Allegra supplied with a kind air. "As in helps prevent the disease."

"That it does do. But!" He leaned forward and said, "Confidentially, the folks at Green Seal are working on something even better."

"And a useful thing it is, NoCos," I mused. "Coccidiosis unchecked can wipe out a herd of turkeys or a flock of chickens in an instant. Green Seal and its like provide the poultry industry an inestimable service with these additives, Finnegan." Madeline and I exchanged a long look. "You say Victor's involved in some of these public events?"

"You bet," Madeline said.

I turned to Finnegan. "Very well, Gil. The answer is yes."

"Hah?" Finnegan said.

"Yes, I will be the poultry spokesperson for Green Seal Farm Feed. For the period of one year, I think you said?"

Madeline reread the slip of paper with the consulting fee figures and smiled like a sunrise.

"Terrific!" Finnegan bounded toward me like an elated kangaroo, his hand extended. Lincoln got to his feet with a warning growl. I snapped my fingers, and the collie stopped, cocked his head, and then settled back at my feet. Finnegan pumped my hand enthusiastically. Then he shook hands with Madeline and Joe. He hesitated before he shook hands with Allegra— Madeline says Ally's looks intimidate some men—then put both hands around her small one and shook it heartily. "Well," he beamed. "My boss at Green Seal is going to change her mind about me when I tell her about this!"

I glanced out the window. The rain had stopped. A reluctant sun nudged through the bellies of rain clouds. "Yes, well. We must be off, Finnegan. It's after five, and I'm due at this feed seminar of yours in a hour."

Finnegan gave a guilty start and looked at his watch. "Gosh. So it is. Well, thank you, Doc. And thank you, Mrs. McKenzie. We'll see you at the high school, then? In about forty-five minutes? My boss'll be there and you'll want to meet her."

Was the man never going to leave my office? It was time for a strategy I had used to good effect on garrulous pharmaceutical salesmen and intrusive Avon ladies. As Finnegan rattled on,

I advanced. He backed up. He stopped. I advanced again. In a matter of moments, we were all outside.

Joe, Allegra, and Juno dispersed to do evening chores. Madeline and Lincoln followed me. I advanced on Finnegan until he got to his car. I opened the driver's door for him, closed it, and waved him on. His mouth was still moving as he backed out of the driveway and onto Route 15.

"The man provides both entertainment and audience for himself," I said. "I hope I don't live to regret this, my dear."

"He's just trying to get along." Madeline tucked her arm comfortably in mine. She is a queenly woman. I always feel a slight jolt of pride when she attaches herself to my arm. Lincoln paced at my opposite side as we headed toward the house. He is a sable collie. The magnificent mahogany of his ruff is the precise color of Madeline's hair. The sky was clearing to a soft blue. The check Madeline held would see us through another month. I sighed with contentment.

"So what do *you* think is his trouble, sweetie?" Madeline said, continuing a conversation I was not aware we'd been having.

I halted halfway up the steps to the back door, puzzled. "What trouble? Who said anything about trouble?"

Madeline nudged me forward and we walked into the kitchen. The scent of her meat loaf permeated the air.

"Meat loaf," I said. "And baked potato, if I'm not mistaken. Hurrah!"

I noticed she had set the table for two. Of course. Only Allegra and Joe would be home for dinner. The two of us were doomed to the rubber chicken and mushy peas of the Green Seal Farm Feeds Fest. Madeline's meat loaf is one of my favorite meals. "Perhaps we can skip the dinner part. I could arrive after, and deliver my speech."

"Not tonight, sweetie. You had soft-boiled eggs for breakfast."

Madeline's meat loaf is strictly rationed due to wholly unwarranted concerns about my cholesterol. But she was headed upstairs to change for our foray into farm feed, a process that would take some minutes. And since I was attired in shirtsleeves and chinos, perfectly acceptable clothing to deliver a speech on a warm July evening, I could stay downstairs. Neither Allegra nor Joe would notice a missing slice.

"You're coming up with me." Madeline did not make this into a question. In fact, she tugged me past the oven.

"I . . ."

"Of course you are, sweetie. You want to change that shirt. And you were going to tell me what you think it is about Gil, anyhow."

"Finnegan? I have no idea what you're talking about."

She clasped my hand affectionately. "Austin, you always forget about the people part. Something about his boss. Remember? He said his boss was going to change her mind about him now that you've agreed to this consultant gig."

"Hm. So he did."

Madeline continued to propel me past the dinner table and up the stairs. "You know, Austin. I think you may just have saved that poor soul's job for him."

"I?" I said, startled.

"Well, it stands to reason Gil must have been screwing up somewhere. You know how whirly he can get. And here he gets to keep his job because of you. I am so *proud* of you, Austin."

She gave me a warm kiss and suggested my seersucker sport coat for tonight's event since the June evening would be warm. And we both went upstairs.

Which left me no chance at all at the meat loaf, of course.

We left for the seminar some twenty minutes later and drove the short hop into Summersville to the high school.

# Two

IN times kinder to farming, feed seminars such as the one hosted by Green Seal were held at the Grange Hall. But the Grange Hall was gone, the property scooped up by developers and replaced by a 7-Eleven quick mart. The cafeteria at the Summersville High School provided a convenient meeting place for those Tompkins County farmers profitable enough to survive our economy.

Madeline and I walked into the cafeteria just on the hour. Summersville has a population of about twenty thousand souls, a sad decline from the glory days of the sixties and seventies. The high school had been built to accommodate a far larger number of students than was currently required. Green Seal had a fair turnout for both the food and the seminar, but the attendees appeared lost in the cavernous space. About a third of the cafeteria tables had been set with plates and cutlery. A large steam table near the podium at the far end of the room wafted the scent of roasted turkey into the air. From the doors open to the kitchen area came the clatter of cans. I rose to my tiptoes and peered over the heads of what crowd there was. Peas. A hairnetted person was emptying large cans of mushy peas into a caldron. But I contemplated the prospect of turkey with pleasure, delighted that I'd been wrong about half of the meal.

Most of the crowd had loaded up on the hors d'oeuvres—pasty cheese squares and bright orange pepperoni—and was already seated at the tables. I surveyed the faces in the room with a sense of satisfaction. We had opened the practice a mere two years ago, and the room held a substantial number of clients. Many of our clinic's clients were in attendance. Orville DeGroote and his pale blonde wife saw us and waved. Joe and I had castrated twenty of his bull calves just last week. The Longwoods sat a little farther down at the same table. They grew Longhorn cattle on a farm some distance from the village. Ike Longwood raised a hand to me and saluted. Madeline followed my gaze and winked companionably at me.

The horse crowd was not in evidence, however. They are a substantial part of our practice. The Green Seal crowd was almost exclusively commercial farmers—and most farmers have an amiable contempt for the recreational use of animals, and a sadly pragmatic attitude toward pets.

There was not a complete lack of sentiment among the commercial community, however. Although very few farmers named the steers, hogs, and wethers that they bred for their own consumption, most swapped the butchered remains of the animals they hand raised for their freezers with neighbors the next farm over.

I caught sight of one notable exception. "The O'Learys," I mused aloud.

Madeline, in the middle of an animated discussion about canning practices with Olivia Gardener, failed to hear me. Rita Santelli, editor and publisher of the *Summersville Sentinel*, heard me all too well.

"What about the O'Learys, Austin? We're eating their turkeys tonight. There's nothing wrong over at the farm, is there?"

Rita was a small, peppery widow in her midforties with a lot of freckles and a pair of sharp gray eyes. She had inherited the *Sentinel* from a distant cousin, and, to everyone's mild amaze, managed to turn a profit her second year. She had recruited me

to write my popular column "Ask Dr. McKenzie." I had a fond-
ness for her, only slightly diminished by her wanton attacks on
my prose style.

"I was ruminating on the degree of sentiment in the farming community. Or the lack of it."

Her eyes followed mine to the table where the O'Learys
had congregated en masse. Lewis O'Leary sat between two of
his sons. Ronald, at Lewis's left, looked even thinner than the
last time I had seen him. Cordwainer, at his right, was the
handsomest man in Tompkins County, or so Madeline has informed me. Jensen, the middle son, was conspicuous by his
absence. The O'Leary women were clustered at one end of the
table. Angela, the matriarch, sat in sour silence beside one of
her two daughters-in-law, Ron's wife, Linda. She owned two
horses and was a client of our clinic. I didn't see the notorious
Maired, Jensen's discontented and—reportedly—spendthrift
wife.

All the male O'Learys had Black Irish coloring, black hair,
blue eyes, and ruddy complexions. Like peacocks, they were
hard to miss in a crowd. Angela and Linda were wrens by
comparison.

"And you mean the O'Learys have zero sentiment? You'd
be right about that." Rita sucked at her lower lip reflectively.
Lewis turned suddenly, and looked over his shoulder at us, as
if he'd heard his name amidst the general clamor. Rita stared
challengingly back, and then asked me, "Do you handle the
poultry farm?"

"I'm not sure who handles the birds. But as chance would
have it, we do take care of Linda O'Leary's geldings."

"Ron's wife," Rita said, as if cataloging the information.
Which indeed she probably was. "The nice one."

"They are slated for vaccinations for tomorrow, as a matter
of fact. The horses, not Ron and Linda. I run into Lewis on occasion, but never professionally."

"His eyes that bloodshot from drinking too much?" Rita
asked.

"It's possible," I said.

"Or d'ya suppose it's just general meanness?"

I wondered how that information was categorized in Rita's
active brain. "Notable Townspeople, Characters of " perhaps.

Lewis jerked his head around, growled at Ronald, then balled his left hand into a fist and clocked the man over the ear. Rita gasped. The room stilled into shocked silence, then into a louder uproar than before, as everyone pretended they hadn't seen Ronald's humiliation. Madeline touched my shoulder and said, "Good heavens!"

I grasped her hand firmly in mine. Madeline was fully capable of marching over and telling Lewis what's what. This possibility had occurred to Rita, as well, for she said, "Don't even think about it, Maddy. Ron's forty-two years old, if he's a day, and he could take Lewis in a New York minute if he wanted to. It's pretty obvious he isn't going to do that."

"Just look at that boy," Madeline said. There was a glint in her eye that I knew well. She was angry. "He may be forty-two years old on the outside, but *he* still thinks he's six on the inside. That boy's got tears in his eyes. That man's a disgrace. What's he about, hitting his son in public like that?"

"I suppose he belts them in private, too," Rita said with a sigh. "C'mon. The Reverend Shuttleworth's ready to start the prayer. Let's sit down and oh, please *not* with that little shrimp Gil Finnegan, oh rats, it's too late."

And indeed, Finnegan was signaling us with an energy that was hard to ignore. Madeline is never one to shirk her social duty. Finnegan had changed out of his Green Seal coveralls into a shabby sports coat and a cotton shirt. He draped his sports coat over two of the folding chairs, presumably to reserve a spot for us. It was unnecessary, as the seats around him were unoccupied. Madeline settled next to him, I settled next to her, and with a sulky air, Rita sat directly across from the three of us.

"Hiya, Rita, meter maid," Finnegan said.

Rita rolled her eyes at Madeline.

"And, Doc, I want you to meet the boss. You want to put your purse on the seat next to you, Rita, so we got a spot for her when she gets here?" He cast a nervous look over his shoulder. The Reverend Mr. Shuttleworth's arrival had been the signal for everyone to be seated, which left the entire cafeteria open to view. Just as young Shuttleworth began his ecumenical invocation, an attractive, hard-faced young woman in a tailored suit and high heels clicked briskly into the hall. She stopped, cast an appraising eye over the assembly, then tapped her way over to the four of us. Young Shuttleworth stopped in the middle of his petition to the Almighty, waited until she seated herself next to Rita, then concluded with a firm "Amen" to which we all dutifully responded. The end of the prayer was a signal for a general rush to the steam table.

Unperturbed, the young woman thrust her hand out to me and said, "You must be Dr. McKenzie."

I shook it.

"This is Dr. McKenzie," Finnegan said, as if she hadn't spoken. "Dr. McKenzie, this is my boss, Karen Crown. You got my message, Ms. Crown? The doc here's signed on for one year."

"Yes," Ms. Crown said. "So I hear." Her sleek brown hair was cut in an uncompromising bob. Small gold hoops were affixed to her ears. Her severely cut suit was in marked contrast to the overalls, plaid shirts, and print dresses worn by most of the seminar attendees. She was as neatly groomed as a show horse about to enter the ring.

Since Finnegan's social skills were on a par with those of a well-meaning—but clumsy—draft horse, I said, "May I introduce my wife, Madeline? And Rita Santelli, publisher of the *Summersville Sentinel.*"

Karen nodded at Madeline, and said to Rita, "You're here to cover the seminar, I hope."

"That's right," Rita said cheerfully.

Karen smiled. "It'd be very nice to see a story about how much Green Seal contributes to the local economy on the front page. Below the fold, of course. I don't suppose I can expect miracles."

Rita smiled right back. "A feed seminar? Not front-page material, I'm afraid." She tapped the digital camera she wore around her neck. "We'll get plenty of pictures, of course. But I limit any coverage of an event that's essentially advertising to copy about Summersvillians."

"We'll need to talk about our ad schedule, then," Karen said without batting an eye. "No front page, no weekly insert."

I settled back in my chair. The ensuing conversation would be interesting, to say the least. Rita's deceased husband was a nationally known journalist whose probity had been without question. Rita herself subscribed to those same elevated ethics. The news was not for sale.

Rita's smile showed quite a few teeth. "Sorry. No can do. You might try the Summersville's swap sheet."

Karen turned abruptly to Finnegan. "Gil. Get these folks some food, would you?" I had the distinct impression that she snapped her fingers. (Madeline informed me later that this was not true.) "See if you can avoid the worst of the turkey parts."

Finnegan fumbled to his feet. Madeline, who was looking at Karen with a fair degree of disapprobation, rose to her feet as well. "I'll just give you a hand, Gil."

Karen waited until Madeline and the salesman had attached themselves to the end of the line at the steam table. "There's no need for Gil to hear these numbers. He's already got the local store over budget." She pulled a little dingus from her purse and poked at it with a long-nailed forefinger. I believe it is called a Strawberry. "The figures here say Green Seal spends eight hundred dollars a week with your paper. Your circulation's what? Twenty-five thousand? Shouldn't think that you're making a profit on sales of the paper alone."

Rita's eyes narrowed, and two spots of red appeared on her cheekbones. Karen snapped the dingus shut. The smile never left her face. She didn't add anything else, but slipped the dingus back into her briefcase.

"And?" Rita said with dangerous calm.

Karen shrugged. "Just thought I'd let you know."

Any intemperate reply Rita might have made was forestalled by the appearance of our dinner. Or supper, as most Summersvillians would call it. Madeline had removed most of the skin from the turkey in front of me and heaped a large quantity of mushy green peas next to a minuscule scoop of mashed potatoes and an even smaller dollop of dressing. At five feet nine and 150 pounds of wiry muscle, I could well afford a larger serving of mashed potatoes. Not to mention a bit of crispy turkey skin. I gazed at my plate in some dudgeon. Madeline's own double scoop of mashed potatoes was covered in gravy.

"... detective," Finnegan said.

I looked up from the gloomy contemplation of my meal.

Rita's glower had been replaced by a smirk. Madeline looked proud. Karen Crown looked skeptical, but interested.

"I was telling the boss about the sniper case you solved a coupla months ago, Doc." Finnegan swallowed a large portion of mushy peas.

"I think I read something about that," Karen said. She glanced sideways at Rita. "In the *Syracuse Herald*."

"Oh, Rita was right on top of that one," Finnegan said proudly. "Way I hear it, the fella from the *New York Times* got most of his info from her reporters."

"That's not strictly true," Rita admitted. "And I had an inside source, so to speak, since Austin let me scoop everybody else. But thanks for the hometown support, Gil."

"It sounds like you did a good job, though," Karen said. "I'll be sure to get a subscription sent to the home office. It's a good idea to keep a finger on the local news."

Rita wiggled her eyebrows. Karen smiled at her and raised an eyebrow in my direction. "And you solved the case, Dr. McKenzie?"

I bowed, without rising from my seat. My first foray into the private investigation business had indeed been a success. "I had able support. My wife discovered the identity of the killer well before I did. And a fair amount of the legwork was accomplished by our two young assistants."

"Your first case?" Karen said, with a slight emphasis on the adjective.

"Austin nailed the Hamlet killer a little after that," Madeline said. Her eyes glowed with pride. "And that was all on his own."

"Green Seal seems to have gotten more than we bargained for," Karen said with a doubtful air. "Are you going to quit being a veterinarian?"

"Not at all," I said. "The two professions are not at all dissimilar, you know. The successful resolution of a murder case is directly analogous to the successful resolution of undiagnosed pathologies."

"Can this guy talk, or what?" Finnegan said in simple admiration. "Tell you what, boss, if we had to pay the doc here by the word, we'd have to double the retainer."

Rita was overcome by a sudden fit of coughing. Perhaps a spoonful of those disgraceful peas had stuck in her throat.

Karen ran one hand through her hair in a somewhat distracted manner. "Yes, well. Dr. McKenzie. Welcome aboard. I've reviewed your credentials—your medical credentials, that is—and Green Seal is privileged to have you aboard. As far as your responsibilities to corporate are concerned . . ."

She was not allowed to finish. Lewis O'Leary, a second plateful of turkey and mashed potatoes balanced on the flat of his hand, caught sight of us as he left the steam table. He veered in our direction like an out-of-control dump truck. "Finnegan!" he bellowed. "You bloody crook!"

O'Leary approached the end of the table. Finnegan, his face pale, swallowed hard and stood up, to demonstrate, perhaps, that he was no coward. O'Leary drew back his arm and mashed the plate onto Finnegan's chest. Gravy, peas, and potatoes dribbled down Finnegan's shirt. Then O'Leary shoved the poor man back into his seat.

Rita, with the insensitive aplomb that characterizes the true journalist, began to take pictures with her digital camera. Madeline's eyes flashed in dudgeon. Karen Crown's mouth was open in astonishment.

I rose to my feet and said sharply, "Sit, O'Leary!" in a tone that has brought more than one recalcitrant animal to heel. O'Leary squinted balefully at me out of his small blue eyes. He pulled one of the folding chairs away from the table, flipped it back end to, and sat down, his legs straddling the seat. I, too, resumed my seat, and said, "What seems to be the problem here?"

O'Leary jerked his thumb in Finnegan's direction. "Last two feed deliveries have been short." He glared balefully at Karen. "Until there's an adjustment on my bill, you aren't seeing one thin dime from me."

Gil shook his head, like a steer bothered by flies. "I don't see how that can be, Mr. O'Leary. I checked the load weights myself before I brought over your last delivery. Frank Carbone helped me verify it. You can check with him."

O'Leary grunted. "Yeah? I'm not saying that you didn't leave the depot with a full load of feed that ought to have been mine. How much you had when you got to my farm is another thing altogether. There's more than a few guys I know rather pay less for what's dropped off the back of the truck."

Karen's lips were a thin, angry line. She avoided looking at
Gil. "Your delivery was short by how much, Mr. O'Leary?"

"Coupla tons at least, you add it all up." He rubbed his
hand along his jaw. "That what you think, Ron?"

Ron, standing behind his father in silence, shrugged indif-
ferently. I noticed that he failed to meet Finnegan's eyes.

"Ron!" his father bellowed.

"Ton, ton and a half maybe," Ron muttered.

O'Leary turned to Karen. "I'm a reasonable man. You
knock a thousand off my last bill, we'll call it square." He
took a deep, satisfied breath. "But I have to tell you, now, that
I've been having some very fruitful discussions with some
fella named . . . what was it, Ron?"

"Ansom Collins," Ron said.

"Eh?! Speak up boy!"

"Ansom Collins," Ron said, more loudly.

O'Leary grinned, "The rep from Whole Farms Foods,
don't you know. Now he took a look at the price per ton you
thieving bums are getting from me, and he was pretty sure he
could go you better."

Finnegan's brow was sweaty. He wiped his hands down the
sides of his pants—so I presume his hands were sweaty, too.
"I just can't believe that, Mr. O'Leary. We've already cut your
price per ton to the bone." He attempted a laugh.

"So you'll make it up in volume, eh?"

". . . And we can't sell you a dollar's worth of feed for
ninety-nine cents and make it up in volume."

O'Leary shook his massive head in mock sorrow. "Then I
guess that Whole Farm Foods can."

Finnegan's look at Karen was despairing. Her face was
stony. "Well," he said helplessly. "We'll see what we can do."

O'Leary got to his feet with a hideous scraping of the
metal chair on the linoleum floor. "You do that." He jerked his
head at Ron, and the two of them turned away. "And you'll not
forget the rebate on this quarter's bill? Fifteen hundred, you
said?"

"A thousand," Finnegan bleated to O'Leary's retreating
back.

Karen folded her paper napkin with care and looked at her
watch. "I've got to get back to Syracuse. There's a district

managers' meeting at eight tomorrow morning." She leaned forward, her face very close to Finnegan's. "I don't want to see one nickel drop in profits this quarter, Gil. Not one. You read me?"

Finnegan nodded and kept nodding as she gathered her briefcase and pushed away from the table. "Dr. McKenzie," she said coldly, "Mrs. McKenzie? I'm glad you're on board with us. And Rita? I'm sure that any story you write about this evening's seminar is going to be a positive one? We're going to be reviewing our advertising budget at tomorrow's meeting." She paused. "Along with recommendations for downsizing. This whole upstate area's proving to be quite a profit problem for us. Quite a problem." She nodded at us and clicked sharply out of the cafeteria.

"I do think," Madeline said after a long moment of silence, "that some coffee and pie might cheer everybody up. Rita and I'll go get us all some."

"Cheer everybody up?" Finnegan brushed futilely at the mess on his shirt. "I'll tell you what's going to cheer everybody up." He stared at O'Leary, who was standing in a group of farmers, head thrown back in laughter. "When that old devil's dead."

# Three

~~~~~~

MY disquisition on the efficacy of the feed additive NoCos in the prevention of coccidiosis in farm animals was well received. Although, as Madeline pointed out, it would have behooved Green Seal to offer caffinated beverages after dinner. Stupor is a well-known aftereffect of a carbohydrate-laden meal. A troupe of dancing elephants would have failed to wake a few of my more elderly listeners. But there were a sufficient number of questions from the audience to assure me that my points had gotten across. Madeline and I left the cafeteria just on nine o'clock, well satisfied with my first appearance as the Green Seal spokesman.

It was a beautiful evening. We were on the cusp of July. The rains through June had been heavier and more frequent than usual and the plant world had gone berserk. The air was redolent of the scented petunias and early lilies. The trees thrust branches thick with leaves against the moonlit sky. We got into our Bronco and set off for home.

Madeline was unusually silent.

I, too, was less conversational than usual. The uproar

caused by Lewis O'Leary had effectively put paid to the rest
of my meal. I felt as if I'd had no dinner at all. Madeline
roused herself from her musings to note that we were headed
down Main Street. "Which isn't the shortest way home,
Austin, of course." I could feel her perspicacious eye on me in
the darkness. "Are you thinking . . . maybe the Embassy?"

"I was, my dear."

The Monrovian Embassy is a dive. But it is a dive that
serves the best battered onions and juiciest hamburgers in
Tompkins County. It is a rare treat, the Monrovian Embassy.

She sighed. "I have to say that was the most inadequate
meal I've had for some time."

"It is because we generally eat at home, and you are a
splendid cook. And the atmosphere was not at all conducive
to a pleasant meal."

Her hand closed over mine affectionately. "Maybe it's because you went on and on about the importance of a succulent
feed for livestock in that terrific talk of yours, but I swear my
stomach thinks my throat is cut."

I made a neat right turn into the parking lot in back of the
Embassy, narrowly missing a pickup truck racing south out of
the parking lot. I put my hand out to keep Madeline from
plunging forward and braked hard.

"Bloody fool," I said. I looked into the rearview mirror.
"That looks like Finnegan's truck. He must have been drowning his sorrows at the bar."

Madeline squeezed my hand. "I haven't got a sorrow in the
world, sweetie, but I wouldn't mind drowning in a pitcher of
cold iced tea."

I parked, escorted my wife from the Bronco, and we
headed toward the dim lights of the Embassy.

During term time, the Embassy attracts students from
nearby Cornell University, in addition to the regular crowd of
Summersvillians, and it can be difficult to find a booth, even
late on a Monday night. But this was high summer, and the
students were absent. When we walked in the front door, it
was to a subdued jazz trio playing in the corner, and a fair
number of empty booths and tables.

The Embassy is unembellished. A long, battered wooden
bar occupies the length of the east wall, and a row of booths

rests against the west. Rickety tables lie helter-skelter down
the center aisle. At the back, the center door leads to the
kitchen, the door on the left to the bathrooms, and the door to
the right to the parking lot out back. The decrepit appearance
of the place is due to Rudy Schwartz's total indifference to appearances (and, gossip has it, to the health code of the state of
New York).

Madeline spied our favorite booth in the back and swooped
toward it like a sloop in full sail. She was wearing an outfit
that is a favorite of mine: white slacks that show off her ad-
mirably rounded hips and a loose purple top embroidered in
gold thread about the neck. I paused briefly to admire her—
and muse on my luck in marriage. A rudely familiar voice
broke into my thoughts.

"Yo! Austin!"

Madeline, too, had heard those unmistakable tones. She
stopped at the booth just before our own and exclaimed with
delight, "Victor! And Thelma! How nice to see you here!" At
Thelma's muttered invitation, Madeline slid next to her and
disappeared from my sight.

I came up and sat down next to Victor, who greeted me
with a punch in the arm and a lubricious look at my wife's
cleavage.

Victor Bergland is some ten years younger than I and was
the college committee's first choice to take over the chair in
bovine sciences at my retirement. Based on his work in the
spontaneous transmission of bovine encephalitis, not to mention his dabbling in the anomalies of azoturia myocitis syn-
drome, I had to agree that—academically—Victor was more
than an adequate replacement for me.

Victor has a long face, with a large, banana-shaped nose,
and full head of wildly wooly hair. He bears an uncanny resemblance to the better breed of goat. I nodded a greeting to
Thelma. She is a rather sour-faced person. When she gets ex-
cited (which, I reflected with some glee, is not often. Poor Victor!), her voice takes on the overtones of a mandrill monkey.

"Back from the high school gig, Austin? I hear the feed
company shoehorned you into a kiddie talk. How it'd go?"

"Victor feels these public affairs can limit your scope if
you aren't very choosy about where you appear," Thelma said,

in her macawlike way, "In his *Frontline* interview, Victor felt that Heywood Braun really failed to grasp the finer points of mad cow diseases."

"What finer points would those be?" I asked with some curiosity. It was even more curious that Thelma was tooting Victor's horn for him. They both had a more combative approach to marital relations. "I mean, the brain's infected with prions, the cow exhibits the usual symptoms, and boom, it's dead."

Thelma patted her hair in a rather fussy manner. "Victor feels that *Frontline* had an obligation to dig deeper into the issues, so to speak."

"No, I don't," Victor said. "And stop mentioning *Frontline*, Thelma. Everybody's sick to death of hearing about it."

Despite the limitations of his rather overbearing personality, Victor has his good points. But modesty isn't one of them. And he is never rude to Thelma. Thelma proud of Victor? Victor rude to Thelma? And modest to boot? I was intrigued.

"*I'm* not sick of it," Thelma said loudly. "And Madeline hasn't heard about it at all, so how could she be sick of it? As for Austin . . ."

"Austin'd like to hear about it, too," Madeline said.

"I would not," I said frankly. "What I would like is to order the Monrovian Special. I didn't get any dinner."

"Get your slides mixed up and spend the dinner hour sorting them out again?" Victor boomed. "Ho-ho-ho."

Ho-ho-ho, indeed.

"My talk was quite well received," I said. "And I am not a Luddite, Victor. I gave a PowerPoint presentation."

"Austin was brilliant," Madeline said, "and there were tons of questions, after. That's not what made him miss his dinner."

"Well?" Victor demanded. "What happened?"

I raised a hand to capture Deirdre Montoya's attention. I tried to recall a time of day when I had been in the Monrovian Embassy and Deirdre had not been there waitressing. I could not. She was always there. At the moment, she was deep in conversation with some fellow gloomily nursing a beer. She caught my eye, pointed to the sign advertising the Monrovian Special, and nodded when I held up two fingers.

The ordering accomplished, I returned to the discussion of the feed seminar, which had been rolling along without me.

"O'Leary's a tough customer," Victor said to Madeline. "You say he clouted the oldest boy over the ear?"

Madeline sighed. "He did. And then came and raised a rumpus at our table."

"He was raising a rumpus in here not twenty minutes ago," Thelma said waspishly. "Be thankful you just missed him. He's a horrible man."

"He came here after his appearance at the high school?" I said with some curiosity. "Are you certain?"

"It was him," Victor said, who is a slouch in the grammar department. "Unmistakable. Had a row with his other boy over there." He nodded toward the bar where I saw that the man in earnest discussion with Deirdre was indeed Jensen O'Leary, the one son who had not been at the seminar. "And then Cordy,"

"The good-looking one," Thelma interposed.

Victor raised his voice over hers, "Cordy came barreling in and it looked as if we were going to have a real brouhaha. But Rudy Schwartz banged out of the kitchen after the first glass broke and tossed 'em all out. Jensen came back inside after a bit and resumed drinking. I don't know what happened to the old man. Went home, I expect."

"You know who I feel sorry for?" Thelma asked, "His wife, that's who I feel sorry for. That wife must have a hard life. A hard, hard life. I shouldn't be surprised if he beats her, too." She sniffed and folded her napkin into a perfect rectangle.

Madeline tilted her head to one side. It was unusual to hear Thelma expressing sympathy for anyone but herself. Not unthinkable, but rare.

"Farming's a tough life," Victor observed. "And that sort of farming's on its way out. Maybe Lewis beats his wife out of frustration."

In her affectionate way, Madeline occasionally reminds me that I tend to be tone deaf to all human communication. But even I could sense that unspoken messages were flying like mad between Victor and Thelma. And not very courteous ones, either.

Deirdre placed two Monrovian Specials on the table. One hamburger was not only bunless but rested next to a large pile of coleslaw. The other dripped with bacon, cheese, fresh onion, and the juices of a well-larded steer. Crisp, golden French fries were attractively tangled with the beer-battered onion rings.

I looked at Deirdre, who rolled her eyes Madeline's way. Madeline looked at me. Her face softened. She placed a small portion of potato and onion on my plate.

"Factory farming," Victor added, although no on had encouraged him to continue with his opinion. "There's a great deal of public outcry over factory farming."

I tested the hamburger. It was delicious. The beef was undoubtedly from a feed lot. I looked at Victor's plate. The remains of a salad sat there. Victor usually loves the Monrovian Special. Had my old friend turned vegetarian on me? I took a large, satisfying bite of hamburger.

"Like the old days, Austin."

"Eh? What's like the old days?"

"Student protest," Victor said with satisfaction. "After decades of teaching students intent on making the most money for the least amount of effort, we're finally getting some good, solid concern for the environment, animal welfare, human rights." He blew out his cheeks in a puff of satisfaction. "And about time, too."

I picked up an onion ring and set it down again. Time was out of joint, so to speak. In all the years I'd known him—and Victor and I went back a long way—I had never once known him to take the slightest interest in politics. Victor even eschewed academic politics, not out of conviction, but because protozoa at the end of an electron microscope constitute his essential *raison d'etre*. I narrowed my eyes to get a better look at him and got another jolt of surprise. "Victor. Your hair is darkening."

He smoothed it. "Nonsense."

"Victor," I said somewhat heatedly. "Your hair is darker than it was when I saw you last week."

"I told you about that vitamin supplement I'm taking. I even recommended it to you. But would you take my advice? No!" He threw up his hands, "Heaven forbid. I'll tell you what, Austin. You try these supplements yourself, you might grow a bit more thatch on the old rooftop. And what there *is* of your hair might get some of its youthful color back, like mine is."

"I've never heard such nonsense in my life," I said. "And that includes your lamentable spoken locutions. Don't look now, Victor, but your modifier's dangling."

"Boys," Madeline said in her let's-calm-down voice. "I believe Thelma and I would like some coffee."

"I beg your pardon, my dear," I said. "I'd be delighted to get you coffee. As soon as I get Victor here to see some sense."

"Don't bite your mustache, Austin. And let's ask that nice Deirdre for the dessert menu. And what was it you were saying about modern-day protest, Victor?"

"Yes. Well. A few of my students have set up a committee and asked my support as faculty advisor."

"And the nature of this committee?" I asked.

"Organized Outrage Over Factory Farming."

I mulled over the acronym. "Is this group inclined to violence of any kind?"

"Eh? Of course not. Lucinda . . ."

"Who is Lucinda?"

"Lucinda Whitby. The young woman who is the moving force behind OOOFF." He pronounced the *O* with a shortened diphthong. "She is in my second-year seminar Disease Control in Small Poultry Flocks."

"That is a misleading title for a seminar," I pointed out. "One doesn't know if the subject matter relates to a limited number of birds or to the study of tiny avian creatures."

"It's turkey and chickens," Victor snapped. "Don't be an ass, McKenzie. Lucinda is interested in the substitution of free-range scavenger flocks for the sort of confinement farming that people like O'Leary go for. She has had quite an influence over the content of this seminar."

"Scavenger flocks?" Madeline said a little doubtfully. "You mean wild turkeys?"

"Precisely. There are turkey types that thrive as village birds. The Spanish refer to them as *guajolote*. There is a New World species called *criollo* that have retained their ancestral self-reliance and are widely used by farmers in Mexico. Lucinda believes that—"

Thelma smacked her hand flat on the table, a habit I've always found intensely annoying. It does, however, get one's attention. "I am not feeling well, Victor."

"What?"

"I said it's time to go home."

Victor fumbled to stand upright, forgot he was seated in a booth with me on the outside, and sat down again.

"Do let Victor out of the booth, sweetie," Madeline said.

She and I both got up. Victor and Thelma scrambled out of the booth in that crablike way that such furnishings demand. And without another word, they were both out the door.

"How very odd," I said.

"You think so, sweetie?" During the foregoing conversation, Madeline had managed to acquire both a cup of coffee and a piece of Rudy Schwartz's amazing lemon pie. I saw that she had not forgotten me. Not only did I have a cup of coffee but a piece of lemon pie, too.

"Well, what's all this, then?" I said with deep pleasure. "Thank you, my dear. What's the occasion?"

She set down her fork and smiled at me. When Madeline smiles like that, the world is a brighter place. "Have I told you lately how much I love you?"

"There is no need," I said, "but thank you all the same. This still doesn't explain what's gotten into Victor."

"Austin. For heaven's sake. Put it together. Hair dye. This sudden interest in politics. And he's given up meat! Did you see that vegetarian plate he ordered? Next thing you know, he'll be buying a sports car and signing up for the gym." She ate a large forkful of pie. "Victor Bergland, my love, is having an affair."

"An affair?" I smoothed my mustache. "I am astonished, Madeline. And you know I do not use that word lightly. It means, literally, 'struck down in stone.'"

"Yes, dear."

"Are you sure?"

"I am, dear. Or at least Thelma is. I didn't tell you the whole of my conversation with her at the grocery store. She— umm . . . came across a series of pretty explicit e-mails . . . not sexy explicit . . . romantic explicit."

"My goodness." I ruminated. Then I said, "From whom?"

"Well, that's obvious, this Lucinda Whatisis, that's who." She shook her head. "I'd never thought I'd see the day when Victor took up student protest. Austin? No good is going to come of this."

"Does the pie tribute relate to this?"

"We've been married twenty-two years next month,
Austin. And you've never given me a moment's heartache. So
I suppose the pie tribute relates to this, although . . ." She
sighed. "A truly responsible wife would take better care of
your cholesterol. I hate bein' the food police, sweetie. Especially when you enjoy my cooking so much. But go ahead. I
swear I won't let you fall off the wagon the rest of the week."

I insisted that we share the pie, which appeared to mitigate
Madeline's guilt over allowing me the treat and we spent the
remainder of our evening at the Embassy listening to the jazz
trio and sipping a little brandy.

We came home to an untroubled house. Lincoln greeted us
with a wide yawn from his post by the back door. The light on
in the bedroom adjacent to the clinic in the barn showed that
Joe was studying late. The light in the upstairs bedroom at the
house was off, which meant that Allegra was sound asleep undoubtedly with Juno the Akita at her feet and Odie the house
cat on her pillow.

Madeline headed straight for bed. Lincoln and I wandered
outside. Away from Madeline's calming presence, I became
agitated all over again at the thought of Victor's affair.

In all our years as friendly adversaries, he had never com-
plained about his marriage. Victor was a vociferous com-
plainer when he felt the occasion warranted it, and not at all
furtive about it. Their oldest son had been a pain in Victor's
backside since he'd given up a scholarship to Yale to head out
to LA to be a rock star—a possibility unhampered by a total
lack of musical talent, apparently, since the boy was at least
making enough to cover expenses. And he bellyached end-
lessly about the current dean, the paucity of grants, the
tenured idiots he was forced to manage as chair of his department. But in all that time, he had appeared contented in his
marriage to the mandrill-voiced Thelma. And now this pursuit
of misspent, furtive love. And a graduate student, at that. A
girl, perhaps, close to Allegra's age.

What sort of girl would fall in love with my bumbling,
ursine friend?

I ruffled Lincoln's ears. "It is all profoundly disturbing, Linc."

Lincoln whined and nosed at the palm of my hand. The antidote was no further than a pasture away, however. The relationship of animal to man is straightforward and uncomplicated by deceit and misdirected lust. I would pay a good-night visit to the horses.

I went into the house to procure a handful of carrots and headed out to the paddock to Harker, Andrew, and Pony. I passed Madeline's vegetable garden, abundant with tomatoes, squash, cucumbers, parsley, onions, garlic, and any number of richly colored peppers. Oriental lilies and roses from Madeline's flower garden released their scent into the night.

Calm settled my perturbed spirit.

Upon coming to the paddock, I rested my forearms on top of the gate and whistled. There was the soft three-beat thud of cantering horses. Andrew reached me first. A Quarterhorse, and some sixteen hands high, his long legs give him an advantage over thirteen-hand Pony. Her greed, however, is far more determined than his, and he got one bite before she shouldered him out of the way and hogged most of the carrots for herself.

Perhaps there was a lesson here for Victor.

# Four

〰〰〰

"ARE you acquainted, Allegra, with a young woman named Lucinda Whitby?"

Our household rose early. It was seven o'clock, and another fine July morning. Morning chores had already been done, the patients attended to, the stalls mucked out, our resident animals fed. We were ready to begin the day. Joe had changed his barn clothes for a clean T-shirt and rumpled shorts, headed for a summer course in parasitology. Allegra wore a neat pair of cotton overalls, ready to accompany me on calls. Both were eating Madeline's homemade granola, slathered with fruit and yogurt, with evident enjoyment. So was Madeline. Given a choice between what was essentially horse feed and sticky oatmeal, I was consuming oatmeal. Until my inquiry about Lucinda Whitby, we had been sitting in contented silence, Lincoln at my feet, Juno at Madeline's, and Odie atop the woodstove.

Allegra paused, a spoonful of fresh blueberries halfway to her mouth. "Yes. I mean, I know who she is. She's in my Small Ruminants class."

Allegra is a first-year student in the veterinary program. Small Ruminants is a required course for first-years. Victor's poultry seminar was for second-year's. I was bemused.

"She's older than me, though."

"I," I corrected automatically. "She's older than I."

"Right." Allegra gave me a sunny smile. "Anyhow, she flunked it first time through. So she had to retake it."

"She's got a thing against factory farming," Joe said, "if we're talking about the same person."

"*I've* got a thing against factory farming," Allegra said immediately. "In a perfect universe, there would be no factory farming."

"Who said I approved of factory farming?" Joe said.

"The way you said it said you did." Allegra set her jaw and deepened her voice to a poor imitation of Joe's baritone, "Like, 'she's got a thing against factory farming, the fool.'"

They glared at each other. And I see I must digress yet again. The McKenzie Veterinary Practice had been in a growth pattern. A rather slow growth pattern, at the moment, I must admit. Faced with two superbly qualified applicants, and only one poorly paid position, we had offered Ally and Joe an opportunity to job share. The fact that the job sharees had loathed each other on sight was unfortunate, but not cataclysmic.

I looked at my wife and raised my eyebrows in a rueful expression. Although the initial animosity Joe felt for Allegra (rich kid with an indulgent daddy) was equaled by the irritation Allegra felt whenever she dealt with Joe (smart city kid with a chip on his shoulder), the two had reached a rapprochement of sorts early on. Which is not to say there weren't occasional flare-ups.

"But this Lucinda is really rabidly against factory farming?" Madeline prompted. "Did I hear something about a protest organization?"

"That birdbrain?" Joe said. He speared a slice of ham from the platter in the center of the table. "She couldn't organize her shoes."

"As usual, Turnblad, your facts are wrong," Allegra said.

"It's not a fact, as such. It's an opinion."

"Well, your opinion's uninformed. And yes, Maddy, Lucinda's started this committee against factory farming. They

staged a protest down at the Green Seal warehouse just before
the semester ended. She and this other guy flung themselves
in front of the delivery truck."

"For heaven's sake," Madeline said. "That sounds pretty
birdbrained to me."

Allegra conceded this point with a nod. "Yeah. You're
right. The truck didn't run over her or anything, because she
was in class the next morning looking just fine."

"How *does* she look?" Madeline said with unfeigned interest. "I mean, what does she look like? Is she pretty?"

Allegra looked at Joe in a mildly inquiring way. "Not really. She goes for this retro sixties look, which is so over, I
can't begin to tell you. Long cotton dresses, gross sandals.
And her hair's so long it must be a pain to wash it, because she
doesn't seem to much."

Joe speared a second piece of ham and said briefly, "She's
hot."

Allegra snorted.

Joe shrugged. "What can I tell you? The girl screams sex."

"And I suppose you're an expert," Allegra snorted again.
"Have you even *had* a date in the last six months? I think not.
You spend all your time sucking up with extra projects for this
class, extra credit for that class."

"I don't have a rich father to pay the bills, do I?"

Allegra blushed beet red. Joe was, in fact, on partial scholarship, and his studiousness was a matter of necessity. Cornell
is one of the most competitive schools in the nation. But Joe,
too, was being unfair. Allegra paid for her own tuition out of a
small legacy left by her grandmother, although no one knew
that but Madeline and me. But for that insult, I believe Allegra
would have apologized. As it was, Allegra snapped, "Fine!"
and flounced off to make sure the clinic van was equipped for
the day's calls. Joe grabbed the dirty dishes and stalked stiff-
legged to the sink. He washed and dried them with dispatch,
thanked Madeline for his breakfast, and stamped off to his di-
lapidated Ford Escort to go to class. Juno, her tail wagging
frantically, raced around in circles, certain there was something she could do to clear the atmosphere, she just wasn't
sure what. Odie yawned and washed her face. Lincoln put a
paw on my knee.

"It appears the cease-fire of the past few weeks is at an end," I observed.

"Ally got a letter from Connecticut yesterday."

I raised my eyebrows in inquiry. "Her mother wrote to her?"

Madeline shook her head. "I don't know. She hasn't talked to me about it yet. But every time she gets a letter from Connecticut, she gets whirly for a few days. Let it alone, sweetie. These things have a way of working themselves out."

My wife's wisdom notwithstanding, I thought perhaps I would broach the subject of fractious families with Allegra on the way to our first farm call of the day—routine vaccinations of the two horses owned by Linda O'Leary. I waited until we had been on the road some minutes. Lincoln rode peacefully in the rear seat. Ally sat staring out the passenger window. Her thoughts were obviously miles away.

Allegra's father had been involved in Byco, one of the three largest financial scandals of the decade, and was currently spending one to four in a country-club prison in California. Her younger sister and mother were living in reduced circumstances in Connecticut. This much I knew from articles in *The Economist*. Information that Madeline and I had gleaned in a roundabout way told us that Allegra used most of her legacy from her grandmother to care for her younger sister, saving for herself only enough for vet school tuition.

What we knew from Allegra herself was that a year ago, at the height of the Byco indictments, she believed that her father had conspired to murder her event horse Harker for the insurance money. Allegra had not yet forgiven him.

The best way to settle a shy young filly is to approach from the side in an unthreatening manner. As soon as Lincoln, Allegra, and I loaded into the van and were under way, I said, "This will be your first visit to the O'Leary farm, I believe."

Allegra already had the patient file open on her knee. "Yes. We've got two sets of vaccinations to do. Rabies booster, Potomac fever, rhino, encephilitis. And there's two geldings. One's an Arab," She wrinkled her nose. Arabs can be a handful if underexercised and overfed. "And the other's a Morgan. The owner's Linda O'Leary." She frowned. "That name's familiar."

A better opening could not be asked for.

"She's married to Lewis O'Leary's son Ronald."

"That's the guy that slapped his son around at the feed thingie last night?"

"The same."

"Yikes." Allegra perused the file further. "Uh-oh. This is a PIA?" She glanced over and twinkled at me. "There's a little note at the bottom."

On rare occasion, I impose a Pain in the Ass charge on those clients who prove rude, recalcitrant, or badly brought up. Rarer still, I impose the fine for an unruly animal. "Mrs. Ronald, as she's known in the village, to distinguish herself from Jensen's wife, Maired, is an extremely pleasant woman. The PIA charge is not on her account, nor I may add, on her horses'. Although the Arab is spoiled," I reflected, "and we will need to employ the twitch. No, the PIA is for Lewis, who routinely objects to my bills."

"Linda's father-in-law?"

"And Ron's father, which may be more to the point." I slowed a little to allow a confused squirrel to decide whether to run across the road or not. "Lewis may be wicked. And he is quite possibly the worst father I've had the misfortune to meet. I haven't met yours yet, you see. But Linda doesn't spend much time or energy worrying about what she can't change. She is quite a nice woman. And happily married to Ronald. Lewis? He is what he is."

There was a stiff quality to Allegra's silence. I braked and signaled to turn into the vast hatchery barns where this branch of the "nice" O'Learys lived.

Allegra sat bolt upright as she took in the spread of the place, her sulkiness forgotten. "Holy crow."

"O'Leary's Poultry Farms," I said. "The largest turkey grower in the eastern United States. They handle eight hundred thousand turkeys a year, from egg to carcass. And this is merely a third of it." I came to a stop at the barred gate and both of us studied the grounds. "The grower's located at the home farm, two miles from here. And the brood operation where the eggs are laid is two miles in the other direction. Jensen and Maired are in charge of that. The eggs are sent from the brood operation here, to the hatchery. The poults are sent from the hatchery to the growing barns in large trucks." I got out of the Bronco and retrieved my carrying case from the rear hatch.

"Are all those buildings filled with turkeys?" Allegra asked in awed tones.

"Little ones, yes."

Five long, aluminum-sided one-story buildings surrounded a small ranch house and horse barn. "Three hundred thousand of them at a time." I pulled plastic booties out of the wrappings and tossed Allegra a pair through the driver's window. "The domestic turkey's autoimmune system has been compromised in favor of rapid growth. They spread more diseases than kindergartners in flu season. So we will have to disinfect before we go onto the grounds." An outdoor spigot was located to the left of the barred gate. I took the stainless steel bucket from the back of the van and filled it with a solution of water and Betadine. I sluiced all four wheels with this disinfectant, and then tapped the vehicle horn three times. There was a long pause, and then the gates swung open with a turkeylike shriek.

Allegra pulled on the plastic boots as we drove through. I drew up to the small, four-stall barn that held Linda's geldings and waited until Linda bounced out of the farmhouse and jogged toward us, ponytail flying.

"Something's wrong," Allegra said.

"Eh?"

"I mean something's really wrong. With Linda O'Leary. If that's Linda O'Leary." She scrambled out of the Bronco and took several steps toward Linda, who, I saw now, was in a highly agitated state.. Her face was pale, her eyes were wide and staring, her pupils were dilated. Her thin frame shook with deep, shuddering breaths. If she had been a horse, I would have administered a light anesthetic. As it was, I jumped out of the car and stood there as she rushed up to me. She clutched her cell phone on one hand. With the other, she grabbed my lapel. "Thank god, oh, thank god. I'm so glad it's you. He's dead, Dr. McKenzie, he's dead!"

Allegra put her arms around Linda and said, "Shhh, shhh, shhh," which apparently is as effective with people as it is with horses since Linda made a visible effort to calm herself.

"Come and sit," Allegra coaxed. "Here in the van." She drew the frantic woman over to the passenger side, where she'd left the door wide open. Linda settled sideways in the passenger seat, her feet braced against the running board.

"Now, give yourself a chance to catch your breath," Allegra said kindly.

Linda closed her eyes briefly, and then sighed. "Okay," she said. She looked at Allegra. "Thanks. I'm Linda O'Leary."

"Ally Fulbright," Allegra said. "Are you okay? Is there anything we can do?"

"And who," I asked with some curiosity, "is dead?"

The word almost set her off again. Linda stared at the open cell phone in her hand. She lifted to her ear, then snapped it shut. "Why, it's Lewis," she said in a bewildered way. "Lewis is dead."

# Five

~~~

THERE was, Linda said, no one to drive her to the scene of the death, and she was in no state to drive herself. She refused to consider waiting until her husband left the site and came home. "I have to be with Ron," she said over and over again. "I have to."

"Then we'll take you," Allegra said, "Won't we, Dr. Mac? There aren't any urgent calls on the docket this morning, as far as I can tell."

"Nothing that can't wait until this afternoon," I said. All farmers were resigned to the fact that a veterinarian's time was not his own, and that a 10 a.m. appointment was at best an educated guess about the actual time of arrival. Until we develop an ambulance system for animal emergencies, it must always be so.

Allegra nodded. Her young face was serious with responsibility. "I'll call the morning appointments to let them know we'll be late. And here, Mrs. O'Leary, you sit up front with Dr. Mac. I'll be fine in back with Linc."

Linda sat in the front seat next to me, dazed into quiet. Ally settled in back with Lincoln. I cleared my throat. "And where would we be headed?"

Linda rubbed her face with both hands. "They found his body in the Dumpster in back of the Embassy. The W and S guys. That's where Ron called from. Simon Provost called him."

Jan Walters and Art Sobreski were the Summersville garbage collectors. My old friend Simon Provost is our police lieutenant. And if Lewis O'Leary's body had been dumped in the Embassy Dumpster, I'd wager my best set of scalpels that this was a case of murder. I drove us to the scene of the crime in silence. It took us less than fifteen minutes to reach Main Street.

The citizens of Summersville are on the whole a peaceable group. Yellow police tape girded the Embassy's parking lot, and the expected crowd stood quietly behind it. A lone police cruiser was parked on the sidewalk in front of the restaurant's door, alarm lights flashing silently. The rear of our volunteer ambulance obstructed the single southbound lane. Two uniformed policemen stood at the entrance to the parking lot. Near them, Ron O'Leary sat on the curb, his head in his hands. There was no sign of either of the other two brothers. And Lewis's new widow, Angela O'Leary, thankfully, was nowhere in sight. Nigel Fish, Rita's lead reporter, was very much in evidence, however. He roamed the boundaries of the yellow tape like a retriever after an inaccessible duck.

Linda was out of the van almost before I came to a stop in front of the Williams's Pharmacy. The crowd parted respectfully for her as she ran toward the disconsolate figure of her husband. I parked the van and descended into the street. Allegra was quick to follow, and Lincoln was quick to follow her. I approached the patrolmen, both of whom were known to me from my first foray into life as an amateur dick, as we PIs occasionally refer to ourselves.

I hailed the nearest patrolman. "Arnie. I see we have a situation here."

Arnie Kiddermeister was the youngest of the Kiddermeister clan, most of whom embark on police work after graduating from high school. He stood in regulation fashion, his hands behind his back. His eyes were drawn irresistibly to Allegra who, despite the heat and her coveralls, was as pretty as ever. I took the opportunity afforded by his momentary inattention to duck under the yellow tape.

"Uh," Arnie said, "Dr. McKenzie. Lt. Provost said specifically not to let you in there."

I did not turn around, but withdrew my Honorary Deputy badge out of my wallet and waved it over my shoulder.

"Hey!" Nigel Fish shouted. "Hey! How come the local vet can get in there and the press can't?"

Fish, who seemed unacquainted with my position as a Summersville deputy, did require an explanation. I strolled back to the yellow tape and proffered my credentials.

"You've got to be kidding me." According to Rita, Nigel has just turned thirty, although his balding head and splodgey middle make him look older. As an investigative reporter, he is not half bad. He aspires to a position on a newspaper with greater reach than the *Sentinel*—such as the *New York Times* or the *Wall Street Journal*. He is, therefore, as competitive as a sow after molasses when on a story and inclined to trample those in his way, a characteristic of successful reporters, I believe. A national career was not an impossibility.

Nigel returned my badge with a skeptical sigh. "Okay. How did this come about, Dr. McKenzie? You going to give me a quote?"

"The deputization was an acknowledgment of my modest contribution to the solution of the sniper case," I said. "As you may recall . . ."

"As *you* may recall, Dr. McKenzie, I deputized you for the duration of the case." The badge was plucked from my grasp. Simon Provost had snuck up on me from behind. I plucked the badge back. "Has the murderer been brought to trial?"

"You know darn well the lawyers are still jockeying." Simon resembled those retired gentlemen who make a career as a greeter at Wal-Mart. He has a tired face, rounded shoulders, and a hangdog expression that is quite deceptive. Despite his intransigence regarding the support of the local citizenry—such as myself—in the investigation of his cases, he is quite a competent policeman. "We'll be lucky to get a trial date sometime this year. The defense attorney's bombarding the prosecution with all kinds of case law."

His expression became even more hangdog. "So what are you doing here, Dr. McKenzie? As if I didn't know."

"I am here to offer my support," I said promptly.

"And we don't need it. Thank you very much."

I rose to my tiptoes and peered over his shoulder. The Embassy, along with most of this side of Main Street, is set along a curve in a small tributary that leads let to nearby Cayuga Lake. The parking lot had the best view of the water. The lot itself was empty except for the Dumpster, and an old Lincoln Continental that belonged to Rudy Schwartz, the Embassy's owner.

Several individuals wearing latex surgical gloves and harassed expressions poked about the Dumpster. A stepladder had been placed at its side. A police photographer perched on the uppermost step, his camera aimed into the receptacle's depths.

"I see your scene-of-the-crime people are hard at work," I said casually. There was, I knew, a considerable amount of downtime during investigations such as these. Simon couldn't proceed without the most basic of forensic information: an estimated time of death, a cause of death, trace evidence such as hair and skin that could lead to the apprehension of the perpetrator. Simon was cooling his heels until the SOCO crew was finished. And undoubtedly starved for professional conversation.

"I take it there is a perpetrator?" I added.

"You mean did Lewis O'Leary smack himself in the back of the head and leap into the Dumpster at the back of the Monrovian Embassy? Probably not."

"So there is a murderer to be found."

Simon drew a long breath and expelled it in a sigh.

"Ron O'Leary apparently told his wife that one of the W and S disposal crews discovered the body?"

Simon nodded. "Yeah. And it's a good job that they took a look in the Dumpster before they unloaded it. The deceased was right on top of the green plastic bags from the restaurant."

"There was no detritus *on* the body?"

Simon rubbed his hand across his face. The morning was well advanced. It was hot and getting hotter. "De-what, Doc?"

"Trash," I said succinctly. "If there wasn't anything on top of the body, then it must have been placed there sometime after the restaurant closed at two."

"That had occurred to me."

"And if there was trash on top of the body it must have . . ."

"The time of death," Simon said testily, "seems to have been between midnight, when Rudy slung a pile of garbage bags into the bin, and two, when Rudy put the last of the trash out before he closed up. The body was sandwiched between the two."

"And how advanced is rigor mortis? Or has it passed off altogether? It is now . . ." I looked at my watch. ". . . nine-fifteen. Rigor passes off after ten hours or so. I ask only so that you can get a head start on determining whether he was killed here or elsewhere."

Simon looked skyward with a resigned expression. "Doc. You're a good guy. I even found a lot of your contributions in the sniper case pretty darn useful. But this is a police matter. As soon as the guys here are finished and I can sign off on getting the body out of here, I have to go talk to Angela O'Leary and start to get some idea of when and where her husband was last night. And I have to tell you, Doc. Talking to newly made widows is not my favorite thing. Not by a long shot."

One had to respect the difficulty of Provost's position. I inclined my head to acknowledge his point. Then I ducked back under the tape and made my way through the crowd to Allegra. She and Linc were sitting on the curb. Her knees were drawn up to her chin, and she rested her chin on them. Her face was solemn. Lincoln saw me first and walked over to greet me. Allegra uncurled herself and got to her feet.

"Did the lieutenant say anything?"

I shook my head. "It's early days yet, my dear. We are to continue with the day's appointments, and I will discuss the case with the lieutenant later, after the forensic evidence begins to come in."

"So we're on the case?" Allegra said eagerly as she strapped herself into the passenger's seat.

I checked to see that Lincoln was safely wedged in the backseat, then strapped myself in. "Yes," I said. "Simon may not know it yet, but we are on the case."

"OH, no." Madeline set my inch of whiskey and a pot of tea on the kitchen table. "Don't tell me we're on another case.

What did Simon have to say about your inter . . . I mean your offer to help?"

It was four o'clock, a time of day when the two of us recuperate from our day's labors with a modest amount of food and drink. In the summer, we sit on the front porch and discuss the events of the day since breakfast. It was pleasant here on the porch. The farmhouse is situated so that we looked out over a fair portion of our thirty acres. Most of our land is in hay. Hedgerows of aspen, willow, oak, and beech divide our two ten-acre fields. An inefficient way of grass management, to be sure, but one that allows us the maximum amount of bird life nesting in the trees, and a healthy population of silver fox, rabbit, raccoon, deer, and an occasional mink.

A gentle breeze swept the scent of all this greenery past my appreciative nose. Lincoln dozed near the porch rail and Odie sat on the alert at the southwest corner of the porch for the splash of minnows in the small pond at the foot of the lawn.

Madeline had spent the morning picking fresh strawberries and hadn't learned of O'Leary's murder until her lunch with Lila Gernsback. She'd spent the remainder of the afternoon freezing the strawberries, and although we had spoken by phone, the two of us had not thoroughly examined the matter.

"Are we on the case?" I repeated. "Well, yes. In a manner of speaking. Simon has not yet advanced to the point in the case when he can appreciate my usefulness to the investigation."

Madeline tugged thoughtfully at the curl over her left ear. "Well, I'm sure he will, sweetie. But although you have a *wide* range of expertise . . ."

"Thank you, my dear."

". . . from being able to fix any old piece of machinery on this farm, to being able to fix any sick animal within three hundred miles of here . . . not to mention the fact that you can cut, ted, and bail twenty acres of hay in two days. But just what is it that you can help the lieutenant with? I mean, this seems to be a case of murder, Austin."

I sipped at my Laphroaig and regarded my wife with a sapient eye. The sniper case had been fraught with a certain amount of danger. I could tell where her thoughts were headed. "This is a case with fascinating potential, my dear.

But we are not dealing with a villain who kills for the sake of slaughter. If you're afraid for my safety, you needn't be."

Madeline set her rocker moving a little more vigorously. "I am worried," she admitted. "I'm never happy about getting involved with murder."

"But not all murderers are irrationally violent, as was the case with the sniper. As to the nature of this crime? It calls to mind that great tragedy *Lear*."

"*King Lear*? As in William Shakespeare?"

"The very one." I picked up a cracker spread with goat cheese from our local co-op and bit it in half. "A father with three sons vying for the throne. A substantial kingdom to be divided. And then . . . murder."

"I remember that the old fellow dies," Madeline said with a puzzled air, "but wasn't he nice?"

"Nice?"

"I mean. You felt terribly sorry for Lear. All he wanted was proof of his children's love, and although he went about it in a pretty stupid way, he wasn't mean as a snake." Madeline bit into a goat cheese–filled cracker with decision.

Inside the house, the phone began to ring. Madeline, mulling over the parallels between that great tragedy and our current one, didn't seem to hear it.

"And Lewis O'Leary was mean as a snake. It's not awfully humane of me, Austin, but from what I hear, a whole pile of people had reason to knock him off."

The phone continued to ring. Modern technology has its uses, I will go so far as to admit that. But the irruption of a shrilly ringing phone on a peaceful conversation is not one of them.

"I can think of at least two people unrelated to O'Leary with sufficient motive to kill him," I admitted. "But the probabilities that Lewis was knocked off by one of his relatives are quite high. You know the statistics."

"Mm. So maybe your expertise in Shakespeare isn't going to be as helpful to Simon as we thought." She broke off and sat upright. "Austin, is that the phone?"

"Yes."

"For heaven's sake." She started out of her chair just as the ringing stopped and sat back down again. "Now, that's a shame," she said reproachfully, "What if it'd been some poor animal that needed us?"

I always forget about that. After forty years in academe, when I was only available when I wanted to be, it is difficult to get used to the fact that my current occupation requires me to be on call. "I do beg your pardon, my dear. Undoubtedly, whoever it was has left a message. I will retrieve it."

I went into the house and passed through our living room to the kitchen. At the time of my marriage twenty-two years ago, the house had changed little from the small, uncomfortable Victorian it had been when built in 1862. Madeline had picked up a sledgehammer and changed all that. She knocked the living room, parlor, and keeping room into a single continuous space, updated the kitchen, and painted the walls a pleasant sunburn sort of pink. The living room held a saddle-colored leather sectional couch that faced a brick fireplace. This led directly to our large dining-room table—at which we were able to seat twelve or more in a pinch—and into the kitchen itself, which was dominated by the woodstove that kept us warm in the winter time.

The telephone was atop the counter that separates the kitchen proper from the rest of the living area. The message light was blinking, but before I could retrieve the information, the phone rang again. Mild guilt over the missed call led me to pick the receiver up and speak in less than my usually brusque tones: "McKenzie."

A shout assaulted my ear: "Doc? Is this Dr. McKenzie?"

"Lower your voice, man," I demanded. "I can't understand a word you're saying."

"Thank god, thank god." A sob came over the line. "You've got to help me."

I now recognized the voice. "Gil?"

"It's Gil," he said. "Gil Finnegan. You know, the guy from Green Seal."

"You've sold me feed for ten years," I said testily. "Of course I know who you are. What's the matter with you?"

"I'm in jail," he said bleakly.

"Hm."

"I'm in jail because they think I offed that old bugger O'Leary."

"Hm," I said again.

"And you've got to help me, Doc. They let me make this phone call to you."

"You used your one phone call to call me?" I was quite flattered at this demonstration of trust.

"Hah? Oh. No. I got a lawyer coming in and I called my wife and I had to let the kids and my mother know, so I've been making a lot of phone calls."

"I had no idea the constabulary allowed you more than one phone call."

"I've got my cell," he admitted.

"Your cell phone?"

"Right."

"They didn't take your cell phone away from you when you were arrested?"

"I haven't been arrested. I'm in jail. But I haven't been arrested."

Oh, the power of the misused preposition. "You mean you are *at* the jail."

"Yessir."

"They've brought you in for questioning regarding the death of Lewis O'Leary."

"Yessir."

"And what would you like me to do about that, Mr. Finnegan?"

"Don't do that, Doc. Don't call me 'Mr. Finnegan.' You call me Mr. Finnegan when you're pissed off at me, like the time I got the goat feed mixed in with the horse feed."

"It would have killed the horses," I said sternly. "Rumensin is toxic to equines. A mouthful would have killed them all. You are an idiot, Finnegan."

"It's even worse when you call me Finnegan!" he wailed. "What I want you to do is find out who really killed that old fart O'Leary."

"You mean," I said. "That you are requesting my services as an investigator?"

"I am, Doc. Please. Everybody talked about those two cases you solved for weeks."

"Three, actually," I said, "If you count the case at the Inn at Hemlock Falls."

"I'm in this all alone," he said tragically. "I called a coupla detectives out of Syracuse already, but they all want what they call a retainer. You don't want a retainer, too, do you, Doc? I haven't got any money. After this, I probably don't have a job." Another sob vaulted its way down the telephone line.

"You *are* retaining me, or attempting to. A retainer is the act of recruiting the services of a consultant such as myself. It is not the exchange of currency."

Finnegan's silence was puzzled.

"Let me clarify this. We need to be quite clear, Finnegan. You are presuming that my services are free?"

He hiccupped, and then said, "You mean you charge, too? Just my luck. There's only one lousy detective in Summersville and I got to pay him? Jeez. Sorry, Doc. I didn't mean that. It's just that if I got to pay somebody, I should probably go with like, a pro. Okay. Fine. Well. Like they say, thanks for listening."

"Hold on," I said. I mused for a long moment. "Perhaps we can come to an accommodation, Finnegan."

The silence was expectant.

"I could, perhaps, make an exception for an old friend."

"You mean you could find out who killed Lewis O'Leary for free?"

I considered those great fictional detectives who had never once seen a paycheck for their services. Gregor Demarkian, for example. The man refused to obtain a detective license and refused fees of any kind. Peter Wimsey. Miss Marple. Their names are legion, and their deeds heroic.

"Yes," I said. "I will find out who killed Lewis O'Leary. For free."

# Six

〜〜〜

AFTER a quick trip to the village for suitable supplies, I announced the arrival of our first official client at dinner, with highly satisfactory results.

True to her promise to provide cholesterol-free food after the debauch at the Embassy, Madeline had prepared tofu with lentils. (A saving grace was fresh tomatoes from the garden.) I proffered the bowl of Alpo-like provender to Allegra and said, "The investigatory arm of the McKenzie Veterinary Practice has its first active client."

The news pulled Ally from her glum contemplation of the oil cruet. "We have an investigatory arm?" she asked.

Madeline raised both eyebrows in apparent dismay. "Sweetie! You're kidding!" She sighed. She tugged at one auburn curl in a worried way. "You aren't thinking of giving up the veterinary practice?"

"Not at all. But diversification is the key to growth."

We looked meaningfully at one another. Both of us had faith in the profitable future of McKenzie Veterinary Practice, Inc. (Practice Limited to Large Animals). But the way was

proving more difficult than we had anticipated. The success of
the veterinary school at Cornell, the physical beauty of our surroundings, and the reluctance of many newly hatched DVMs to
leave the nest contribute to an oversupply of clinics in our area,
and a subsequent dearth of clients. On the other hand, while
there are many large animal vets to choose from near Summersville, there were, as Gil Finnegan had pointed out, no detective agencies other than ours.

Joe swallowed a large mouthful of tofu and said, "You
mean a paying client?"

I sidestepped the payment issue with a literal truth: "We
are on retainer."

"It's the O'Leary case," Ally said with a touch of interest.
"It's got to be. Whoa. Did one of the sons call and ask for your
help?"

"No. Gilbert Finnegan is the accused. Or at least he feels he
is about to be accused," I amended. "He spent the latter part of
the afternoon in the village pokey. Provost let him go, but he
was asked to keep the police apprised of his whereabouts."

"Aha. They told him not to leave town." Ally had the first
genuine smile I'd seen since the arrival of the letter from her
former home. "Did Gil do it?"

"I have no idea. I doubt that he would have begged us to
find the true killer if he had."

Madeline had maintained an impressive silence. She rose
to her feet, went to the refrigerator, removed a pitcher of
lemonade, and brought it back to the table, all with an air that
alerted us she had something to say. She sat down, put her el-
bows on the table, folded her hands underneath her chin, and
regarded us gravely. "A detective agency."

"It does seem to be a natural outgrowth of our current activities."

"Our current activities are dangerous enough, sweetie."

There was some truth to this. A veterinarian spends a good
deal of time castrating lively young bulls, wrestling recalcitrant cows, and subduing irritable swine.

I pointed out the obvious. "Our current clients are always
much larger than humans, and far less prone to think before
they act."

"He's got a point, Maddy," Joe said.

"I can't recall the last time I saw a bull with a gun," my wife said tartly.

"I should think there's little chance of gunplay, my dear."

"There's a big chance of that, Austin. You remember what happened at the end of the sniper case."

There had, indeed, been guns at the end of the sniper case. But they hadn't been pointed at us.

"Would we have to carry guns?" Ally said with a frown.

I smoothed my mustache. "Pack heat, as I believe the expression is?" My dear wife's concern for our welfare had to be taken into account. But I was prepared for this. "No, Allegra, we would not. As a matter of fact, we will take an active stance against use of weapons of any kind. I have come up with a motto that sums up the objective of Cases Closed, Incorporated, to that effect."

"Cases Closed? That's what we are going to call ourselves?" Joe made a "not bad" sort of face. "Sums it up, I guess. I mean, we can close a case one way or the other, I suppose."

"It's a name that inspires confidence," Madeline said loyally. "And there's no doubt in my mind that we'll solve every one we'll get. And if we aren't going to carry guns, or beat up on people, I'm all for it. What's the motto, Austin, darlin'?"

" 'Best in Peace,' " I said with a fair degree of pride.

There was a short silence, then a joint murmur of approbation.

"With a view toward closing our first case expeditiously, I've purchased the essentials of an investigator's kit." Conscious of the attention of the entire table, I began to pass around my purchases of the afternoon. "First, a cell phone cum camera for each of us."

There was a second silence, this one of shock. My disaffection for cell phones—noxious emblems of a technology age dedicated to noise, few restraints, and nosiness—was a byword in our village.

"I admit to an unreasonable prejudice. I have relented. The cell phone is a useful adjunct to any detective's operations. Suppose one of us is abducted? Folded into the trunk of a vehicle and spirited away? This little mechanism"—I held my own cell phone aloft—"emits a signal that allows the police to track one's whereabouts."

Madeline, a trifle pale, moved as if to speak.

"I can't see any of us getting kidnapped, really," Ally said. "Honest, Maddy."

"The camera feature is also useful for recording evidence or interviews with witnesses."

All three of the new employees of Cases Closed examined their cell phones with varying degrees of admiration.

"The next useful piece of equipment is this laser measuring tape." I held up this interesting gizmo with pride. "Precise details of the scene of the crime are easily obtained through the use of this device." I laid the laser tape to one side, and withdrew four large magnifying glasses from the shopping bag. "These need no justification. And these," I upended the bag. Four packages of resealable plastic bags tumbled onto the table. A dozen small steno pads fell out last. "The steno pads are for case file notes. The plastic bags are for evidence. The clinic is already equipped with latex surgical gloves, which we will all use when collecting evidence to prevent any contamination of the site." I surveyed the mound of detective tools on the table with pride, and then distributed the items around the table. "I would call this a very good start. As time goes on, we may be in need of various disguises, should our operations call for any undercover work. And I expect that both you and Joe, Allegra, will be able to perform searches on the Internet as needed. But for now, I can't think of anything else we need to open for business."

"A license?" Joe suggested.

"In due course. For now, my status as a volunteer deputy should suffice."

"Provost is okay with this?"

"Private investigators can be a valuable adjunct to law enforcement. Particularly departments that are as underfunded and undermanned as the lieutenant's. I believe Simon will welcome the appearance of Cases Closed on the scene."

"It would be a great help to the community to discover the identity of Lewis O'Leary's murderer," Madeline said. "But are you sure Simon himself feels that way, Austin?"

I waved my hand, as if to sweep away any purported objection from my colleague in crime.

Joe leaned back in his chair. "So, we're good to go with

this. O'Leary's the guy they found in the Embassy Dumpster with his head bashed in?" Joe asked.

"Yes."

"Are we going to give this case a file number, or anything?" Allegra asked. "I mean, if we're taking case notes, I'm assuming there's going to be some sort of a filing system. And does it have a name?"

I thought a moment. Then, inspired by the numerical system for ear tags, I suggested: "We will begin with CC004, to reflect the three murders successfully investigated before the present case."

Everybody took a moment to log this number into their steno pads.

"And we should name the case. Like we did with the sniper murders," Ally said eagerly.

"We didn't name the case the sniper murders," Joe objected. "That was your boyfriend, Nigel Fish."

"Nigel Fish is *not* my boyfriend," Ally said crossly. "Plus he's as old as the hills."

Rita Santelli's star reporter had conceived an enormous crush on Ally upon meeting her for the first time. He had been remarkably persistent in his requests for a date. Ally had been remarkably consistent in turning him down.

I reflected on Lewis O'Leary's character. "We'll call it the Case of the Tough-Talking Turkey. Now. To work. The protocol we used to discover the sniper murder seems appropriate. We will identify the symptoms first, and then arrive at a conclusion as to the nature of the pathology that resulted in O'Leary's death. The symptoms are to be found in the categories of means, motive, and opportunity."

"What about suspects?" Joe asked. "Do we have any idea who might have wanted to knock him off?"

"Not at present. But I have an idea on how to start." I tossed my napkin onto the table and rose. "We will repair to the Embassy Dumpster itself to investigate the scene of the crime."

"But, sweetie, we haven't finished dinner." Madeline looked at the overflowing crock of tofu in distress.

"It's pretty good cold," Ally said.

Joe shoveled the remainder of the serving on his plate

down his throat and pushed himself away from the table. "And I'll be ready for another helping by the time we get back."

"And I," I prevaricated, "will be far hungrier later."

Madeline wrapped the wretched stuff up in tinfoil, and we were off to the scene of the crime.

# Seven

❦

CENTRAL New York is the home of the Finger Lakes, a series of five large and five small freshwater lakes covering five counties, of which Tompkins is one. The whole of Tompkins County is awash with spectacular gorges, streams, and delightful ponds, the result of the passage of glaciers through this part of the continent millennia ago. The village of Summersville is particularly picturesque, as it is set along the banks of a tributary of the Cayuga River, which itself feeds into Cayuga Lake. The five of us—Lincoln accompanies me almost everywhere I go—loaded ourselves into the clinic Bronco and set off for the Embassy just as the sun was setting in a perfect glory of yellow light. The green of the countryside, the blue of the waters, the brilliance of the sky were exceptionally intense. I relaxed behind the wheel with a sense of wonder at the amazing luck that had landed me here, at the epicenter of this wonderful country, with a woman like Madeline at my side, and a burgeoning career as a detective before me. I turned into the Embassy parking lot in a perfect welter of content.

Which was mitigated somewhat by the sight of Simon Provost's battered Chevy Lumina parked just outside the yellow scene of the crime tape that still surrounded the deadly Dumpster.

"Hm," I said. I parked the Bronco and the five of us descended from the vehicle to the asphalt surface of the parking lot.

Simon himself was propped against the hood of his vehicle. Arms folded, chin lowered to his chest, he contemplated the trash bin and the stream that flowed beyond it.

There was an opportunity here, and I was not loath to take it. "It may be politic," I said after a moment's pause "to have a quick bite in the restaurant until Lieutenant Provost leaves to go home to his own dinner."

Madeline cast a shrewd glance my way. "Austin, you've never backed off of anything in your life. You just brought us down here 'cause you won't eat that tofu."

I raised my hand in protest. "Not at all, my dear. Simon has frequently commented on the public annoyance offered by my contributions to his investigations."

"He always ends up coming around. You hate tofu," Madeline continued, inexorably, "and you like Simon and it's as clear as clear to me what you're up to. Fried onion rings is what you're up to."

Alerted, perhaps, by the resonant tones of my wife, Simon looked up from his brown study and raised his right hand in salute. "Hey, Doc. Mrs. McKenzie. Stop by for the burgers?"

"Tell you what," Madeline said into my ear, "I'll take the kids inside, get a beer and we'll chat Deirdre up. She must have some useful information about last night." She waved the steno pad at me. "We'll take notes."

"Excellent idea," I approved. The three of them sauntered around the corner and disappeared. Lincoln and I walked up to the yellow tape.

"Oh, come on in," Simon said with a resigned sigh. "But leave that tote of yours outside, okay? And the dog, too. Just in case."

I was conscious of indignation. "It is not a tote."

"Yeah? Then what is it?"

"It contains the basic tools for an investigator's kit."

Simon sucked his lower lip and regarded me thoughtfully. "It does, huh."

"I do see the advisability of keeping Lincoln away from the area, however." I turned to my dog, held my palm out, and turned it over. Lincoln dropped into a model sit-stay. I slung the kit over my shoulder and stepped over the yellow tape. "Any results from the preliminary review of the corpse?"

"Yeah." Simon turned back to the contemplation of Dumpster. "O'Leary was killed somewhere else, and his body dumped here."

"Interesting," I observed. "Do you have a time of death?"

Simon waggled his hand in a "maybe, maybe not" gesture. "Nine-ish."

"Nine-ish."

"Give or take an hour."

"Naturally."

"He was at that to-do you were at last night, right?"

"He was, indeed. He and two of his sons and their wives. And Mrs. O'Leary."

"You remember what time he left?"

I considered. "It was some little time before my speech. Ten minutes, perhaps. He waited until the dessert course, gulped it down, then gathered the rest of the family together and walked out the door. I confess I was somewhat relieved. He is both rude and interruptive, and I had little desire to deal with that in the course of my discussion. I spoke from eight-fifteen to eight-forty-five."

"All of the O'Learys left?"

I thought back. "I believe that Ronald and Linda stayed for the speech. Yes. I'm certain of it. Cornell's been supporting a coccidiosis study at their growing barns for the past two years, and I had occasion to ask him about the course of the results. Ha!" I added, suddenly.

"Ha?"

"There was a weedy young fellow with him. Looked a great deal like a Narragansett Bronze. The graduate student in charge of the data collection, I believe."

"Like a what?"

"A Narragansett Bronze is a rare breed of turkey. It is the result of a cross between—"

"I got it, Doc. So this kid that looked like a turkey . . ."

"He wasn't a kid, precisely. In his late twenties, if I'm any judge. At any rate, Ronald began to volunteer some very interesting information about the results of this new coccidiacide . . ."

"The what?"

"It's an additive to the feed that prevents a systemic infection in poultry. The current additive used by Green Seal Feeds is effective to a remarkable degree. But it doesn't eliminate the spread of the disease altogether. This new product apparently does."

"And?"

"And the young man . . . Krippendorf, that's it, tugged at Ronald's sleeve to prevent him from disseminating too much information."

"So then what?"

"So I concluded my speech—to general torpor, I'm afraid—and Madeline and I left."

"Who'd y'all eat with at the dinner?"

"It could hardly be called dinner," I said indignantly. "Mushy peas and reconstituted mashed potatoes. The turkey was quite good, however. But we sat with Gil Finnegan and his district manager. Karen Crown." I narrowed my eyes at him. "But you know all this, Lieutenant. As I understand it, you interrogated Gil for some hours this afternoon."

"Uh-huh. And Finnegan? When did he leave?"

"Gil followed Lewis O'Leary out the door. I believe he meant to speak to him."

"About what, d'ya think?"

The words were on the tip of my tongue: about the accusation of grain thievery Lewis had flung at him, naturally. Which would lead Simon to inquire, what accusation? Which would land the first official client of Cases Closed in the soup, so to speak.

"He didn't say."

"This is what happens when people get evasive, Doc. Their eyes shift back and forth. Their body language gets a little edgy."

"You don't say."

"Fact."

"There was," I amended cautiously, "a slight *contretemps* at the dinner table."

"The deceased accused Finnegan of ripping him off."

"That he did, although," I added with some annoyance, "the 'deceased' was alive, well, and kicking on all eight cylinders when he did so."

"And how did Finnegan react to that?"

"With outrage," I said promptly. "It was clear to the meanest intelligence that the charge was trumped up. Although."

"Yeah?"

"It may not have been clear to Karen Crown."

"This is the district manager for Green Seal."

"She's new in the post, I believe. Most of us here are well aware of O'Leary's business tactics."

"True enough." Simon wandered past the Dumpster and onto a narrow strip of grass that bordered the tributary to the lake. I wandered with him. Lincoln, far too well trained to utter a vocal protest, cocked his head in mute appeal. His ears tuliped forward. I nodded and he sprang to his feet and bounded to the water's edge. "You and Madeline left the high school about when?"

"Nine o'clock or so. There was a short discussion period after my speech. We came here, of course."

"You did?"

"We were both hungry," I admitted.

"So you got here about what, nine-ten, nine-fifteen?"

I was dismayed. I knew what was coming. I prepared myself to keep a steady gaze and calm demeanor. "About then."

Simon rubbed the back of his neck. "That'd be about the time of the murder."

"Apparently."

"You see anything? Hear anything?"

"There were cars leaving the parking lot, of course." I looked him straight in the eye.

"Uh-huh. Any one you notice in particular? I have to tell you, Doc. That when people lie to me, they usually look me straight in the eye."

I tried to recall a case in which any of my favorite fictional detectives had been faced with being both defender of the client's innocence and a witness to the evidence of guilt. I

could not. I sighed. The truth will out. "Yes, we did see someone in particular."

SOME moments later, I joined Madeline at our favorite
booth. She was polishing off the remains of a Monrovian
Reuben, a specialty of the house rivaled only by the great
hamburger itself. She was alone.

"Is Lieutenant Provost with you?"

"He had business elsewhere." I sat down. I looked about
the bar for Deirdre. She was in earnest discussion with Joe and
Allegra. But with the sixth sense that characterizes all great
waitstaff, she sensed my presence and raised an eyebrow in
my direction. I pointed at Madeline's plate.

"Elsewhere? Was he going to go find some more suspects?"

"Not exactly."

"Then what was he off to do, Austin? I thought he'd come
in and have a nice cold drink with us. It's not like him to hare
off without saying bye-howdy." She swallowed the last bite of
corned beef, sat up straight, and looked at me, her blue eyes
large with dismay. "He's not gone and solved the case already,
has he?"

"He *thinks* he may have," I said. "But he is wrong."

"Who does he think did . . . oh, no. He asked you about the
argument Gil had with Lewis at the high school, didn't he?
And then he asked you if we saw anything suspicious when
we got here last night and you told him we thought we saw
Gil's pickup. Didn't you?"

Deirdre placed a large platter of salad in front of me. A
slab of grilled chicken lay athwart the lettuce. I looked at
Madeline over the rim of my glasses. She smiled at Deirdre.
She smiled at me. And then she said with a startled look, "My
goodness, Austin. You just got our client arrested for murder."

WE returned home in a reflective mood. Joe and Allegra
greeted the news of Gil's pending arrest with philosophic reserve. "Although," Joe said as we settled at the dining-room
table for a strategy session, "there's always the chance that he
did it."

"Gil Finnegan bash an old man over the head with a base-ball bat? I can't see it," Madeline said. She placed a plate of oatmeal cookies in front of Joe and then sat down next to me.

"O'Leary was in his late sixties," I said, "which is hardly elderly, my dear. And we are not sure about the murder weapon."

She covered my hand with her own. "Of course it isn't, sweetie. When I look at you now, Austin, what I see is the man I saw twenty-two years ago in the admin offices of the cow barn at Cornell. You haven't changed a bit."

"Is that where you met, Maddy?" Ally asked. "At the school?"

"Madeline was the Xerox repairman, or woman, I should say." I smiled with the memory of the first time I'd seen her. Her auburn hair had been pulled in a knot at the top of her head. Toner had smudged her cheek, making her eyes bluer than usual by contrast. She hadn't yet assumed the queenly proportions that she had now, but her figure had magnificence, then, too. Admiring professors surrounded her. Victor had been among them. The old goat.

"Was it love at first sight?" Ally asked.

Joe made a noise of disgust.

"Well, I don't know about that," Madeline said.

"It was for me," I said.

"Austin stomped into the room bellowing about some lost samples of bovine back fat." She started to laugh. "He walked right up to Victor lookin' ready to tear him limb from limb and he stopped dead."

"He stopped dead when he saw you?" Ally said.

"That he did. Stood there with his mouth open and a lot of chicken feathers on his tie."

"I'd been injecting eggs with bovine sera," I said. "I'd been face-to-face with chickens for weeks."

"Did you stop dead at the sight of him, too, Maddy?" Ally asked.

Madeline's laugh subsided. A soft smile curved her cheek. "No. Not at the time. But it didn't take long at all." She rapped her knuckles on the table. "Enough of that. You two had quite a talk with Deirdre. Austin had quite a talk with Simon. We need to pool this data. We need a plan."

"Well." Ally glanced at Joe. "We picked up a lot of gossip. I don't know if you'd call it data, as such."

"Deirdre's the kind of woman who thinks reality TV's unscripted," Joe said cynically. "And her imagination inflates the littlest thing into a freakin' big deal."

"She's not that bad," Ally said. "You're peeved because she made a pass at you and you didn't know how to blow her off with any class at all."

"Deirdre wouldn't know class if it hit her with a truck."

"Your idea of class *is* to hit somebody with a truck."

"Stop, now," Madeline said calmly. "She was servin' Jensen O'Leary at the bar last night. Austin and I both saw her. And the Berglands both saw Cordy O'Leary and his dad mix it up not half an hour before the two of us got there. She must have heard and seen something that happened for real and that wasn't the product of an overactive imagination."

Joe shrugged acceptance. "I guess. If you boil down what she told us . . ."

"He means we should ignore all the comments like, 'he looked ready to kill him right there on the spot,' and 'You should have seen the hate in his eyes,' " Ally said.

"Right. Basically, Jensen came into the bar about six-thirty. He drank beer. Deirdre served him three, she said, over a couple of hours, which isn't much at all, so saying the guy was a crazy-ass drunk . . ."

"We know we can ignore all that," Ally said.

"Right. So. Lewis comes rolling in a bit past eight-thirty. He starts yelling at Jensen, 'Where the hell have you been,' 'How come you weren't at the Green Seal supper,' yada, yada, 'You no-good SOB.' Typical fatherly behavior."

Madeline raised her head and looked at him. The bitterness in Joe's voice was unmistakable.

"So Jensen just sits there and takes it. Then Cordy comes rolling in. I guess his mother had sent him to get Lewis back home. Cordy starts in on his father, 'You lying SOB,' yada yada."

"Lying?" I said. "Did he say what his father lied about?"

"Not that Deirdre could tell us. We asked. Then Lewis started in on somebody called Maired. Called her a slut and worse."

"Maired," I said. "Jensen's wife."

"Yeah?" Joe smiled grimly. "Well, she's not a favorite of Lewis's, I can tell you that. Then Rudy Schwartz comes rolling out of the kitchen."

"Deirdre went to get him when it looked like it was going to break into a real fistfight," Ally said. "So she missed some of the yelling."

"And Rudy told them to take it outside. Which they did."

"They went into the parking lot," Ally said. "Deirdre sneaked into the kitchen and watched them. There was a lot of cussing, but nobody threw a punch. Cordy got into his truck. Jensen went back into the bar. Lewis stood there looking at his watch."

"As if he were waiting for someone?"

Joe shrugged. "Hard to say, I guess."

Ally shrugged, too. "Anyhow, Rudy made Deirdre get back out on the floor and she didn't see what happened after that."

"And this was about what time?" I asked. I had been making notes as they talked.

"Quarter to nine, Deirdre says." Ally craned her neck and looked at the time line. "Sheesh. All this stuff seems to have happened within the space of an hour."

"Or less." I leaned back and contemplated the time line. "Provost places the time of death between eighty-thirty and nine-thirty. Provisionally."

"Won't he be able to get any closer after the full autopsy's done?" Madeline asked.

"Probably not," Ally said. "I haven't had a lot of post-mortem stuff yet, but it'd be tricky to pin a death any closer than that."

"Too many variables," Joe agreed.

"And Provost says the body was moved," I said.

"Well, of course it'd been moved," Madeline said. "How could you kill somebody in a Dumpster? I mean, why would the person be in the Dumpster in the first place?"

I gazed at my wife in admiration. Simplicity is the hall-mark of genius. "You are absolutely right, my dear. But there is a curious fact. And that is the placement of the body."

"You mean that it was between the loads of garbage," Ally said. "Yeah, well, we asked Rudy that. And he said he took the last load of garbage out at two, just before he locked up and went home."

"Before two a.m.," I said. "And after midnight. Where do you suppose it resided for three hours?"

I made a note.

"Won't the forensics tests give us some idea of that?" Joe asked. "I mean, there's no way that a killer could get rid of all the trace evidence."

"It certainly should." I made another note.

"So that's what we learned from Deirdre." Joe leaned back in his chair and clasped his hands behind his head.

"We have a great deal of work to do," I said with satisfaction. "The very first thing is interviews. We need to establish where Gil Finnegan was from the last time Lewis O'Leary was seen alive to six o'clock in the morning, when the boys from W and S garbage collection discovered the body. And we need to know where Lewis O'Leary was from eight-forty-five, when he was in the parking lot, looking at his watch, until the time of his death, and from the time of his death until the appearance of the body in the Dumpster."

"I hate to think on it," Madeline said. "But do you suppose he was lying on the ground somewhere in that lot when you and I got there about nine-fifteen?"

I looked at her with sympathy. "I have no idea, Madeline. I hope not." I tossed the pen onto my pad. "What I do know is that it's after ten, and time that the two of us went to bed. We'll need an early start in the morning. Joe, what's on the call sheet for tomorrow?"

Apparently there was no need to look. "An autopsy out at Best's Boers. It's a goat. They've got it in the cooler. They left a message on the voice mail service and I called them back and arranged it for eight o'clock."

Autopsies on small ruminants take an hour or less, depending on the loquacity of the grower. Frank Best was a taciturn man. "So with luck—" I began, only to be interrupted by the phone. I stood up and looked at the flashing button. It was the clinic line, not our private number, which meant that at best it was Gil Finnegan begging to be set free and at worst a client who needed my services at this ungodly hour of the night. I reached for the bloody thing. Before I could pick it up, Allegra darted past me and said into the receiver: "McKenzie Veterinary practices. This is Allegra. May I help—" She stopped in midflow. She listened. Her face turned white. She replaced the receiver into the cradle with a crash and turned to Madeline. Her face was set in stone.

"There'll be someone at the front door in a few minutes. Don't let them in. Don't tell them I'm here." Her eyes grew brilliant with tears. She turned on her heel and walked up the staircase to her room. She paused halfway, and said, "Please."

A few moments later, she slammed her bedroom door closed. The sound reverberated through the house.

Juno, curled in her basket by the woodstove, was startled into waking. She jumped onto the floor and looked at each of our faces in turn, her eyes anxious, her tail wagging furiously.

"Juno," I said. I pointed up the stairs. The dog whirled in a circle, then raced up after her mistress.

"Well," I said into the astonished silence.

The doorbell rang. Once, twice, and then once again. In unspoken accord, all three of us—four including the redoubtable Lincoln—went to the front door. Joe pulled it open and stepped back.

I'd seen the man standing there three years ago. On television. With his lawyers, going in and out of the courtroom. He'd been dressed in natty suits. Well-tailored pinstripes with rep ties and immaculately laundered shirts.

The man in front of me was not the man he had been before. A faint stubble shadowed his chin. His hair was long and in need of a washing. His chinos were rather the worse for wear and the T-shirt he wore carried a logo that read Elaine's Good Eats.

"Hi," he said. "I'm looking for Allegra Fulbright."

"My goodness," Madeline said. "You must be her father."

# Eight

〰️

"SORRY to trouble you," Sam Fulbright said, "but I need to borrow a bit of cash for the taxi."

I looked past his shoulder. The Summersville Cab Company consists of two drivers and one vehicle. Dougie Watson is the night man. He leaned out of the driver's window and waved at me. "Hey, Doc."

"Hey, Dougie," Madeline responded. "How're you doing these days?"

"Can't complain," Dougie said.

"And Myrna? Her arthritis any better?"

"Not so's you'd notice," Dougie responded gloomily.

This particular village ritual over, Madeline got down to business. "This man asked you to bring us to our house?"

"Said you'd be good for the fare." The light over our porch is a powerful one. I could see the lines of worry in Dougie's face.

"Surely," Madeline said briskly. "How much is it, Dougie?"

"Fifteen'll do it. Price of gas is sky-high these days."

"And another fifteen will take him back to town?" Joe stuck his hand in his back pocket and brought out his wallet.

Sam Fulbright licked his lips nervously.

Dougie looked doubtful. "I s'pose so. Where d'ya want me to drop him?"

"The Super Eight," Joe said briskly. He cast a hard, unforgiving look in Fulbright's direction. "Or that little motel just off of Cayuga. The Siesta."

Fulbright made a small gesture of resignation. "Don't bother with the return trip. I'm thumbing it these days." He closed his eyes, and then opened them as widely as possible. "If I could just see Allegra for a few moments before I go back on the road?"

Madeline always knows what to do in situations of this type. I looked at her for guidance. She bit her lip, tugged a curl into place over her ear, and said, "I'm sorry, I don't think so," just as Fulbright pitched forward and fainted on our front stoop.

"Oh, dear," Madeline said. "Oh, phooey." She knelt by the man's side and gave his cheeks a brisk slap. Fulbright's eyes fluttered open. "Sorry," he said. "It's been awhile since I've eaten."

"Well, hang it anyway," Madeline said crossly. "Austin, give Dougie the fare. Joe, give me a hand getting Mr. Fulbright here into the kitchen."

"But, Maddy."

"Don't 'but, Maddy' me. We'll give the man some dinner and a hundred dollars and send him on his way. But we can't leave the big jerk in a heap on our doorstep."

Joe's brow darkened, but he grasped Fulbright by the shoulders, heaved him to his feet, and propelled him into the house. He may have been a little rougher than necessary settling the man into a chair at the dinner table, but Fulbright remained upright.

"There is a good deal of the lentil tofu left, I believe." I said. "Quite nourishing."

Madeline snorted delicately through her nostrils, like a mare expressing distaste at a rotten smell. Which was not inapt since the unfortunate Fulbright did indeed smell as if a shave and shower had been several days in the past. She slapped a bowl of her excellent beef stew in the microwave, brought a loaf of her onion rye bread from the bread box, and removed the plate of fresh tomatoes we'd had at dinner from the refrigerator and placed them on the table.

Joe turned one of the dining-room chairs back-end to, straddled the seat, and sat down. He stared at Fulbright without any expression at all.

I found myself badly in need of a Scotch. I poured a generous two fingers into a highball glass, and, with reluctance, a mere half inch into a glass for Fulbright. I set it in front of him as Madeline placed the heated stew on the table.

The man was clearly hungry, but his table manners were gentlemanly for all of that. He ate quietly, with little fuss, but with the dedication of the genuinely famished. None of us spoke until he had finished the stew, the bread, and the tomatoes, and settled back into his chair with the Scotch in hand.

"There are," Madeline said tartly, "shelters for folks without any resources at all."

Fulbright nodded. "I've seen my share of those. But nothing south of Syracuse. Unless there's such a facility in the village."

"Just Father Caspian at the Church of the Holy Mother of God," Madeline admitted. "So things have come to that, have they?"

"They have indeed."

"No relatives to help you out? No friends?"

He shook his head briefly.

"You could get a job." I jumped at the sound of Allegra's voice. It was as frigid as any wind from the Arctic. She came down the stairs at a glacial pace, her eyes cold, her mouth set in a hard and stubborn line.

Fulbright half rose to his feet. "Ally. Princess."

Madeline snorted. I snorted. Joe sneered.

"Don't you dare call me that," she snapped.

Fulbright sat down. He swallowed hard.

"Well," Ally demanded. "About the job?"

"I intend to. I meant to." He looked down at his shabby, dirt clothes with a bewildered expression. "But people won't hire you when you look like this. Not even at Valu-Mart."

Madeline opened her mouth to speak and then closed it.

Allegra advanced through the living room and into the kitchen. She stopped very near to me and broke the silence. "What do you want?"

"Just a chance to get on my feet again. I didn't know what it would be like. I hadn't any idea. I wasn't prepared for . . . all this."

"To be broke?" Joe's amused voice broke into this little melodrama with a salutary and entirely welcome effect. "Come to think of it, it is something that requires a little practice. Guys like you, with no street smarts? I'm pretty amazed you made it out this way."

"Where did you come from?" Madeline asked.

"Oh, Schuylkill is my guess. Right?" Joe grinned. "The minimum security prison?"

Fulbright rubbed the back of his neck. It didn't seem possible to me that any human being could look as tired as he did.

Allegra slipped her hand in mine. It was very cold. But it was Madeline she appealed to. "What do I do now?"

"We'll let him have a bath and a bed. And we'll decide about it in the morning. You go on up to bed yourself, Ally. We're all too tired to deal with it right now. As soon as I get him set to rights, I'll come up and we'll talk."

I confess my hopes of an early bedtime with my wife were well and truly dashed. It was after midnight when she and Lincoln finally came into our bedroom. I looked up from the copy of *Cows Today* that I had been perusing for the past hour and more and flung back the comforter. "Come and lie down with me, my dear."

She yawned. "Three minutes," she said. "I just need a quick shower. I swear the man has cooties."

"Lice?" I said with interest. "Really?"

Madeline stuck her head through the half-open door to our bathroom. "Really. I took everything he was wearing and dumped it out in the burn pile. And I gave him some of your old clothes, the ones I was going to take to Goodwill."

"You put him in the junk room?"

This is a small room off our kitchen that holds a collection of rubber boots, cast-off umbrellas, and decades-old copies of *Science*. (Madeline got rid of our copies of *National Geographic* years ago.) There is a small cot in there, a relic of our camping days. The sound of the shower drowned out any reply she made. A few minutes later, she drifted into our room, the scent of lilacs trailing behind her, wrapped in a silk robe and nightgown I had given her recently, for no reason at all other than the fact that purple suits her down to the ground. She settled next to me and tucked her head comfortably into the side of my neck.

"You spoke to Ally?"

I felt her nod.

"Is there anything we should know?"

"No." Madeline gave me a violent hug, then sat up in order to turn out the bedside light. "You'd think these guys would know better, Austin."

"What 'guys' would that be?"

"These high-flying, money-mad executives. You can't turn on the TV or read a magazine without some story that shows you chasing money and ignoring your family is going to lose you the love and respect of your wife and children and these guys go ahead and do it anyway. I guess they think that it'll happen to everybody except them. So here's Ally's father, down on his luck, trying to lean on a family he's despised for years, and it's the same-old, same-old and I could just spit." She snapped out the light and settled against me in the dark. It took a few minutes, but I could feel her indignation seeping away. "The thing is, it's all new to her, the poor kid. This kind of pain is all new to her."

# Nine

BREAKFAST was an unsettled and silent affair. Madeline's eyes were shadowed with fatigue. Joe brooded. Fulbright made no appearance. We didn't see Ally at all. It was her morning for routine barn chores, which are accomplished between five and six o'clock and she had returned to her room by the time I came down for breakfast.

The dour atmosphere affected the dogs. Lincoln kept close to me. Juno pattered downstairs, left most of her kibble in her dish, and pattered back up. Only Miss Odie—with the detached insouciance that characterizes *felinus domesticus*—remained untouched. Were Odie a person, Madeline believes that she would take the form of a bad-tempered Chinese empress.

Joe loaded the autopsy kit into the Bronco, and we set off for Best's Boers well before eight o'clock. The forecast was for rain later in the day and the air—like my mood—was thick and humid.

George and Phyllis Best's goat farm lies west of Summersville. Its two hundred acres are spread over a series of small hills that overlook Cayuga Lake. It is a spectacular setting. The shabbiness of the farmhouse and surrounding buildings makes little difference when the eye is occupied with the intense blue of the lake and the splendor of the hills.

The house—an elderly double-wide trailer—is set well up the side of the tallest hill at the end of a winding drive. In the wintertime, it's impossible to get to the place without a four-wheel-drive vehicle. I slowed down to negotiate the curves while Joe retrieved the client file from its folder.

"Quite a few visits over the past couple of years," he said as he paged through the file.

"Goats are taking little creatures," I said. "But they are prone to a variety of ailments." We drove around a sharp curve and the small farm lay before us. A herd of kidlings cavorted in the driveway. I slowed the Bronco to a crawl.

"Jeez, Doc. The goats are out."

"Goats are always out. Any goat farmer will tell you that if a fence will hold water, it will hold a goat."

Joe grinned. I was glad to see it. He had been far too somber this morning. I felt my own glowering mood lift a trifle. "We are to perform a necropsy on one of the goats?"

He paged through the file. "Yeah. When Mrs. Best called yesterday I told her to stick the body in her chest freezer until we came out. She didn't seemed fazed by that at all."

"They've been in goats for twenty years. Before that, it was sheep for thirty."

"Hm. There's a note here I haven't seen before in any patient file. It says PNB." He glanced at me. "This anything like the PIA?"

"That's Madeline little joke. It stands for Post No Bills. And the reason you haven't seen it before is because we rarely use it." I pulled to a stop in front of the tin-roofed shed that was the principle shelter for George and Phyllis's herd. The kidlings swarmed around the drive like a hive of four-legged bees. Baby goats put me forcibly in mind of cocker spaniel puppies, particularly baby Boers. They are brown and white and have long floppy ears. We watched them leaping in the sunshine, and my mood lightened still further. "The Bests are frequently cash short. They pay when they can. And they are meticulous farmers." I gestured at the farm around me. The three tin-roofed sheds that housed the goats were neat and well kept. Healthy goats grazed peaceably in well-maintained pastures. Boers are a handsome breed and these goats were fine specimens of their kind, with glossy coats and well-rounded rumens.

But the wire fences were patched with bailing twine and plywood. The tin roofs were rusted through the coats of cheap paint. An ancient Ford tractor sat on blocks in the middle of the yard. "You know as well as I do that small family farms like these are a thing of the past. When the Bests pass on, some chucklehead from Long Island will buy the two hundred acres and turn it into a vineyard selling exceptionally bad wine."

Joe wasn't convinced. "But we don't charge them at all? It's a good thing we're diversifying. Kind of hard to keep the practice going if we don't get paid."

"This morning," I said, "we will be paid in information and rewarded by the sight of a well-kept farm devoted to the welfare of the animal. Money is only one kind of value, Joseph. Besides, this will give you some hands-on field experience. I'd like you to conduct the autopsy yourself."

George and Phyllis emerged from the shed at the same time. I knew for certain that Phyllis had just turned eighty. George was some years older. Years of hard physical labor had gnarled their bodies. Years of work in the outdoors had weathered their complexions. Both had snow-white hair and wire-rimmed spectacles. George sported a full white beard. For the past ten years, they had posed as Mr. and Mrs. Santa Claus in the Summersville Christmas pageant.

But their own lives were not untouched by tragedy. They had lost their oldest son in a tractor accident many years before. Their one surviving daughter was a sour-faced old crock who'd just retired from the high school as a special education teacher. Louise hated farm life in general and goats in particular. She'd been after her parents to sell the property to developers for years.

Joe and I got out of the Bronco. Joe went to the rear to retrieve the autopsy kit. I hailed the Bests, and shook hands with George, whose normally cheerful face was glum. Phyllis shooed the kidlings back into the shed and greeted me with a worried smile. "Sorry to call you out, Dr. McKenzie. George says to tell you right up front that we haven't seen a bill from you for the last visit and that you be sure and get that out to us. And this one, too."

"I'll speak to Madeline," I said. "But it was my impression that you are paid up."

Phyllis set her jaw. "We don't take charity here, Doctor, I thought we made that clear from the beginning. George is meticulous about the bills. And we make enough to get by."

"You do, indeed," I said. "Phyllis, you haven't met our clinic assistant. May I introduce Joe Turnblad?"

"Aren't you a good-looking young man," Phyllis twinkled up at him. "But too thin. And Mrs. McKenzie is such a good cook, too! Have you been with doctor long?"

"Just about two months, Mrs. Best."

"Call me Phyllis, dear." She turned to me and set her hands on her ample hips. "Now about the bill, Doctor."

"This call is in something of a practicum for Joseph," I said. "A field study, as it were. The costs, of course, will be assumed by the clinic, since you will be doing us a favor by allowing Joe to conduct the farm call."

The slant to her jaw became more stubborn. She looked at George, and her face softened. "George says okay. As long as it isn't a handout. We pay as we go, here."

"Nothing of the kind, Mrs. Best," Joe said briskly. "It isn't every day that I get a chance to conduct a goat autopsy."

"Looking forward to it, are you?" she said with a pleased air. "I like a boy who enjoys his work."

Joe scratched his head. "Yes, well. Can you tell me what happened to the goat?"

"She just keeled over yesterday afternoon. Put her head right up and died."

"How old was she?"

"Goodness. Let me think. Just under five months. She's out of one of my favorite does. Biscuit, over there."

A cream-colored goat with a shadow of Boer brown on her neck and shoulders peered at us through the fence. She bleated dolefully.

"There you are, Biscuit," Phyllis said in comforting way. "She misses her kid."

"And the buck?" Joe asked.

"Art Bailey brought one of his bucks to visit last year. We bred back Biscuit, Lavender, and Paprika."

"And those kids are fine?"

"Oh, yes. They seem to be."

"You kept the body cool?"

George nodded.

"You want we should bring her out?" Phyllis asked.

"Let's find a flat spot well upwind of the shed," I said. "A picnic table would be ideal. Joe, you might give George a hand with the carcass." I picked up the autopsy kit. Joe followed George into the garage attached to the Bests' little house and emerged with the body of a doeling wrapped in a large green garbage bag. Phyllis led us to the backyard. I took the disposable tarp from the kit and Phyllis spread it over the table. Joe and George slung the dead goat on top. I searched through the kit for the scalpels and handed them to Joe. George, still silent, retreated to his wife's side and took her hand.

I removed the garbage bag and conducted a visual inspection of the body first. The ophthalmologic tissue was pink. The nostrils were clear of mucus. The rumen was well defined. I placed my hand over the rear quarters, which were well fleshed. "She's in good shape, Phyllis."

"We're worried about worms. It's been so wet."

Parasites are of particular concern to goat growers. Unlike other ruminant species, caprines have little or no resistance to a horrifying variety of intestinal pests. And once a parasite population infests a pasture, only the snows of winter will act as a disinfectant. An epidemic of deer worm or *Haemonchus* would devastate the Bests.

"We'll know soon enough." I stepped back from the carcass and nodded to Joe to begin.

The physical process of a field autopsy is simplicity itself. The belly side of the carcass is opened from throat to stern. Tissue samples are taken from all internal organs, and fluid samples extracted from the bladder, heart, and gut. The specimen jars in an autopsy kit are labeled heart, lung, liver, and so on. I set the specimen jars in a tidy row at the head of the picnic table and observed the deftness with which he made the long incision. The interior of the animal was neatly laid open to view. It is a marvel to me to contemplate the splendid construction of animals. Heart, lungs, liver, rumen, spleen—that all the organs work together is one of God's marvels.

The boy knew what he was about. I moved back to give him room to work and stood next to George and Phyllis.

"You heard about the tragedy yesterday," I said, after a suitable pause.

"We sure did." Phyllis shook her head. "Awful thing. Just awful. Of course, George always said that Lewis was headed for a bad end, didn't you, George?"

George nodded.

"George said he heard Gil Finnegan did it."

"That remains to be seen," I said. "But yes, Finnegan's been arrested, I believe. I have my doubts as to his guilt, however."

"You do?" Phyllis's eyes rounded in surprise. "Isn't that something? George doesn't think he killed Lewis, either."

There was a pause. Joe snipped carefully around the liver. Conversation appeared to have come to a halt. I searched for a comment that would prompt more information. Madeline had suggested more than once that I pay more attention to the sensitivities of my fellow man, but I was stymied. How would I get the infernal woman to gossip? Finally, a thought occurred to me. "Phyllis? You and Angela O'Leary are both members of the Auxiliary, are you not?"

"Yes. Yes, we are. I've got banana bread in the oven to take to the poor soul this afternoon."

"So you haven't yet had her reaction to her husband's death?"

Joe paused in his dissection of the heart. His shoulders shook. With laughter, I believe.

"Well, I'm sure she's very sorry about it all," Phyllis said with an air of bewilderment.

Joe dropped a segment of the aorta into a specimen bottle and said, "Why do you think Finnegan's innocent, Mr. Best?"

I suppose my question was clumsy by comparison. Joe's seemingly casual inquiry was far more productive. Phyllis relaxed and said chattily, "Oh, George says it's more than likely one of the boys that did Lewis in."

"One of the sons," I said in an attempt to empathize. "Terrible thing. Terrible. Hard to believe, patricide."

"George doesn't think it's hard to believe at all. The way he treats them is just a scandal."

"But he's been treating them badly for years, by all accounts." I smoothed my mustache. "Why pick the man off now?"

Phyllis looked earnestly at George, who raised his eyebrows and then shook his head. "Well, there's all that worry about the money. Angela says they're just barely keeping body and soul together. Although George thinks that hard to believe. I mean, just look at all they've got over there. Why, the place is huge."

George made a noise like a garbage disposal.

"Well, that's certainly true," Phyllis said. "That Cordy running around with Cheryl. There's a motive for you."

Although George seemed to be in clear and unambiguous conversation with his wife, I was temporarily at sea.

"Cordy's the handsome one," Phyllis said. "And he's what they call a swinging bachelor."

Joe's shoulders shook again.

"He spends a lot of money on his women, Cordy does, and George's question is: where does it come from? Only place all that money could come from is that turkey farm. George thinks Lewis must have found out Cordy was taking money behind his back—Lewis's back, that is—and spending it on girls like that Cheryl."

I reflected. "But which Cheryl would that be?"

"From the bank. Angela's never liked her. That little piece is just after what she can get, and like George says, who better to help Cordy steal that money from his daddy than a bank clerk?"

George hadn't spoken a word yet, as far as I could determine. Perhaps he communicated on a frequency heard only by dogs and his wife. He cleared his throat and Phyllis punched her husband in the arm. "Go *on* with you. She is a sexy little piece, I'll give you that. But it's a fact that Angela's wondering if there's something funny going on at the bank. She told me so herself. And if maybe Cordy and Cheryl have cooked something up between the pair of them to rob Lewis and Angela and Lewis found out about it, well, I'm surprised Cordy didn't get his own head blown off before he blew off his daddy's."

"Good heavens," I said. "Lewis's head wasn't blown off, Phyllis. He was struck over the head. With a blunt instrument, to borrow police parlance."

"You know, Doctor, I don't understand one word in twenty from you sometimes, but if you're saying that George was mistaken about the blowing off the head part, I do understand that. I don't know were George gets these ideas," Phyllis confessed. "Our Louise says her pa's addicted to gossip."

"Here we go, Mrs. Best." Joe backed away from the picnic table and held the surgical scissors aloft. A small piece of bright red tissue dangled from the blades. "This is a malformed aortic valve. Could it be a heart attack, sir?"

"Possibly," I said. "It is never wise to theorize in front of the facts. We wouldn't know for certain until the necropsy results are complete."

"Is that a good or a bad thing?" Phyllis said anxiously. "A heart attack. It's bad for the doeling, of course. But it's a big load off George's mind if it isn't those scary worms. At least we don't have to worry about the rest of the herd. So is a heart attack that killed her?"

"Hard to say at this point." I walked over to the carcass and peered into the cavity. Muscle and organs were a healthy pink. Parasites drain the animal of blood. Anemia is usually the proximate cause of death. The liver, spleen, and lungs in particular would have been as pale as wax had parasites been the cause. "It is highly unlikely that the cause of death was due to parasitic infection. I can probably set your minds at ease about that. If death was indeed due to a heart attack, this may be an anomaly."

George rumbled.

"An anomaly is something that only affects this animal," Joe explained.

"So we don't have to worry about the rest of the herd getting the anomaly disease?" Phyllis said.

"Probably not," I said. "Unless this is a genetic deformity passed down from the doeling's parents. I would say the odds are small. I'll reserve judgment until the tissue samples have been biopsied."

"Oh, dear." Phyllis patted her cheeks in a distracted manner. "It's never easy, is it?" She sighed, gently. The kidlings, having wriggled free from their pen again, bounced into the backyard and started to eat the bean plants in the garden. George shooed them away by waving his hat. Phyllis watched them bounce out of the yard. The relief on her face was plain to see. She turned to me. "Please, Dr. McKenzie. Won't you and your young Joe have some coffee? I made you some of that zucchini bread you like so much."

"Thank you, we will."

George gathered up plastic tarp and wrapped the little carcass into a tidy bundle. Phyllis disappeared into the house. George disappeared in the direction of the shed. I pulled at my mustache in satisfaction. "You did very well, Joseph."

"Thank you, Doc. It's the first necropsy I've done alone."

"I wasn't referring to that. Although it was neatly and cleanly done. No, I was referring success of our foray into the detective business. We now have a motive to explore. And if it is indeed a fact that Cordwainer and his poopsie have been stealing from his father, we'll have two suspects to add to our list." Phyllis emerged from her back door with a plate loaded with the promised delicacy. The loaf was dripping with freshly churned butter. "Perhaps more possible motives will emerge over the zucchini bread."

But the Bests had no further murder-related gossip to offer. George did suggest a possible lead, however. The word in town was that Jensen had just discovered his wife Maired was having an affair with Cordy.

"Which just confuses the issue, doesn't it?" Joe asked. We were headed back down the winding drive to the highway. "You'd expect Jensen to whack his brother, not his father."

"What a family," I mused. "Betrayals of all kinds, all over the place. You know, the rumors of the affair may not be true. Small towns are notorious hotbeds of gossip. And Summersville is a small town. But it's all grist for our mill." I signaled and pulled onto Highway 15. East would take us back home. West would take us to Ithaca and the Tompkins County courthouse, where our client currently languished. I headed west.

"We're going to interview Gil Finnegan?" Joe asked after a moment.

"We are. We are in need of some hard facts before we proceed any further. Where was Gil at the estimated time of death? Where was he in the interim between the death and the disposal of the body in the Dumpster? Besides, I want to save myself a trip to Syracuse. As I understand it, he'll be held in the county jail until the arraignment, and then he'll be shipped out to Syracuse to await the trial. My last discussion with him was fraught with sobs. I didn't get much out of him at that point. If he sobs during out interrogation today, Joseph, we must think of a diversion to keep him coherent."

"I'll try to come up with one." Joe stretched his arms over his head and grinned.

# Ten

~~∞~~

THE last time I'd been in the Ithaca County Courthouse, the old cut-stone building had been a hive of reporters, TV people, and members of various law enforcement agencies. On this Wednesday morning, the atmosphere was less frenetic, but an aura of urgency hung about the place all the same. Men and women in pin-striped suits hustled briefcases up and down the shallow steps. Uniformed patrolmen lounged in the halls in that hunched, wary fashion that seems to characterize the urban police professional. Knots of worried-looking civilians in T-shirts and the repellant footwear known as flip-flops formed isolated clusters, like soldier ants on a foray for food.

Joseph and I passed through the metal detector and followed the signage through the building and down a set of stairs to the basement. A grim-looking young woman in a blue uniform sat behind bulletproof glass, reading a report of some kind. I rapped smartly on the glass barrier, and she glanced up with porcine indifference. "Yeah?"

This is a greeting that nettles me considerably. My night's sleep had been shortened by the incursion of a former felon into my home. This same felon was going to unsettle my peaceful home for some undetermined length of time—not to mention the hurt he had already caused a child Madeline and I held in considerable affection. My black mood of the early morning returned like a crow to carrion. "Do not 'yeah' me, young woman," I snapped. She looked blankly at me, then from side to side, as if to find someone to signal "get a load of this!" The person she found was Joseph, who leaned past me and said with a consciously charming smile, "Hey, there."

She turned pink. Joe has that effect on young women, and even, I have noticed, on women much older than himself such as Madeline's best friend, Lila Gernsback.

"Help you?" she said to Joe.

I rapped on the glass again. She turned her gaze to me reluctantly. "What!"

"I am here to see Gilbert Finnegan, that's what." I delivered my best admonitory glare, which, I must admit, seemed to have no effect at all. She swiveled her piggy little eyes back to Joe. "Name?"

"Austin McKenzie," I said sternly.

She flipped through a blue binder. "I don't have any Auster Mc-whatever here."

"You do," I said firmly.

"I don't," she said. "And if you aren't on the list of approved visitors, you're not getting in."

"Now, see here, young lady. And I used the term *lady* advisedly . . ."

"Doc." Joe grasped me by both shoulders and set me gently aside. "Stand over here for a sec. Okay?" He returned to the reception desk and the bellicose receptionist. "Maybe you can help us . . ." His gaze traveled down to the ID dangling from her breast pocket. ". . . Janet. It is Janet, isn't it? Or can I call you Jan?"

"Jan," she breathed, with a sappy look on her face. "Maybe your name's on this list. What is it?"

"Call me Joe." He rubbed the back of his neck and gave her rueful smile. "I'm a detective."

Janet's brow wrinkled in through. "Plainclothes? I haven't seen you around her before."

"Private."

"Private? You're a private detective? Jeez. I don't know, Joe."

"Gil Finnegan's retained us to represent him on the O'Leary murder case."

"Huh. Yah. Well."

"You can call back there, can't you?" He jerked his thumb in the direction of a steel door carrying the legend TOMPKINS COUNTY JAIL.

Janet called. After an interminable wait, we were searched, forced to march through yet another metal detector, and then shown into a small room with a linoleum floor, no window, a battered metal table, and two chairs. After another interminable wait, a uniformed policeman came in with Finnegan, who looked much the worse for wear after one night in the clink.

"You gotta a half hour," the patrolman said. "Then I haul him back. I'll be right outside the door if he gives you any trouble." He hitched his pants up, scowled at us all in a way meant to be menacing, and left the room.

Joe folded his arms and leaned against the far wall. I remained sitting. I gave our first official client the once-over.

Gil was in a pitiable state. He was not dressed in prison garb, but in an unironed short-sleeve cotton shirt, jeans, and a brand new pair of tennis shoes with no laces. He had clearly been provided with some sort of shaver and a bar of soap, but his hair was lank and his face was sweaty. He sank into the chair on the other side of the table and said. "Jeez, it's good to see you, Doc. You, too, Joe. After I talked with you yesterday, I wasn't sure that you were going to take my case. You are going to take my case, aren't you? That's why you're here, isn't it? You're going to find out who really killed that old fart O'Leary."

I glanced at the closed door. "It might be politic to refer to O'Leary as Mr. O'Leary and not 'that old fart' in future."

"Politic," Gil repeated.

"Advisable," I said by way of clarification. "And speaking of advisability, we need the name of your lawyer."

"My lawyer. Well, that's kind of a problem, see? I don't really have the what d'ya call it, funds for a real lawyer. So they gave me one for free. Like I didn't have funds for a real detective. So I got stuck with you guys."

Not twenty-four hours ago, the man had been pleading for my help! I frowned at him. "What you have is a public defender. Who is paid by the state of New York. You do not have a lawyer for free. It is costing somebody something. As is the use of my agency's services." I sat back in my chair. It doesn't do to belabor the point with people like Finnegan. "And does your lawyer have a name?"

"Julie something. Julie Cavanaugh."

"Do you have her card?"

"Yeah, Doc. Sure. Right here." He proffered it to me. I made a note. I returned the card to him, flipped my notepad to a fresh page, and said:

"Begin."

"Begin?"

"I want you to start at the beginning, go on, and then stop." (This offhand literary allusion surprised a chuckle out of Joe.) "I want you to tell me precisely what you did after you left the high school cafeteria at eight o'clock."

"The night of the murder, you mean."

During my career as professor of bovine sciences, Victor Bergland had spent many evenings encouraging me to be "more responsive to student needs," by which he meant I had to suffer fools gladly. I never have. I never will. I looked Gilbert Finnegan straight in the eye and reminded him that New York had the death penalty and that if he didn't focus on the task at hand, he was bound to swing. Or fry. Or shuffle off this mortal coil via whatever method the state deemed humane at the moment. And that if he didn't provide me with lucid answers to direct questions, he just might leave this world a lot earlier than the state intended, since I would kill him myself.

"The problem is, of course," Joe said as we wended our way back to Summersville an hour later, "that the death penalty in New York is only for cop killers and some kinds of premeditated murder."

"My opinion on the probable outcome of his future acted as a motivator," I responded. "So, phooey on his sensibilities. And he gave us what we needed."

Joe looked at my notes and chewed on his lower lip.

**CASE NO.: CCOO4**
                              **Murder Night: Finnegan's activities**

8:00 p.m.: follows V to parking lot. Sees V drive off. Sits in truck and "thinks about things."

8:15 p.m.: cell phone call from V who demands his presence at the Embassy by 8:45.

8:22 p.m.: tire blows on F's pickup truck. F pulls over in a cul-de-sac by Winston St. Changes tire. Sees no one.

9:10 p.m. (approx.): races into parking lot. V not there. Races out of parking lot. (Verified by A and M McK.)

9:20 p.m. (approx.): back in the Winston St. cul-de-sac. Sits and "thinks about things." Falls asleep.

2:45 a.m. (approx.): drives home via Rte 332 and Rte 15. (Verified by witness for the prosecution at 7-Eleven.)

3:00 a.m. (approx.): arrives home to angry wife. (Prob. not a likely witness for the defense.)

7:00 a.m.: arrives at work at Green Seal.

"I'll tell you something," Joe said. "That's the lousiest set of alibis I've ever seen. The poor schmuck is toast. You *sure* he didn't knock off O'Leary?"

"You think he hit O'Leary over the head in the parking lot, dumped him in the back of his pickup truck, drove off, and sat for several hours until it was safe to go back to the Embassy and throw the body in the Dumpster? That's what the police think."

"Why the Dumpster?"

I assumed the question was rhetorical. "Why indeed. Why not the river? Or weight the body down and toss it in the lake? Why not any number of things? My old friend Provost has not created a rational theory of the crime, which has led, of course

to Finnegan's erroneous arrest. As to Finnegan's guilt—I am
not sure of anything at the moment. We are considerably
handicapped by the dearth of forensic data."

"The cops have that."

"The cops have that," I agreed. "And so should his defense
lawyer, don't you think? What is the address on that card?"

"One-forty West Seneca."

I frowned. Not the most salubrious part of Ithaca—but
then no part of Ithaca is actually blighted. I made a U-turn
at the infamous Octopus intersection and headed back down-
town. We arrived at 140 Seneca in fairly good time. The contrast between summertime traffic and the months when the
students infest the town is considerable. Had we attempted the
same trek in September, it would have taken us three times
longer.

The law office of J. P. Cavanaugh, Esq., was located between a down-at-heels student apartment building and Thayer's
appliance store. The building had once been a single-family
house of less than 1,000 square feet, judging by the outside.
The three wood steps leading up to the front porch had been
recently painted dark blue. The clapboard siding showed signs
of inexpert repair and the frames of the windows flanking the
front door were in sore need of wood putty. A pot of Martha
Washington geraniums bloomed next to the porch railings.
I opened the screen and applied the brass knocker firmly to
the door itself.

A faint shout came from within and Joe and I walked inside.

The living room had been converted into a reception area.
There was a fireplace at the north end, and windows on the
other three sides of the room. An unoccupied desk sat under
the east-side windows. A half-open door to the right of the fireplace led to a kitchen. A door on the other side of an archway
that bisected the room was firmly closed. It opened abruptly,
and a very beautiful woman walked out. She had long, silver-
blonde hair wound into a tight bun and eyes of an unusual violet. She was blessed with what I've heard called an English
complexion, smooth and porcelain clear, with a faint blush of
peach on her cheekbones.

I have always preferred mahogany hair and blue eyes, myself. But beside me, Joe quivered as if he had been stung.

"Ms. Cavanaugh" I said.

"No. I'm so sorry. Julie's not here."

The creature's voice was as lovely as her complexion, "soft, low, an excellent thing in a woman." And like my Madeline, she was a southerner.

"I'm Bree Beaufort. And I'm holdin' down the fort for Julie for a few days. A family emergency, I'm sorry to say. Can I help you gentlemen?"

Joe gurgled. I grasped him by the arm and set him firmly in the chair that stood by the fireplace. "I don't know if you can, Miss Beaufort. We require Ms. Cavanaugh's services as an attorney. Specifically in her capacity as public defender."

"Julie's not a public defender as such, Mr. . . . ?"

"I beg your pardon. I am Austin McKenzie. This is Joe Turnblad."

Joe muttered something that may have been "Hi."

"Well, Mr. McKenzie. Julie does take on a few cases for the defense attorney's office. Are you inquiring about a specific case?" She waved gracefully at the couch. "If you are, please have a seat, and I'll see if I can help you. I'm covering the office in Julie's absence and I was reviewin' some case files just now."

"You're an attorney?" Joe managed.

She smiled at him. "Newly minted, I'm afraid. From North Carolina. My daddy thought it'd be a good idea to take the New York bar in case I got a job offer up here, and I've just been sworn in, as a matter of fact. I was takin' a little time off to visit Jules. Now, which one of you is in need of a representation? Is this a criminal case?" She turned that violet gaze on to Joe. "Are you about to be arrested?"

Joe leaped from his chair and shouted, "No!" He ran his hand through his hair and took a deep breath. "That is to say, Dr. McKenzie and I are here on behalf of one of our clients."

The violet gaze switched to me. "*Dr.* McKenzie?"

"He's a vet. A veterinarian. I am, too. Or I will be, in a year or two. And we're detectives. Both of us. And veterinarians."

Love was making Joe stutter. I deemed it wise to intervene. "We're here on behalf of our client. Gilbert Finnegan."

"Oh," she said. "The murder case. Some information came in on that this morning."

"I thought perhaps we might take a look at the autopsy report," I said.

She smiled. "You did?"

"We did," I said firmly. I indicated the couch with a sweep of my hand. "If we may?"

"I suppose we should."

I waited until she had settled gracefully onto the couch, and then sat down at the other end. "Finnegan has hired us to discover who murdered Lewis O'Leary."

"A veterinarian? And a soon-to-be veterinarian?"

I had the distinct feeling that—in her gentle, southern way—Ms. Beaufort was teasing us. "In our capacities as investigators."

"I see."

"Both the forensics report and the autopsy results would be invaluable in conducting a thorough investigation."

"I'm sure they would." The violet eyes cooled a little. "I'm sorry to have to ask you this, but do you have some sort of identification? And a copy of the contract between you and Mr. Finnegan?"

The look Joe and I exchanged was dismayed. "I am afraid," I said after a moment, "that we have neither. Our foray into the detective business is relatively recent and our . . . er . . . secretary is behind in the paperwork." I sat and turned the problem over in my mind. A copy of this week's newspaper was on the coffee table. The headline screamed: "Local Grower Killed." "What you need is a character reference. Or at the minimum, some sort of verification of our bona fides. Would the publisher of the *Summersville Sentinel* suffice?"

"I believe he would."

"The number is 555–4100. Ask for Margarita Santelli."

Miss Beaufort rose fluidly and walked over to the reception desk. I turned to Joe, who was staring stupidly in her direction. "Did you bring your cell phone with you?"

"What, Doc?"

"The one with the camera gizmo. I thought perhaps we could take pictures of the relevant reports in the event Miss Beaufort does not have access to a copy machine."

"Uh. Yeah. I did." He patted his pocket in an absentminded way. "But I think I saw a Xerox machine in the back office."

"Dr. McKenzie?"

I turned. She held the receiver in one hand, the other covered the mouthpiece. "Ms. Santelli has given you quite a . . . um . . . recommendation. So I'll be happy to give you what support I can from the case file. And she asked me to ask you where this week's column is." She held the phone out to me. "Would you care to speak to her?"

I struck my forehead with the palm of my hand. "The devil you say." The copy for "Ask Dr. Mckenzie!" (the exclamation point is courtesy of the *Sentinel*'s advertising guru) is due Wednesdays before noon in order to make the Thursday print deadline. Recent events had completely driven the task from my mind. "I shall have to speak to her." I rose and advanced to the desk. Miss Beaufort handed the phone to me, held one finger up in a "just one minute" gesture, and disappeared into her office. I held the phone to my ear. "Good morning, Rita."

"Good after*noon*, Austin. What's all this about you going into the detective business?"

"A recent development," I said. "It occurs to me now that you may be interested in an interview with myself and perhaps some of my staff. In my capacity as the founder of Cases Closed, Incorporated."

"At the moment, I'm interested in the copy for the column," Rita said briskly. "But tell me this, in your capacity as the founder of whatchamacallit . . ."

"Cases Closed."

"Right. Do you have the inside skinny on what's happening with the O'Leary case?"

"Naturally."

"Then you don't feed the news to anybody but me or Nigel. Please?"

"I'm happy to support the *Sentinel*, as you know. But I'd like to propose a quid pro quo."

"And what kind of this for that would it be?"

It is always a pleasure to deal with a woman who recalls her Latin. "Hands off my copy," I said promptly.

"I beg your pardon?"

"I confess to a character failing, Rita."

"You? Never?"

There was, I think, a good deal of affection mixed in that

scornful inflection. "You edit my copy with a one-hundred-pound thumb. Last week you even deleted the illustration I sent in. It is outrageous." I stopped and took a breath. I was becoming quite heated.

"The photo you sent in was too explicit for a family newspaper."

"How are my readers to identify *Strongylus vulgaris* through a mere written description? Visual aids are valuable adjuncts to learning, Rita. As a newspaperwoman you should know that. None better."

"As a newspaperwoman, I know that a picture of a lot of wriggly worms in a pile of horse manure is going to turn readers off. So the answer is no, Austin. No deal. You do *not* get free rein to gross out my readers in my newspaper." The sound of a phone slammed into its cradle rang in my ear. I set the receiver into the phone rest, only to have the instrument ring immediately. I picked up.

*"And get me that column by this afternoon!"*

I replaced the phone and looked at it thoughtfully. "How did she know which number to call back?"

"She probably hit star-sixty-nine," Miss Beaufort said as she reentered the reception area. She held a sheaf of papers in her hand. "That automatically redials the last number called."

"It does?" I withdrew my steno pad from my coverall pocket and made a note. That was a useful piece of information for the employees of Cases Closed.

I rejoined Miss Beaufort as she reseated herself on the sofa. "The public defender's office faxed over a copy of the preliminary forensics report and a summary of the autopsy. It looks as if your client died from a subdural hematoma secondary to a blow on the head." She handed a set of the papers to me and one to Joe. "The ME seems to think that a tire iron is the most likely choice for a murder weapon."

"One blow to the back of the skull," I said. "Hm. Probably by a left-handed assailant. Now that is fortuitous."

"It is, isn't it?" Miss Beaufort said. "The incidence of left-handedness in the American population is less than fifteen percent. If you applied that probability to your suspect pool, it might help narrow it considerably."

"It might, indeed."

"On the other hand,"—Miss Beaufort's smile was lightly ironic—"A killing backhanded swing with the nondominant hand is certainly possible."

"Good heavens," I said. "You are probably right."

Joe uttered the first complete sentence I'd heard from him since we'd entered the law office. "How do you know all that?"

"Well, I play tennis, for one thing. And for another, I have a sort of Velcro brain. All kinds of irrelevant stuff sticks to it. Like the incidence of left-handedness." She shook her head ruefully, causing a few tendrils of silver-blonde hair to float around her cheekbones. "Now, take a look at the forensics report. Don't you find a lot of it very peculiar? Not to mention incriminating."

I scanned it. "By incriminating, I assume you're referring to the fact that a tire iron was found in Finnegan's pickup truck. Traces of a blood type similar to the victim's were found on it."

"That's one."

"And traces of a blood type etcetera were found on a tarp in the truck bed."

"That's two."

"And to the presence of turkey feathers on the accused's white cotton dress shirt and the coveralls of the victim."

"Three times and the poor soul's out." Then, "Turkey feathers," she repeated with an odd inflection. "Does that represent some sort of weird talisman?"

"It represents the fact that O'Leary was a turkey farmer," I said.

"Oh. Really?"

"Indeed. And this, the albumen and fetal protein found on the front of his coveralls?"

"Turkey eggs?"

"You are absolutely right. Turkey eggs. The O'Learys grow turkeys from egg to market weight. It's quite unusual to find a hatchery, a breedery, and a grower in one operation. It has always been my impression that they are quite profitable as a result. Which is to say it's not unusual to find this kind of evidence on the victim. One would collect like specimens from any of the O'Learys, alive or dead."

"I see." She tapped the papers into a neat pile and placed

them on the coffee table. "Is there an explanation for this other data? The river water on the pants cuffs?"

"It may help explain where the body lay until its final disposition in the Embassy Dumpster," I said. "The restaurant is set on the banks of a tributary to the Cayuga River."

"So the body was covered by a tarp that was left in the bed of Gil's pickup truck and concealed by the river? I wonder why?"

I made several notes. This was a sagacious woman.

"Would you like to see the scene of the crime?" Joe said suddenly. "I could meet you there tonight. Around six-thirty or so. We could get something to eat. You might want to see some of the village, too."

Miss Beaufort regarded him kindly. "Aren't you just the nicest thing, Mr. Turnblad? But I'm up to my ears in work while Julie's away. Perhaps another time."

Madeline has referred to this sort of response as the southern kiss-off. It occasionally fails with northerners, who are far more direct. It failed now with Joe, who said, "Why don't I give you a call Saturday?"

I intervened before the atmosphere became too painful. I rose to my feet and grasped my love-struck assistant by the arm. "Thank you for your help, Miss Beaufort. We'll be in touch."

She turned her head slightly, so that Joe couldn't see, and gave me a wink. Then she accompanied us the front door. "You'll keep me informed? Things don't look too promising for the poor soul."

I tugged at my mustache. "You can say that again."

# Eleven

THE demands of domestic and clinic life persuaded me to
shelve any further investigatory activity until I had time to as-
similate what we had learned and decide on a course of action.
We spent the remainder of the morning making farm calls.

Joe and I returned home to a late lunch and an empty
house. Both dogs were gone. My wife was not there, either. I
had not been in touch with Madeline all morning—an unusual
occurrence, since we speak several times a day. But I had been
unusually busy. And from the details she left in the note attached to the refrigerator, so had she.

> *Lila needs a hand for a couple of days, so I've taken
> Ally over there. Harker, too. Lunch on second shelf.
> Linc and Juno with me. (No pie for you, Austin!!!!!)*

"Pie," Joe said, reading over my shoulder. I pulled the note
out from underneath the magnet and retired to the table to
think it over. Joe pulled covered dishes from the refrigerator
and began piling them up in front of me. He slapped down two

forks, a bag of rolls, a roll of paper towels, and pried open the
two largest Tupperware containers. The first was chicken
salad. The second was pie.

"What kind of pie is it?"

"Cherry," he said through a mouthful of chicken salad.
Madeline's chicken salad features apricots, celery, and homemade mayonnaise. It is exceptional.

"If you have less than your usual quarter pie, I might have
a piece without incurring the usual recriminations."

"She'd ask if you'd taken a piece and you'd fold," Joe said
with a notable lack of sympathy. "And then she'll give me a
look and I'll feel like crud. But I'll risk it if you want me to."

"There is nothing as irritating as noble self-sacrifice, Joseph.
I'll have the pie. And if she gives you the look, so be it."

Joe obligingly handed over the pie plate. "So Ally's at
Lila's to help out? That's kind of odd, isn't it? And why do
you think they took the horse?"

"Unless all six of her barn stuff have come down with the
flu at the same time, I can't imagine Lila would need barn
help. The most logical explanation is that Ally needs Lila's
help in schooling the horse." Lila, a voluptuous divorcée, was
between husbands at the moment. At such times, she relieves
her boredom by taking on eventing students.

"We've got the arena here."

"True." I folded the note in two and addressed myself to
the chicken salad. "I can only surmise that our unwanted
houseguest is still here and that Madeline has decided that
Lila's house offers a suitable refuge."

Joe looked around the living room. "Then where is he?"

"I have no idea. Perhaps he'll turn up when we do clinic
rounds."

We finished lunch, tidied the kitchen, and went to check on
our resident patients.

The clinic offices are attached to a twelve-stall barn, which
is in turn attached to a large indoor riding arena. When I
bought Sunny Skies nearly forty years ago, a refugee Hungar-
ian who'd been in the dressage business had owned the place.
In the early days of our marriage, both Madeline and I rode in
event classes, and we put the indoor arena to good use. But it
had remained unused for many years. I had considered reno-

vating the space to accommodate more patients. But then Allegra came to work for us. She brought her horse Harker with her. The horse had taken a year or more to recover from a bad fall, and she had just recently begun to school him in the hope of fitting him up to ride again and the indoor was an ideal place to reaccustom him to work. I must admit to a certain amount of disappointment that the space had not—as yet— been needed for purposes of expansion. But, as Madeline frequently reminds me, it takes time to build.

Pony, Andrew, and Harker occupy three of the twelve stalls attached to the arena when they are not turned out in their pastures. The remaining nine are for any of our large animal patients that require extended care.

Currently, none of our large animal patients did.

But the clinic cages were full, thank goodness. Although the phone book lists us as a farm practice, we do take in house pets. Two cats and one Labrador Retriever were recovering nicely from hysterectomies. A pet mallard suffering from pesticide poisoning was not. I made the necessary phone call to the client's mother, and we put the boy's pet down. It would be a far happier world without pesticides. Joe attended to the dressings on an injured ewe, and I checked the answering service for messages. There were none.

These activities took something less than an hour. We saw nothing of Sam Fulbright. A quick look into the junk room off the kitchen showed that the cot had been slept in. His knapsack had been stuffed under the bed. A check of the downstairs bathroom told us the shower had been used. But there was no sign of the man himself. Joe took himself off to the university library, and I settled down to toss off a draft of this week's column "Ask Dr. McKenzie!"

The column invites the animal owner to write in with questions that should be properly answered by professionals such as myself. It is part public service and part, although I have not confessed this to Madeline, a means of bringing the attention of the public at large to the scope of the services offered by our practice. I had been humbled to realize how secure a place academia had provided for us; the laissez-faire world outside those secure environs can be a dog-eat-dog sort of place.

The first letter was in a twenty-four-pound rag content envelope in heavy cream.

Mrs. Charles Hunt The Reaches Summersville, New York

07.02.06

*Dear Dr. McKenzie:*
*I am the owner of a pedigreed German shepherd who was sold to me by a supposedly reputable kennel in Germany that has won dozens of awards in breed shows. I have had the dog for three months and in that time it has destroyed a genuine Louis XIVth table, torn up the carpeting in my sunroom, and chewed up three pairs of very expensive shoes. What makes me even madder is that the dog will not allow anyone to get near me. We have tried giving the animal "time-outs" by locking it in its run. We have also used the electric collar to train it to no effect. I believe the kennel has sold us a dog of bad character, and that the dog should be put down. Can you please give me your criteria for euthanasia? That is, when should a supposedly "healthy" animal be put to sleep? My husband will abide by your decision.*

*Sincerely yours,*
*Ripped Off*

I like to think that a hallmark of my column is a certain sense of humor. My response to letters like these takes no time at all:

*Dear Ripped Off:*

*If you are asking for my criteria for owner euthanasia, which is more appropriate in this case than thinking about putting down your pet, it is tripartite:*

*1. Buy a large, muscular, intelligent dog bred to do a challenging job like security work or drug sniffing.*

2. *Confine the dog to a crate for long periods of time when it becomes bored with nothing to do.*

3. *Blame the dog when it goes half crazy with boredom. Return the dog to the kennel and take a long walk off a short dock.*

*If you are asking my criteria for euthanizing a healthy dog, there are none.*

*Very truly yours,*
*Austin McKenzie, DVM*

I was rather pleased with the colloquialism "long walk off a short dock." And Rita frequently accuses me of stuffiness!

The second letter was in a pink envelope. The address was printed in block letters. An iridescent sticker of a teddy bear had been affixed to the back of the envelope.

*Dear Dr. McKenzie:*

*My name is Erica. I am seven. My big brother is Eric. He is twelve. He says unicorns are a made-up animal. When I said they are real he said I am stupid. Please tell my big brother Eric he is stupid and not me and that you have given unicorns shots like my pony.*

*Love!!!!*

*Your friend Erica*

I laid the letter down and considered my reply. What immediately sprang to mind, of course, was the famous letter to Virginia, a letter that did not lie to the child but focused her attention on the true spirit of Santa Claus. This was exactly the opportunity that I had hoped "Ask Dr. McKenzie!" would provide when I first approached Rita with the idea for the column.

*My dear Erica:*

*Yes, Erica, unicorns do exist.*

*And yes, your big brother Eric is stupid. Everyone*
*should believe in unicorns.*

*Very truly yours,*
*Austin McKenzie, DVM*

The phone rang just as I keystroked the last lines of the letter. It was Rita, her voice several decibels higher than was her
norm.

"Austin, do I have to put an ad for the P and C's special on
artichokes where your column's supposed to be, or what?"

"It is on its way to you momentarily." I saved the file and
logged on to e-mail. "My apologies for the delay. But I spent
the morning at the county jail with Finnegan."

"Yeah?" Rita's voice dropped. "Anything you can tell me
for tomorrow's story?"

"Just that he's innocent." I keyed in the *Sentinel*'s e-mail
address and sent the file.

"Does he claim to be innocent, like they all do? Or do you
have some real proof?"

"There are some inconsistencies in the evidence gathered
by the police that perhaps should have been taken into account
before the arrest was made. In my opinion, the arrest of my
client was precipitate."

There was a pause. I could hear the clicking of the keyboard. "That's pretty good, Austin. Can you give me quote on
these supposed inconsistencies?"

"They aren't 'supposed.' They are quite real. But until the
investigations of Cases Closed, Incorporated, are concluded,
I would like to reserve the details."

"Austin, you are *such* a stuffy old f . . . guy. Can't you just
give me a quote that sounds like a normal person?"

"I am a normal person," I said stiffly.

"You are a . . . hey! Your e-mail just came through. Hang
on a second. Let me open the file . . ." There was a pause. Rita
shrieked. I held the phone away from my ear.

"Austin, is this letter supposed to be funny?"

"I thought it was quite appropriate. Do you want me to tell
the child her brother Eric is right? There are no such things as
unicorns?"

"What the heck are you talking about, unicorns? You can't tell Ripped Off she ought to be euthanized! What's the matter with you? Dammit all, Austin."

I heard the furious clacking of the keyboard.

"There, I've fixed it."

"I thought we agreed that you were going to leave my copy alone."

"We agreed to no such thing. Good grief. You belong in the last century, Austin, you know that? No. Call me a liar. Not this last one, the one before that. Oh." The change in the tone of her voice was noticeable. It is the tone of voice with which women hover over babies. "Oh, Austin, this letter is so *sweet*."

"Thank you," I said, somewhat mollified. "Although I would hope it doesn't sound too sweet."

"Not yours. Erica's." More clatter at the keyboard. "There, I've fixed up your second answer, too. Thanks. Fine. Glad you got it in."

"Rita!" I shouted. "I would prefer that you read your edits to me before—"

"Got to go! Let me know about any breaking details on the case ASAP, okay?" She cut the call off with a clatter. As soon as I hung up on my end, the phone rang again. I regarded it with intense disfavor. I was beginning to feel if my entire existence was being defined by the telephone. It was not a feeling I cherished. I picked it up and said, "Rita. Austin here. I demand . . ."

"Austin?"

"It's you, Victor."

"It's me. Yeah. Look, Austin. I was wondering if we could kind of get together."

"If it's about dinner, Madeline keeps our social calendar. And I'm not going to be free for social obligations until this case is solved. You are aware that my agency has been retained to solve the O'Leary murder."

"No. No, I hadn't been. That's nice."

That's nice? Something was very wrong here. The Victor I knew should have responded to this with a hoot of derision. The Victor I knew never sounded tentative or at a loss, as he did now. The sound of his breathing came down the line.

"Victor?"

"Right here, Austin. Never mind. It sounds like you're busy. Well, listen. I'll catch you later."

"Victor . . ."

And for the fourth time that day someone hung up on me before I could hang up on them.

Puzzled, I swiveled in my office chair and surveyed my empty house. My rolltop desk is situated between the fireplace and the saddle-colored sectional couch that occupied most of our living room. There was almost always someone there. Madeline. The dogs. Joe and Allegra studying, squabbling, or eating.

Something upstairs began to thump down the staircase, like a fifty-pound bag of feed rolling slowly downhill. Miss Odie stopped halfway down, sat upright on the step, and curled her tail around her haunches. We stared at one another. She squeezed her golden eyes shut, opened them, and looked away from me.

There is a myth that animals can't look humans in the eye because they have no soul. This is nonsense. Animals can't look humans in the eye because of what they see there.

"I seem to have failed my old friend."

Odie began to wash her face.

"Nonsense. I'm imagining things."

What would Madeline say? Madeline would demand that I call him back.

I called him back. The phone rang. The answering machine clicked on. The answering machine is a device invented by the rude, the insolent, and the uncivil. My usual response to the perky request to "leave a message after the beep" is a loud raspberry. As I drew breath to leave a request that Victor call me back, someone picked up the phone and said "Hello?"

"Ah. Thelma. It's Austin. I was looking for Victor."

"Victor? You were looking for Victor? Well, when you find him tell him from me to *drop dead*!"

This time I hung up before she could hang up on me.

I sat there, baffled. I am the first to admit that the behavior of animals has always made a great deal more sense to me than that of human beings.

I dithered. I tried to decide what to do. Not a thing occurred to me.

The sound of the back door banging open raised my spirits. My dog trotted in, came up to me, and laid his paw on my knee. My wife followed and gave me a kiss on the cheek. I hadn't seen her since breakfast. It felt much longer than that. It felt like eons.

She dropped onto the couch with a sigh. In the summertime, Madeline wears her hair pinned on the top of her head, sleeveless cotton blouses in various bright colors, and trousers that she variously refers to as clam diggers, Capri pants, or pedal pushers. Today's blouse was striped.

"You look tired, my dear."

"I'm not tired. I'm pissed off."

Madeline is the most equable of women. Her temper is rarely roused. She folded her arms under her bosom and raked the room with a fiery glance. "Well? Where is he?"

"I was just asking myself that," I said eagerly. "Thelma was not at all helpful."

"What does Thelma have to do with the price of bananas in Brazil?"

"It seems that Victor has gone somewhere."

"Victor?"

"Madeline, do you think he may have left her? That is, left the marriage?"

"My goodness." This news seemed to have lifted her out of her snit. "What happened?"

I explained.

"And you just let him go off like that?"

"I did call him back," I said.

"Oh, for goodness' sake!" Madeline jumped off the couch and strode to the phone. She dialed and when the call was answered said, "Thelma? It's Maddy."

And for the next forty-five minutes, I perused the latest issue of *Science*, walked outside to check on the progress of the green beans, picked a bucket of beans, practiced retrieves with Linc, and eventually wandered back to my desk.

Madeline had returned to the couch. Her face was glum. "Well, you were right. He's walked out."

"Just left?" I said in amazement.

"Walked out of the house and into an apartment with this Lucinda Whatsis. Thelma's in a state and a half. She and her mother are going to drive to Atlanta starting right now. They're going to stay with Thelma's sister for a while, give Thelma a chance to take it all in."

"My word."

Madeline put her hands to her cheek. "My lord, my lord. It never rains but it pours." She shook her head. "Golly."

"Isn't there something we can do?"

"Well, you've got to find the poor soul. He's your best friend and he asked you for help."

"I have no idea what to say to him."

"You'll think of something. So you go along and do that, Austin. I've got enough on my hands here." She looked around the living room again. "Have you seen him at all?"

"I just explained, my dear, that—"

"Not Victor! Sam Fulbright!"

"Oh." I smoothed my mustache. "No. But there is evidence that he bathed, at least. Perhaps he left the house early this morning, before we all came downstairs."

"Oh, he was here this morning, all right," she said bitterly. "Ally found him outside with Harker and there was a set-to like you wouldn't believe."

"Outside with the horse? Surely he can't have been plotting to harm it again."

"You couldn't prove it by Ally. Me? I think he was just wandering around outside looking at stuff. But Ally says the insurance policy's paid up until September, and it's clear as day the jerk's down on his luck and he's the beneficiary because he bought the poor thing and she had a screaming fit. So I took her over to Lila's. And Harker, too, to give everyone time to settle down." She sucked thoughtfully at her lower lip. "The tires are low on the horse trailer, by the way. Remind me to take it by the gas station for some air."

"Very well."

"As to where Ally's father is," she muttered to herself, "I have no idea. I thought he was here. I told him I'd be back to talk with him later, so he better not have hared off." Madeline's eyes flashed. "The man needs to be set straight and then some."

I cleared my throat. "I confess to some confusion, my dear. Victor's trouble, Ally's trouble. This unwelcome guest, her father. Shall I throw the fellow out? Shall I search for Victor? What should I do if I find him?"

Madeline's laughter is infectious. She laughed, then she sighed, then she came and wrapped her arms around me. "You know what you need, sweetie? You need a nice, tidy murder to solve. Don't worry about all the people stuff. I'll take care of it. You go ahead and find out who killed Lewis O'Leary."

# Twelve

My wife was right, as always. I am not good at this people stuff. I am good at deduction. The application of deductive reasoning has been a basic principle of my career as scientist, veterinarian, and diagnostician. Establish a clearly defined goal. Apply logic and reason. Verify the facts. And the solution will take care of itself. So it was with a lightened heart and a steady purpose that I sat down at my desk to determine the next steps in the case of O'Leary, the tough-talking turkey. Madeline gave me a hug and retired to the kitchen.

First, I retrieved the police reports from my case and reread them thoroughly.

The evidence, both forensic and circumstantial, was heavily weighted in favor of the prosecution. But the committed scientist does not ignore the value of intuition. Intuition is based on the collection of many observations of the world around us, some of them unconsciously acquired. And my intuition told me that Gil Finnegan was innocent.

To prove it, I had to place the available evidence in context. Yes, Gil's pickup truck had traces of the victim's blood on the tarp in the back. Had the body actually been there? Gil said he drove his truck, slept in his truck, and drove it again from approximately 9 p.m. to 3 the next morning. He would have noticed the weight of a 180-pound turkey farmer in the back. He wouldn't have noticed the tarp.

So who put the bloodstained tarp in Gil's pickup truck? And when?

Gil's clothing had turkey feathers on it, as did Lewis O'Leary's. But Lewis's clothing also had evidence of turkey eggs. The forensics report made no mention of albumen on Gil's clothing.

Had the turkey feathers on Gil's clothing been transferred from Lewis's? Or from somewhere else?

The seat of Lewis's trousers was soaked with river water. But there was no evidence of riverbank grass or plant fauna. If Lewis' body had rested by the river, there should have been.

How and why did river water get on Lewis's pants?

I was aware of Madeline moving about the kitchen. I smelled chocolate chip cookies and fresh bread. I collected my notes and moved from my desk to the dining-room table. "I am beginning to think, my dear, that someone set out to frame Gil Finnegan."

"No fooling?" Madeline paused with the spatula in the air. "Why set up Gil?"

"An excellent question."

"I mean really. It doesn't seem likely, though does it?" She selected two small cookies and placed them in front of me on a napkin. "You have to think of the people part of it, Austin. You always forget the people part. You have to have a powerful dislike of somebody to set them up for murder. And if Gil was set up, that means it was premeditated. Which in New York State means they can stick you full of poison and blammo. You're pushin' up daisies. At the very least the poor soul's going to spend twenty years in prison if he's convicted. There's got to be as powerful a reason to set up Gil as there is to murder old Lewis."

"I don't think much stands in the way of a killer," I objected. "A man angry enough or psychopathic enough to kill one man isn't going to have much of a conscience about putting another in jail for the rest of his life."

Madeline thought about this. I ate a cookie. Lincoln placed his paw on my knee and breathed hopefully into my face. "Not a chance, old fellow. There's chocolate in this."

"Maybe you're right about the cold-bloodedness of the killer." She shook her head sadly. Sometimes "the world is too much with us, late and soon." "Maybe you're right."

"There's a way to check if this is a frame. Gil claimed Lewis had called him and demanded a meeting in the parking lot of the Embassy. There should be a record of the call on Lewis's cell phone."

"How clever of you, Austin!"

I paged through the police documents. Simon had indeed checked Lewis's cell phone records. "Well."

"Uh-oh, I don't like the sound of that."

"There *was* such a call." I smoothed my mustache. It was at times such as this that I wished I smoked a pipe. "Simon has been thorough. I have nothing but admiration for the man."

"Uh-oh. I don't like the sound of *that*. You don't suppose that Gil did it after all?"

"I refuse to believe that the first official client of Cases Closed is guilty," I said firmly. "There's nothing for it, Madeline, I shall have to follow up a few leads that the police have ignored."

"Like what leads, for example?"

I paged through my notes. "I mentioned that this case had the earmarks of a Shakespearean tragedy, did I not? I'll begin where the Bard began. With the offspring of the old king."

THERE is a protocol to death in a town like Summersville. Most villagers are buried by Peterson's Funeral Home. There are two to three days of calling hours. (The length depends to some extent on the notoriety of the deceased.) The times are posted in the newspaper. I put in a call to Artie Callaghan, whose reportorial duties include the obit desk at the *Sentinel*. There were to be three days of calling hours. "Probably," Artie said, "folks want to make sure that he's dead." But, he added, the funeral wasn't scheduled until the following week. "You know what it's like with the autopsies." Artie chuckled. "Takes time to put all the body parts back together."

"True," I said. I thanked him and rang off. I considered funeral protocol: calling hours, embalming, an open casket, all at a cost that would subsidize a small African country. I turned to Madeline and said, "When the time comes, my dear, you recall that I wish to be cremated."

"For heaven's sake, Austin."

"And my ashes sprinkled over the horse pasture."

Madeline raised her eyes to the ceiling. Then she started to hum "Abide with Me" in her mellow contralto.

"Shall we make a condolence call on Angela O'Leary after dinner?" For this, too, was part of the process of burying a Summersvillian. The widow and the rest of the family remain at home until the casket is lowered into the grounds of the Summersville Sailor and Soldiers Cemetery, receiving those members of the community who cared to offer their condolences in a venue other than the musty recesses of the funeral home itself.

"We should make that call in any event," Madeline said. "Let me look and see what I have in the freezer to take with us. I made up two cherry pies yesterday, and unless you and Joe have gobbled them both—yep. There's one left." She closed the freezer door. "You don't think I need to take a hot dish, do you, sweetie? No," she answered herself. "I think the pie's fine. We didn't know them all that well."

After a quiet dinner—Joe had called to say that he would remain at the college until late, I did a quick clinic inspection, checked on the horses, and we got ourselves together to leave for the O'Leary farmhouse. Madeline changed into a cotton skirt of which I am very fond. I relinquished my coveralls and donned a polo shirt Ally had given me for my birthday. We had still seen neither hide nor hair of Samuel Fulbright, although when I checked the junk room off of the kitchen, his cheap knapsack remained under the cot.

"Maybe he's gotten himself run over," Madeline said cheerfully as I rose to my feet after checking under the bed. "That'd solve a lot of problems. And what if there's an insurance policy on *him*, just like there is on Harker? If there is, I bet we could figure out a way to knock him off without anyone the wiser."

I pursed my lips. "I wonder where in blazes the man got to?"

"I'm right here," said a voice behind me. We turned around together. Fulbright stood in the doorway to the junk room. He was wearing an old denim shirt of mine that Madeline had consigned to the ragbag. He wore an old pair of my chinos, too. I am five feet nine, with a fighting weight of 150 pounds. Fulbright is some three inches taller than I. His bare ankles stuck out over the new tennis shoes. His preprison weight had been far more substantial than the figure he presented now, but he still was unable to close the metal snap of the chinos. He had attempted to disguise the resulting gap by blousing the shirt over his belt buckle.

He was a mess. But least he was clean.

"I'd hope you'd decided to move on," Madeline said frankly. "May I ask where you've been all day?"

Fulbright was still a handsome man, despite the puffiness around his face that resulted from a prison diet. Ally had his eyes, which were river green. The arrogance that had been such a part of his attitude during the days of the trial was gone. What he looked like now was shifty. "I went out looking for a job."

"Around here?" Madeline said indignantly.

"And I found one. At the grain store." He spread his hands and looked at them ruefully. There was a fine blister on the palm of one hand. "They needed someone right away, to load grain and drive. The guy before me just walked off the job, I guess."

"The guy before you was escorted off the job, by the police," Madeline said tartly. "You're working at Green Seal? Part of Gil Finnegan's job was to load and drive. I'm hoping that you came back for your knapsack? You found a place to sleep in town?"

"I won't be able to find a place in town until I get a paycheck," Fulbright said quietly. "I'd appreciate it if I might stay here. I do understand what an imposition this is, believe me."

Madeline slung her purse over her shoulder and said, "Phooey!" She glared at him. "All right. Fine. My husband and I are going out. There's leftover pot roast in the refrigerator."

"And there's quite a bit of tofu," I offered. "Very healthy stuff, tofu."

"And mind you leave me a clean kitchen." Madeline shook her head and muttered, "This is a fine howdy-do," which was a sign she was genuinely upset. Madeline gets southern when she is genuinely upset. "The *minute* you get that paycheck, you're out of here."

She fulminated all the way down the driveway and didn't calm down until we hit County Road 334. Then, "Darn it, Austin. I forgot the damn pie."

I swung the Prius in a U-turn without a word, and we proceeded back home.

Our early return startled Lincoln, who was curled in his usual spot on the back steps. He followed Madeline halfway into the house with a worried expression. His tail was set low and he wagged it slowly. When she sprang up the steps and slammed the back door, he turned around and came back to me. I opened the car door and scratched his ears.

Madeline didn't come out.

I got out of the car and strolled up and down the drive. His worry forgotten, Lincoln trotted at my heels.

Madeline still didn't come out.

I looked at my dog, who grinned back at me. If there were anything wrong, he would have sensed it in an instant. Had she decided to change her clothes? Had she given into her fit of temper and coshed Fulbright over the head with a skillet? I was just about to go in to fetch her when she came slowly out of the back door, the pie balanced in one hand.

"Are you all right, my dear?"

She looked over her shoulder, and then got into the car. I rejoined her. Lincoln went back to his post and lay down with a sigh. We proceeded back down the drive and out onto Route 15.

"Well?"

"I guess I didn't make all that much noise going back in. So he didn't hear me. He was sittin' at the table cryin' his eyes out. Sobbin' like a little kid into my pot roast."

"Oh, my." I adjusted my spectacles and concentrated on the road ahead. "What happened next?"

"I gave him a box of Kleenex." She looked out the window at the glorious scenery passing by. "Austin. We've got such a good life. You're such a good man. Sometimes I think we're smart. And sometimes I think we're just lucky. Tonight I think we're just lucky."

By mutual, unspoken agreement, we dropped any further discussion of Samuel Fulbright's deficiencies as a father and proceeded to the wake.

# Thirteen

※～※

O'LEARY'S Poultry Farms began as a forty-acre spot of farmland about three miles due south of Summersville. Most of the farmland in this area of New York yields eighty to a hundred and twenty bushels of corn an acre—a common and convenient measure when a description of the fertility of the soil is needed. O'Leary's acres were set on rocky ground. The topsoil was thin, mostly clay, and the drainage poor. A crop farmer goes bust very quickly on land like that. O'Leary started growing poultry in the sixties, when farm subsidies were substantial and farm loans cheap and plentiful. Whatever else he may have been in life, Lewis O'Leary was a hard worker and a shrewd businessman. By the midseventies, the farm had grown to 200 acres and 100,000 carcasses. By the eighties, he had added a hatchery and a breedery in a successful attempt to cut out any middlemen between the egg and the grocer. The modern turkey, bred to be all breast and no sense, is vulnerable to a variety of infectious, pandemic diseases. Bio-security—and common sense—dictated that the hatchery, the breedery, and the growing barns be located several

miles from one another. The home farm remained the growing
barns, the place where the turkeys matured to market weight,
were slaughtered, frozen, and loaded onto tractor-trailers to
ship out.

The main farmhouse had been built in the 1860s as a tenant
house for a large farm now erased by time and tough times. It
was shabby in a most peculiar way. The roof was sound, the
siding trim, the doors and windows clean and tightly fitting.
But the place had a pinchback air. What grass there was had
been clipped within an inch of its life. Most the drives from
the house to the barns to roads were graveled. There was no
landscaping to speak of. No flowers, no bushes, no trees. Angela had a vegetable garden by the back porch—no respectable Summersville farm wife was without one, but even
that was clipped and trimmed into rigid submission.

"This is an angry-looking house," Madeline observed as
we parked behind the line of cars on the shoulder. "It's an
angry-looking house and an angry-looking place. I wouldn't
want anyone I cared about to live here."

The evening was warm, and the windows of the house were
open to the breeze. The hum of conversation met us as we
walked up the concrete path to the back door. I rapped lightly
on the door frame and we went into the large kitchen. A large
group of women were clustered around the kitchen table.
Casserole dishes, pies, cakes, cookies, and pots of beans covered every inch of counter space. Madeline found a place for
her cherry pie and joined the women. I went through the dining room and greeted the men seated at the dining-room table.
The immediate family sat in the living room, and I proceeded
in. Angela sat in a rocking chair by the fireplace, her face
stony, her hands folded tightly in her lap. Jensen stood with
his hands behind his back, staring out the front window. A
thin, overdressed brunette perched on the edge of an uphol-
stered chair on the right. She was attractive, in a thin-lipped
way. A scowl emphasized the lines around her mouth and on
her forehead. This must be Maired, Jensen's wife, the woman
whose escapades provided fodder for current gossip.

Ron and Linda were seated together on the Colonial-style
couch. Ron sat with knees apart, staring down at his clasped
hands. Linda rose to her feet as I came through the archway

from the dining room. "Dr. McKenzie! How good of you to come and see us. Mother. Here's Dr. McKenzie, come to pay his respects."

If I'd had a hat, I would have tipped it. As it was, I said, "Most sorry to hear of your loss, Mrs. O'Leary. He will be missed."

She nodded and said in a monotone, "Get doctor a piece of pie, Maired."

Maired compressed her lips, but she moved to rise.

"Thank you, no. I've just eaten."

"Get doctor a piece of pie. Maired!"

Maired flinched, but she got to her feet and said, "What about some coffee? Decaf?"

"Thank you. And I take no cream or sugar."

I sat down in the chair Maired had just vacated and again offered the conventional condolence. "My wife and I are very sorry for your loss, Mrs. O'Leary."

"You heard what happened to Lewis. Thrown out like a sack of garbage," she said in that same strange monotone. She raised a hand and rubbed her forehead.

"I did indeed. Dreadful. Just dreadful."

"Thrown out like a sack of garbage," she repeated, "Thrown into the Dumpster like a piece of trash."

"But I believe he wasn't . . . er . . . aware of it."

"That man hit him over the head, tossed him in the pickup truck, and drove him over to the Embassy."

"But I believe Lewis met Gil at the Embassy, didn't he?"

"Lewis met him at the hatchery. That man hit him over the head and tossed him in the Dumpster."

"Oh, Ma," Jensen expostulated. He turned away from the window and stared down at her. "We've been over this before, Ma."

Madeline said it was a shame, the way the looks were portioned out in the O'Leary family. All of them were tall. All of them had black hair and blue eyes. Cordy—according to my wife—looked like a sexy pirate. Ronald looked like the sort of man you would trust to be your daughter's soccer coach. But Jensen was plain homely. His ears stuck out. His chin was nonexistent. And his eyes were small and watery. He blinked nearsightedly at me. "She claims Pa went to the hatchery. She says he wasn't at the Embassy. She says he didn't set foot in the Embassy all that night. She's been saying that over and over again. It's like she's stuck on rewind."

Perhaps she needed the reassurance of an outsider. "A number of independent witnesses saw him there, Mrs. O'Leary. An old friend of mine among them."

Jensen shrugged. "Won't work. She'll just start that crap all over again."

This was puzzling. Angela stared down at her hands. "Mrs. O'Leary," I said gently. "You recall that we met briefly at the high school the night . . . the night Lewis met with this accident. Did you go home with him?"

"I drove her home." Cordy walked up to his mother. He held two cups of coffee. He handed one to me and took a sip from the other. Maired stood behind him. From the way she looked at the back of his neck, I was inclined to believe the gossip I had heard from Phyllis Best.

"Lewis met him at the hatchery. Then he hit Lewis over the head." The words were slightly slurred. Her face had no affect at all. That—and the repetition. A sudden horrifying thought occurred to me. I set my coffee cup on the floor and knelt by her side. "Mrs. O'Leary? Angela?" I tilted her face to the light. There was a bubble of spit at the side of her mouth and the right side of her face was slack. "Ron," I said sharply. "Call an ambulance. I believe your mother is the midst of a stroke."

There was an ensuing bustle, of course. Someone brought a blanket to keep her warm. I took her pulse. The family gathered around me, whispering. I heard Ron, his voice urgent, talking to the paramedics. Then, a spiteful whisper came from somewhere in the crowd, "All she deserves is a vet, the old cow. Cancel the EMTS."

The ambulance was there in less than twenty minutes. The EMTS loaded Angela with dispatch, and then both guests and family stood on the drive and watched the ambulance tear down the driveway to Ithaca. It was almost full dark now, which made the flashing red lights all the more ominous. Linda rode with Angela in the ambulance. Ron followed her in his car.

Maired nudged me. "Will she die, do you suppose?"

Had hers been the voice that whispered?

"I have no idea. My medical training doesn't extend to Homo sapiens. I can only surmise. It appears to be a minor stroke, if that's any comfort."

Maired smiled. She had very white teeth. "Oh, that's no comfort at all." She looked around in a fretful way. "Where's Jensen? I want to get out of here."

Jensen appeared out of the gloom and grasped her wrist. "I've got to go to the grower barns before we go, Maired. Ron asked me to take over the data collection tonight."

"I don't see why you have to do it." She shook her wrist free of his grip and rubbed her arms, as if she were cold. "This whole thing's been a shock. I need a drink. I don't want to go home by myself."

"You could give me a hand in the barn."

She snorted. "Yeah. Right. Well, if you can't take the time to be with your own wife at a time like this, I guess your brother can." She gave him a cocky smile and walked off. Jensen stared after her with quite a hopeless expression on his face.

"The data collection?" I asked politely. "Is this part of the study on the coccidiacide that you're doing for Cornell?"

"Right." Jensen brought his attention back to me and said, more loudly, "Right. Ron said it's easy, but I don't know a damn thing about it. I don't do this side of the business. I drive the truck."

"And he's the turkey killer," Maired called out from the back porch. "That's what Jensen does. He's the turkey killer."

"Maybe you could come with me, explain what's going on with this data collection." Jensen said. He didn't look Maired's way.

I glanced behind me, looking for my own wife. Madeline stood under the porch light, talking to a girl in her twenties with a nose ring and an ivy tattoo twined around one wrist. Her hair was bleached blonde in some areas, and bright pink in others. Jensen followed my gaze. "Cordy's girlfriend, Cheryl."

"My goodness. I understood she was a bank clerk. I must say she doesn't look like a bank clerk."

"Hard to find good help these days."

I have often thought there is a psychic link between my wife and myself. As if she had actually heard my voice, Madeline turned and caught my eye. I moved my head slightly, in the direction of the grower barns. She nodded back, just as unobtrusively. Jensen, his shoulders stiff with impatience, was already headed down the drive to the building labeled GROWER #1. I hastened after him.

A security door and a biohazard sign barred the way into the first barn—the latter had been posted for the benefit of the turkeys, not humans. We both donned white coats, latex gloves, and enclosed our shoes in plastic booties. Jensen pulled open the door to the growing floor, and I followed him inside.

In one sense, turkey growing is simplicity itself. If the poults survive to the age of three weeks, they are brought to the grower barn in trays and placed in a large area several inches deep in clean shavings. Food and water are dispensed in large troughs placed at intervals along the length of the floor. At nine weeks, the birds are guided through the debeaking machine, which trims the beak so that there are no accidental (or purposeful) injuries from bird quarrels. They are also guided though a machine that clips the spurs on their feet. Then they are returned to the floor until the reach market weight, at about three months. At that point, they are dispatched to turkey heaven.

The domestic turkey is famously stupid. Growers who raise their birds outside are careful that the birds keep their beaks down during a rainstorm. Birds have been known to drown.

There was very little noise as we worked our way across the floor. The turkeys were contented; food and drink was available at will, a homicidal neighbor could inflict no injury after being debeaked, and the place was clean and airy. I suppose, as far as the avian universe was concerned, it was a sort of turkey utopia.

Both Jensen and I kept watch for carcasses. The genetic modification that's gone into the development of the modern turkey has resulted in a bird that occasionally keels over for no reason at all. Most large growers expected a 1 to 2 percent loss from a single crop. Jensen found one. I found none at all.

"Quite remarkable," I said. "Has someone been through recently?"

"Not since this morning. The data we're supposed to get has to do with why the buggers died." Jensen carried the dead turkey by the feet. "So we'll test this guy. And we'll see if anybody left me carcasses in the cooler."

A small and efficient laboratory was located at the end of the growing room. Jensen went in first, flipped on the light, and slung the turkey onto the stainless steel countertop. A standard-sized refrigerator stood in the far corner. Jensen opened it and removed two more carcasses.

"This lab is quite well equipped, Jensen."

"Yeah? It's not because of Pa, that's for sure. When they bury him next week, it'll be with his first nickel. I think all this stuff belongs to the program."

There was an electron microscope, a centrifuge, and a clinical chemistry analyzer. I would have welcomed any of this equipment in my own clinic.

"Okay. I'm supposed to get a blood sample, put it on a slide, and check for this virus." Jensen dug into his shirt pocket and withdrew an excellent color drawing of the parasite that infects animals with coccidiosis.

"That's straightforward enough. If you're testing for incidences of coccidiosis, this is the little fellow you don't want to see. Do you have syringes for the blood draw?"

He pointed to a cabinet above the stainless steel sink. I opened the doors and discovered neatly shelved pharmaceutical supplies. I removed a box of glass slides, grasped several needles in their blue plastic casings, and sheathed for a box of syringes. It was on the upper shelf. I reached up, and as I pulled it out, a Petrie dish slid to one side.

I set the syringes and the needles on the counter and picked the Petrie dish up.

The alga inside was host to a most interesting bacterium.

I glanced over my shoulder. Jensen was intent on a document on a clipboard. I slipped the Petrie dish into my trousers pocket, and then began to prepare three syringes, one for each carcass.

"Okay. It says here that we take a fecal sample, a blood sample, and 'conduct a visual inspection of the carcass for any anomalies.' That means something out of the ordinary, right?"

"It does."

The routine was simplicity itself. Jensen asked that I check the fecal samples under the electron microscope. I did so. Two samples were healthy. The third was infected. Jensen scribbled on the clipboard, threw the pencil on the counter, and stuffed the bird remains in to a green plastic garbage bag.

"May I see the information sheet?"

Jensen shrugged. I flipped through the survey. Over the past several months, the there were isolated incidences of infected birds. Very curious. Very curious indeed.

"Thanks, Doc," Jensen said grudgingly. He smiled thinly. "Unless you're going to send us a bill?"

My answering smile was chilly. But I asked him, as we divested ourselves of the biohazard gear in the entryway, who stood to inherit the farm.

"Beats me. All I know is that it isn't Ma. She gets some kind of pension and we have to let her stay in the house while she's alive, but Pa kept changing his mind about who was going to get what."

Most of the condolence visitors had left, and the driveway was empty of all vehicles except Madeline's Prius and the two pickup trucks I identified as Jensen's and Cordy's. There had been a third vehicle parked next to the truck with the O'Leary logo on the door, a red Miata, but it was gone.

"Looks like she took off to get that drink." Jensen's eyes flickered to his brother's truck. "Look. Thanks again." He stood rather awkwardly, clearly ill at ease. "We must sound pretty awful to you. As a family, I mean."

I didn't respond to this.

"But it was him." A spasm contorted his face. Fear—hatred—anger—grief? "He was something, you know what I mean? All that tough talk. Tried to set us all against each other." He coughed. "Well, I'd better get on to the hospital, see what's going on with Ma."

I saw the comfortable curves of my wife silhouetted against the screen door to the kitchen. It was a welcome sight indeed.

# Fourteen

~~~

MADELINE made whole-wheat pancakes the next morning, a welcome change from granola. But it didn't make the atmosphere any cheerier. Breakfast was shaping up to be another glum meal, made glummer by the cringing presence of Samuel Fulbright. Joe cast him one scornful glance, then proceeded to ignore him. Madeline was lost in her own thoughts.

I, on the other hand, was invigorated at the thought of the investigation that lay ahead. The visit to the grower barns had proved most interesting. And Madeline's little chat with Cheryl the bank teller had provided valuable fodder, which required a quick follow-up. A full and interesting day lay before me. I helped myself to a second pancake and said, "I wonder if you can cover Ally's responsibilities today, Joseph. She had been scheduled to draw TB samples from Vanderbyl's dairy herd." These routine chores provide a small but steady source of revenue for our clinic. "I would accompany you, but the game is afoot."

I, like my illustrious predecessor Sherlock Holmes, was hard on the heels of a murderer. My suspicions were rife. The first—the suspicion that someone was deliberately infecting the O'Leary turkeys with coccidiosis—was taking the investigation in an entirely new direction. The second, courtesy of Madeline's talk with Cheryl the bank clerk the night before, offered another. Cheryl had been loud in her opinion that Lewis O'Leary had been cheating his sons. She'd danced around the issue of proof—and I intended to put a stop to that dancing this afternoon.

"Conan Doyle," Samuel Fulbright said unexpectedly.

All three of us looked at him.

He flinched apologetically. "Sorry. You mentioned that the game was afoot."

"Aren't you due at work pretty soon?" Joe asked. His tone was just this side of rudeness. Fulbright's workday at Green Seal began at eight. It took him about twenty minutes to walk the mile into town.

"I'm going to drop him off in a few minutes," Madeline said. "And then I'm going over to Lila's for the morning."

The ensuing silence became uncomfortable. "Yes," I said, just to break it. "My reference was to Sherlock Holmes. You're familiar with the works?"

"I had a lot of time to read in prison," Fulbright said. "And the prison library has a large section devoted to mysteries. A lot of the inmates have law and order concerns."

"I imagine they do," Madeline said with an unsurprised air.

"I understand there is a detective arm to your veterinary practice, Dr. McKenzie?"

"Yes," Madeline said. "There is. Austin's been retained by Gil Finnegan, to prove his innocence in the death of Lewis O'Leary."

"This Finnegan was the head salesman for Green Seal. I'm doing part of his job, is that correct?"

"Yes," I said. "That is correct."

"Well, if I hear anything relevant. I'll let you know." He cleared his throat. "If you'll excuse me, I'll just take care of these dishes."

Joe looked at me. I looked at Joe. We both looked at Madeline. She raised an eyebrow as if to say, he's trying. She said aloud, "I'll see ya'll later."

It was another fine July morning, and I got on the road with the wind in my face and my spirits high. The only way to improve the day would be to have my dog at my side. But my calendar was full of appointments, and I disliked leaving the dog in the car, particularly on days as hot as this one was going to be.

I had taken the Petrie dish filched from the grower lab into my own clinic the night before. My suspicions were confirmed. The Petrie dish was filled with live coccidia parasites. Joe, drawn not at all reluctantly from a text on parasitology, had agreed with me.

"Someone is deliberately infecting the turkeys," I said. "It's very odd."

"Are you sure?"

"Think about it, my boy. One or two turkeys out of one hundred thousand come down with a highly communicable disease? I mean, you can talk about natural resistance all you want, but that sort of data beggars the imagination. No, someone is doing this on purpose, to skew the data."

"But why?" he'd asked. "If the study's to confirm the usefulness of this new feed additive, who's going to benefit by a bunch of false results?"

*Cui bono?*

Who, indeed?

My first stop this morning was to address that very issue. I had an appointment with Alan Krippendorf. My last was to interview Cheryl Bauman. The interval in between was open. A detective must be prepared to follow where the evidence leaves him at any moment.

The college directory listed Krippendorf's home address. I was familiar with the area, a side street off West Seneca, crammed with older homes converted into student housing. Postdocs were woefully underpaid—it is undoubtedly part of the job description—but even at peasant wages, Krippendorf should have been able to afford better housing. I pulled the Bronco into a curbside spot between a battered Honda and a Harley-Davidson motorcycle and surveyed his premises. I sidestepped a cushionless couch that sagged on the sidewalk, ready for trash pickup, and went up the splintered front steps to the screened-in porch. I made out a dim figure slumped inside.

"Dr. McKenzie?" Krippendorf got up from a plastic lawn chair situated just inside the screen door. "I'm happy to meet you officially, so to speak."

I looked up at him. He was quite tall, extremely skinny, and he still reminded me of a Narragansett Bronze. I shook his hand. It was clear that there was no privacy possible on the screened porch, and by the way he stood defensively in front of the front door, it was just as clear that Krippendorf didn't want me in his apartment. "There's a Java Joes one block over," he said. "Somebody told me that you were quite the coffee drinker when you were chair."

This was meaningless twaddle, but I nodded. He picked up a battered book bag, and we set off for the coffeehouse. "I've got a couple of copies of my résumé here, in case you needed more than one," he said, with a glance at the book bag. "But I figured I'd wait until we sat down to give it to you."

I looked sharply at him. "Your résumé?"

"Well, yeah. I heard that you're working for Green Seal, now? Kind of a spokesman, I guess?"

I had almost forgotten that in the excitement of the past few days. I had been remiss in not responding to Karen Crown's messages. And Madeline had deposited the check. We rounded the corner to West Seneca. "Yes. But my duties are not particularly onerous. I'm to give a few speeches." I smoothed my mustache. "Kiss a few babies. That sort of thing."

Krippendorf stopped in the middle of the sidewalk. A young woman carrying a load of plastic grocery bags maneuvered around him with a loud "t'cha!" "You mean you aren't interviewing me for a research job with Green Seal?"

I could see the outdoor tables in front of Java Joes a block ahead. I could do with a strong cup of coffee. I gave Krippendorf a shove to get him moving and said, "Why would you think that?"

"Well, you're hand in glove with Gil, aren't you? I mean, I heard that you're sniffing around trying to save him from this murder rap and since he's locked up I thought maybe you were coming with a message from him."

"I suppose you could say that I'm Gil's emissary, that's true."

"I thought so!" He looked at me sideways. There was something sly about that look. I frowned at him and pointed to a table situated well away from the clusters of coffee drinkers at Java Joes. "Shall we sit there? We do not want to be overheard."

He nudged me with his elbow and winked. "Gotcha, Doc."

I took a ten-dollar bill from my wallet. "This is a self-service place, I believe. I'd like a large regular coffee, black. And please get something for yourself."

"I'll just give you a copy of my CV. You can take a look while I get the coffee. " His grin was filled with hope. I took the manila folder he withdrew from the book bag, sat down, and flipped through it.

The young man had a fair number of publications to his credit. Most of them were in the area of poultry science, one about the chemical mechanism for evenly dispersing additives through grain, one about the equation for a sort of super coccidiacide, the same one, presumably, that was being tested at O'Leary's growing facility. And the journals in which the articles appeared were respectable.

Krippendorf's postdoc advisor was my old colleague John Wu. That put paid to any suspicion I'd had that the results of the study at O'Leary's were being skewed with the consent of the college. John was as upright as a Hoover.

Krippendorf set my black coffee down on the table, seated himself across from me, and sipped at a huge, whipped-cream-covered concoction. "Before he—well what happened, happened, Gil and I were talking about a job for me at the Green Seal lab in Illinois."

I sipped my coffee. It was excellent. I would have to remember to buy a pound for Madeline.

"You know. The research lab."

"I'd guessed that, yes."

"Gil was supposed to get back to me with some kind of salary offer."

I raised my eyebrows in inquiry.

Krippendorf licked his lips. "This is . . . I mean. You have talked to him about me?"

"I spoke with him less than two days ago," I said, truthfully.

He relaxed, visibly. "So. Well. Did he mention any number to you?"

"I believe he's waiting to hear what your thoughts on the matter might be."

This was out-and-out prevarication, of course. But I had an ugly suspicion of just what young Krippendorf was up to.

"Ha." He relaxed. "Well. I can't just hand the thing over to you right off the bat. I mean, I've got a department chair that's on my ass like you wouldn't believe. And I've already got the sheepskin, so to speak, so I don't have to worry about that. But it's not going to do my reputation any good to have a failed postdoc in my past." He laughed. "I mean, you and I know the additive works just great, right? But we can't let the college know that or they'll want to take a piece of the action. So it's only fair that I be reimbursed for that."

" 'That?' " I repeated with a questioning air.

"Yeah. The . . . uh . . . smudge on my reputation."

I regarded the young swine over the rim of my spectacles. I sipped my coffee. I thought about what to do next.

I would go undercover. I would assume the guise of a streetwise crook.

The decision made, I leaned forward and said, "I hear you, partner. And I'll get back to you. But I can safely say, we are talking six figures, here."

"Six!" He sat back, dismayed. "No. Oh, no. We're talking up front a million and a piece of the action. You tell him that. I told that fool Finnegan that."

My mind reeled. Of course! Krippendorf was trying to sell the feed additive to the largest feed company in the United States. Green Seal's sales in poultry feed were huge. Millions *were* stake.

And Finnegan was smack in the middle of it.

My mind teemed with possibilities. If Lewis O'Leary had discovered Finnegan was part of the scam that was being run in his grower shed, what would have happened next?

What if Finnegan had killed Lewis O'Leary, after all?

If Krippendorf had discovered that Lewis knew all about the scam—had Lewis threatened to turn him in to the college authorities? The man would have been stripped of his doctorate. More likely, had Lewis tried to hold Krippendorf up for a cut of the action? Either scenario offered Krippendorf a strong motive for murder.

I bit my mustache. I sipped my coffee. I looked at Krippendorf, who frowned back at me. The man certainly had the face of a villain.

I made a field decision. I would say no more until I'd held Finnegan up by his heels—so to speak—and shaken more information out of him.

"Dr. McKenzie?"

I snapped back to the moment. "Yes. I heard you. Partner. A gig this big . . ." I spread my hands wide. "Going to take some doing."

"Sure. Sure. I hear you."

"Good. You'll excuse me, then? While I get the ball rolling?"

"You bet." Krippendorf shoved himself away from the table, preparing to get up and follow me. "No!" I said. I had to make a noticeable effort to suppress the horror in my voice. At the moment, I didn't want to be within a country mile of this scoundrel. As it was, I had to forcibly restrain myself from dumping the contents of my coffee cup over his deceitful head. "Stay here and finish your . . . whatever that repellant mess is." I lowered my voice. "We . . . ah . . . probably shouldn't been seen together."

"Right. Gotcha. Thanks, Doc." He winked. I regarded him stonily. I thought about leaving a tip for the busboy, and decided against it. It would undoubtedly end up in Krippendorf's pocket. When I had a chance to talk this over with Victor, he would hit the roof. It would be a most satisfying conversation. For once, we would both be in total agreement. This boy was a disgrace to our profession.

Except that Victor had walked out of the home he had shared with Thelma for thirty years, to move in with his poopsie, and I felt quite awkward about knocking on the door of what was probably a love nest.

Madeline's advice had been to leave it alone. So I had left it alone. But it had been with a heavy heart that I'd set thoughts of my old friend aside, to wait for the time when he would call me again.

But this situation was urgent. This had all the elements of a scandal that could damage the school for some period of time.

I walked rapidly back to the Bronco. It wouldn't do to speculate about Finnegan's possible guilt, just as it wouldn't do to condemn my old friend out of hand for disloyalty to his marriage. It was bad science to theorize in front of the facts.

But the next person I had to talk to was my miserable excuse of a client.

And then I needed to talk to Victor.

# Fifteen

~~~~~

"YOU think maybe Krippendorf killed Lewis O'Leary?" Gil said, stupefied. "Gosh. The thought never crossed my mind, Doc. Otherwise I would have said something."

"I have no idea at this juncture whether Krippendorf killed anyone," I said testily. "But surely you must see how this looks?"

Gill rubbed both hands over his face and shook his head.

I am not a violent man. Disputes should be settled by clear, rational discussion. What is man, if not a rational creature blessed with a nature that can quell the impulse to violence that suffuses the spirits of man and animal alike?

But I wanted to clout Finnegan over the head with a large stick. And then aim a kick directly at the seat of his trousers. I did neither. Instead, I sat in the visitor's room of the Syracuse County Jail and drummed my fingers on the filthy top of the table that separated us. "How in the name of God did you get involved in something like this?"

Finnegan wriggled uneasily in his chair. He was dressed in regulation prison orange. He'd been moved from the Tompkins County holding pen to the proper state facility in Syracuse the day before, and I was hot and irritated from the battle with Syracuse's lousy traffic.

"It's like this. You know how bad business has been, lately."

"Agribusiness is tough all over," I said unsympathetically.

"Did you know I used to be the county manager for Green Seal?" Gil said. "Until it all started to go wrong. We started losing a couple of thousand a month. I have no idea why."

"Didn't your main office come in to give you a hand?"

He looked at me wistfully. "They said it was me. Just plain mismanagement. It was a big place to handle, Doc. We had two drivers, a kid in the back to load the stock, three cashiers . . . we were pretty big."

"Go on."

"I got paid pretty good . . ."

"Well," I corrected him crossly. "You were paid well."

"Like I said. And you know, I could afford my house and five acres, an RV, the whole thing. The American Dream. That's what me and the wife had. And then, well, the smaller farms moved out and sold to vineyards. And we got the Whole Farms Foods guys nosing into my territory. And corporate started cutting staff like you wouldn't believe. So," he said, with a great deal of indignation. "Things changed. You wouldn't believe how things changed. You know where most of the store profits come from these days? It's not from the sale of the corn or oats or the feed for the goats and the sheep and the birds. It's from what they call hobby stuff. Retail stuff. Bird feeders and pet food and dog collars and lawn furniture. Stuff for camping, too. Tents. Air mattresses. Coleman stoves. We aren't a farm business anymore. We're a freakin' Wal-Mart. And we're not any good at that, either. So I went from being district manager to store manager. I had to drive a truck. I was the one that had to run the grinder and the loader. And if that wasn't enough, they cut my pay. So I went from something to nothing. Just like that." He snapped his fingers. "And then Alan come by and talked to me about adding this supplement to the grain deliveries I make out to O'Leary's every week, and I may not know much, Doc, but I know turkeys. And I see how these turkeys don't keel over like they did."

"You mean the death losses decreased considerably," I said dryly.

"Yeah. Whatever was in that stuff, man, it's golden. It was golden. So Alan and I send this memo to corporate . . ."

"Do you have a copy?"

"In my desk at home, yeah. My wife, Bea, can show you. About, I wrote them about how I got this kid who's come up with this great idea to cut death losses, like you said. And from Alan, he wrote that he's this scientist at Cornell working on this additive in his spare time, like."

"What?" I said sharply. "His spare time?"

"Yeah. He cooked this thing up himself, see. And he's looking at how much you college professors make and all the boring stuff you have to do, and he's looking at what he can come up with on his own and he's figuring, see, like, he can make a mint more money and have a better time of it, too. And me? I'm looking pretty darn good to corporate and wasn't that a mercy."

I held up my hand. Gil mumbled to a stop. "You think the formula for the coccidiosis additive belongs to Alan Krippendorf?"

"Sure." Gil shook his head in a pitying way. "He couldn't sell it to Green Seal if it didn't, now could he?"

"And what was . . . er . . . corporate's response?" There is no such thing as a corporate. And if there were, it would be inanimate and incapable of a response. But I bowed to the primary dictate of successful interlocutory behavior: go with the flow.

Gil nodded vigorously. "Oh, they were interested. They were very interested. They said the next step was for me and Alan to come on down to Illinois and talk to them. Thing is, Alan wanted some idea of how much he could cash in on this. Can't say as I blame him. So we were kind of going back and forth over that."

"Do you have copies of this correspondence?"

"Sure do. Like I said. Just ask Bea."

I felt considerably calmer. Gil was a boob. But he was an innocent boob.

"Course, then O'Leary had to go and stick his oar in."

This was promising. "Oh?"

"Yuh. Lewis was giving Alan some kind of heat about signing off on the data collection. Alan needed that sign-off so he could present his findings for his postdoc. that's what he said. Alan, I mean."

"And Lewis and Alan got into an argument over the indemnity agreements?" I brushed aside Gil's puzzled expression. "The sign-off?"

"Lewis? Lewis didn't know a thing about our plan to take this to corporate. It was Cordy that stuck his oar in. Said he could get the old man to sign, but that he wanted . . . I don't know. Something like tobacco."

"Something like tobacco?"

"A payoff, like."

"You mean a quid pro quo." I sighed. Greed. Greed. I glanced at my watch. I would have to hurry if I were to catch Cheryl Bauman before the banks closed.

And as I had surmised to Madeline, we were back to Lear and his wicked children.

BY the time I negotiated the idiotic labyrinth of the parking garage and found my way onto the ramp to I-80, I decided that the key to tracking down the perp, as we investigators call the guilty, was timetables. Timetables and alibis. I had to track both Krippendorf's and Cordy's activities from quarter to nine to three o'clock in the morning. And to do that, I had to question them and the people around them.

How would I do it? Citizens are required to answer questions from the police; nobody had to answer mine.

The obvious solution was trickery. That and manipulation. Investigation was clearly bad for one's character.

Cheryl the besotted bank clerk with the obvious place to start. But to get her to betray her lover might be some task. I would have to lie in order to gather the next necessary bits of information, that was clear. And as Madeline has frequently pointed out, I am not much of a liar.

I had anticipated a need for disguises. I had not anticipated the need for outright duplicity. I took 81 south back to Ithaca and turned the problem over in my mind. Was there an ethically substantive difference between:

a. Donning a wig and a fake tattoo to discover damaging facts about a suspect,

b. Presenting one's self to a suspect and lying through one's teeth about why one was asking questions,

c. Presenting one's self to a probable innocent, and prying damaging information out of a person by more lies,

d. Getting a minion—Joe or Allegra—to do it for me?

I could not think of any valid reason to interrogate Cordy O'Leary or his girlfriend wearing a wig and a fake tattoo.

And if the man were a patricide, I could not, in conscience, send Joe or Allegra to do the dirty work. Cheryl might be as dangerous as I thought Cordy might be.

So I *would* have to lie outright, and lying is a skill I hadn't practiced much. For one thing, I just wasn't very good at it. And even if I had been, what is a scientist's life but a search for the true and the valid? Lying was against every principle I held.

There was a third possibility: that Simon Provost had already interrogated members of the family about their whereabouts and that the relevant information could be obtained from him. But I couldn't think of one reason why Provost would turn the information over to me. And information was the keystone of a good investigation.

I glanced at the clock on my dashboard. Ten minutes after three, and I had had no lunch. I could begin my new role of deceiver by taking the tattooed Cheryl out for a sandwich.

I took the exit to Route 15, and in a depressingly brief period of time, arrived in the parking lot of the Summersville Farmer's Bank. The bank closed, on weekdays, at three-thirty in the afternoon. I parked, exited the Bronco, and rapped on the glass doors. Naomi VanDerPlanck, (a third cousin of that same VanDerPlanck who refuses to anesthetize his bull calves when I castrate them), gestured at me from behind the door and mouthed: "We're closed."

I rapped again.

Naomi looked over her shoulder, shrugged, and unlocked the door. She stuck her head out and said, "We're closed, Dr. McKenzie. Is it something urgent?"

"I am here for my lunch appointment with Cheryl."

"Cheryl Bauman? Really?"

"Really."

"Okay." She turned around, disappeared into the bowels of the building, and returned, followed by the sullen young woman with the striated hair that I had seen the night before.

"Doctor here came to take you to lunch," Naomi said.

"I am conducting an interview for my column for the *Sentinel*," I said. "You are aware of my column, 'Ask Dr. McKenzie!'?"

"No," she said rudely.

Naomi looked surprised, but she said, "I read it all the time. It's a riot. I always tell people, you want to start the week with a good laugh, you start it by reading Doctor, here."

I assumed Naomi was referring to my lightness of touch, since I was not aware of any true comic intent in my column. I smiled deprecatingly.

Naomi bounced up and down. "Are you going to write about her cockapoo? It's about Cindy, Cheryl. What fun. If you're cashed out, I guess you can go."

Cheryl shifted the wad of gum in her mouth from one side to the other. The idea of leaving early clearly appealed to her. She shrugged. "Okay."

I stepped aside to allow Cheryl to exit the building. "We will go across the street."

"The Gothic Eves?" she said in a voice laden with sarcasm. "Oh, yippee. Like I don't eat there every single day."

The Gothic Eves (sic) is run by a pleasant middle-aged woman named Rosalie Cummings. It was originally conceived, I believe, as a sort of teashop. But the residents of Summersville were indifferent to scones and Devonshire cream, so Rosalie expanded the menu to include more substantial items like chicken salad sandwiches, spaghetti carbonara, and spinach lasagna. About a dozen small round tables cluttered up the space. The café curtains at the windows, the tablecloths, the napkins, and Rosalie's apron were all made of the same cotton print. The subject, of course, was roses. A bookshelf lined one wall, filled with paperbacks of the more sensational kind.

Cheryl and I entered a restaurant empty of customers. Rosalie bustled out at the sounds of the bells over the door. I ordered a cream tea. Cheryl ordered a Diet Coke. Rosalie bustled back to the kitchen. Cheryl chewed her gum and regarded me with unexpectedly shrewd eyes. "So, what's this about a newspaper story?"

I eyed her back. Duplicity be damned. "There is no newspaper story." I shook a rose-colored napkin out and placed it on my lap. "You are aware of my close relationship with the Summersville police department?"

She blinked. "Yeah?"

"And you may have heard that once again I am investigating a murder. The murder of Lewis O'Leary, to be precise."

"So?" She rolled the gum to the other side of her mouth.

"So I have come across information potentially damaging to you. I'd like to discuss it."

She closed her mouth with a snap. She flushed bright red. "What d'ya mean. Damaging to me?"

"You have a relationship with Cordy O'Leary?

"Yeah. So what?"

"There have been some questions raised about the access to the farm's accounts."

Cheryl caught her breath. It was a young, vulnerable gasp. Tears began to roll down her cheeks. My heart failed me. Detecting can be a dirty business, even when you are on the up-and-up.

Rosalie brought a tiered cake stand filled with sandwiches and baked desserts, a pot of hot water, tea bags, and a large Diet Coke. She patted Cheryl briskly on the shoulder and said, "Buck up, kid. It can't be that bad," and hustled away again. Cheryl continued to cry, the silent tears rolling down her cheeks with much the same smeary effect on her makeup as rain on a windshield.

"How old are you, my dear?"

"Twenty-three."

I was shocked. Cordy was in his midforties. She looked

older. The makeup perhaps. Certainly the tattoos. But she didn't look *that* much older than twenty-three. It was a shame horsewhipping went out in the last century but one. I bit back an angry comment and said, "If my wife were here, she would suggest that you try one of those tiny éclairs."

Cheryl blew her nose, took a long sip of her Coke, and reached for the cream puff.

"Now. Why don't you tell me all about it?"

"He's the hottest-looking guy," she said. "I mean, he's *hot*. All my girlfriends are ready to scratch my eyes out since we've been, like, hanging out together."

"How long have you been dating?"

"Oh, quite a while," she said with a wise air. "Six weeks and four days. We're coming up on our two-month anniversary."

"I see."

"He said maybe he'd get me a diamond ring to celebrate."

"He did?"

And how, I asked myself, was Cordy going to afford this diamond ring on the pittance his father paid him?

"And then he said maybe not. Cordy can be quite a kidder." She scrubbed her cheeks with her napkin, leaving a smear of beige goo on the roses. "I don't mind at all."

"And when did he bring up the issue of the farm's accounts?"

"Oh. Well. I guess I was kind of kidding around about it, you know? How Mr. O'Leary never let anybody but Dave handle his deposits and that."

"And that" is a locution that has always puzzled me. It appears verbal shorthand for "and all that sort of thing." And if it is, did it mean that Dave, whomever he might be, handled business other than deposits for Lewis? It is an intensely annoying imprecision.

"And who is Dave?"

"The assistant manager and that."

I bit my mustache, but said with restraint. "So you were curious about why Mr. O'Leary wouldn't deal with anyone but Dave."

"Well, *yeah*-ah."

"Sorry to be so obtuse," I said dryly. "Have another éclair."

She had two. "I mean there's nothing for us girls to do all day but put money in, put money out, put money in . . ."

I held up a hand to forestall a repetition as dreary as her days. "I understand."

"So we kind of talk about it, you know? About who has what. I mean, for example, everybody pretty much likes you and they *love* Mrs. McKenzie, so when you go into the overdraft, we all, like, kind of worry."

Twenty-something bank tellers speculating on the state of our finances? I blenched.

"And it's the same with the O'Learys, except we hated him."

"Lewis."

"Lew-isss," she mocked, reminding me briefly of that great fictional detective Endeavor Morse. "God. What an asshole. So, like, Cordy likes to hang at the Embassy and he never has any money for more than a couple beers and it's like, so unfair. So I checked."

"And?"

"The old fart had like, tons of money tucked in that account. And he was the only signatory." Then she added, kindly, "That's like, the person signs this card and only that person's signature lets you into the account."

"Thank you."

"You're welcome. So I told Cordy." She stopped talking and swallowed hard, as if the éclair had stuck halfway down her throat. The tears started rolling down her face again. "I'll get busted if you tell anybody I did this. I'll lose my job."

"You will if you helped Cordy take any of the money out," I said.

"Good grief." I was glad to see that she was appalled at the idea. "You're not pinning anything like that on me! I never did such a thing. Never! Cordy asked me . . ." She bit her lip. "That is, Cordy called up the other day and asked if what I'd told him was still in it, and it all was."

"And how much was it?"

"Three million five hundred thousand and twenty dollars and forty-six cents."

# Sixteen

❦⟋⟍❦

"How much?!" Madeline's voice came over the cell phone like the blast of Gideon's trumpet.

I held the infernal thing away from my ear and repeated the amount.

"You don't have to yell at me, darlin'. I can hear you just fine. And I'm just floored."

"You don't have to yell at *me*."

"Hang on a minute, sweetie . . ." She turned away and the decibel level dropped to merciful levels. "Ally says I'm doin' cell yell."

"What?"

"*Cell yell!* It's when you talk louder on the phone than you really have to."

The pain in my eardrum was excruciating. "I'll be there momentarily, Madeline. Shut down the phone!" I dropped the dratted thing into the cup holder on car console, suppressing a fervent desire to crush it under my heel, despite its usefulness.

I was only a few minutes away from Lila Gernsbeck's farm. At my urging, Cheryl had given me a fairly complete account of how she had spent the evening and early morning at the time of Lewis's murder. (At home. With her parents and two girlfriends who'd spent the night viewing horror films. Which seemed to put her in the clear as a possible accomplice to the murder.) She had just finished the remainder of the cherry scones when my cell phone had rung. With Cheryl's assistance, I'd managed to answer the call. It was Madeline, calling from Lila's, and there was a problem with one of Lila's geldings. So I'd thanked Cheryl, assured her that she was not going to be arrested for snooping as long as she kept the news to herself and never did it again, and set off for Lila's. Once on the way, I decided that the news of the amount of money in Lewis's bank account was too astonishing to keep to myself, so I had rung Madeline back. It worked. I suppose if I got the hang of it, the cell phone wasn't the worst piece of technology ever created.

Lila's twenty acres lie off Route 332. She has a large indoor arena, a twenty-stall barn, and a magnificent old center-entrance Georgian house. The buildings are set well back on a graveled drive. Two large fenced pastures protect her facility from the road traffic. Both held horses. Ally's horse Harker was in the one on the east side of the drive, and he raised his head and whinnied at the sound of the Bronco's engine. Horses are unique creatures, far more sensitive to the five senses than human beings give them credit for. Juno recognized my vehicle, too, and she raced happily down the drive, her tail waving like a pennant in a stiff breeze.

Lila, Ally, and Madeline stood in front of the arena door. Ally was in breeches and paddock boots. She looked as if she'd just come off of a marathon. Lila was clad in what Madeline calls her "Divorcée Available" garb: tight jeans, a low-cut T-shirt of some slinky material, and lizard-skin cowboy boots. Although not as magnificently proportioned as Madeline's, Lila's figure is quite curvy. I am absolutely terrified of her, as are most men over fifty. She is a positive danger to men with a cardiac condition.

Lila waved strenuously and yoo-hooed at the car. I waved back, parked, and got out to greet my wife and errant assistant. Ally gave me a brief, hard hug. I looked closely at her. She looked as if she had been getting some sleep. Best of all, she looked relaxed. The hard riding and comfortable hospitality at Lila's clearly agreed with her.

"Austin!" Lila said, enveloping me in a hug of her own. "Maddy's been telling us all about the murders."

"It's just the one." I reflected a moment. "So far."

Madeline looked alarmed. "Good grief. Do you think someone else is going to get killed?"

"I considered dispatching Gil Finnegan to his Maker this morning. I may yet. But no, I don't anticipate another death. Unless Lewis has written something peculiar into his will and left the money and the farm to the Summersville mayor. Then we'll have to prevent an assassination attempt."

"I'm surprised no one knocked the old bastard off before," Lila said. "And don't count on his leaving his money to the boys. The old skinflint didn't allow one of those boys to go to college. Can you believe it? Stuck on a turkey farm all their lives, with no other job skills to speak of? And somebody like Cordy, especially."

Madeline cocked her head to one side and said, "Hm. I know that tone of voice of yours, Lila. Like Cordy especially what?"

Lila smirked.

"Oh, Lila, not Cordy."

Lila's grin widened, rather cheekily, I thought. "Best-looking man in Tompkins County. What do you want me to do? Retire to a nunnery?"

"Stop biting your mustache, Austin," Madeline said absentmindedly. "And close your mouth. Lila Eileen Gernsback, you are something else. So how did all that come about?"

I'd overheard accounts of Lila's escapades before. "Allegra," I said sternly, "aren't you needed in the barn?"

All three women turned, looked at me, and burst into laughter. Madeline wrapped her arms around me and kissed me heartily on the cheek. Then she turned back to Lila and said, "How long were you two . . . you know. Involved."

"Oh, couple of weeks. He's not a bad guy, but that family of his . . ."

I could stand it no longer. "He's twenty years younger than you are, Lila."

"Austin, *I'm* twenty years younger than you are," Madeline said. "Go on, Lila."

"But," I began.

Then three women all looked at me again. "Austin," Lila said, "if you're even thinking about saying what you're thinking, button it up. Honestly, Madeline, how do you stand it?"

"Well," Madeline said comfortably, "it has its compensations." She wriggled her eyebrows. And all three women burst into laughter again.

"I am going to check on the horse," I said stiffly.

"Hang on a minute, sweetie. I'm sorry. I do sincerely apologize. But you get so fusty sometimes. Lila, you were saying about Cordy's family?"

"Well, Ron's marriage was the saving of him, I'll say that. Linda's a peach. And she let all the bushwa the old man handed out roll right off her back. But the other two boys suffer some, let me tell you. And that Maired. Phut!"

"Bushwa like what?" Madeline said in a very interested way.

"Sunday dinner with the *whole* family every single week. And after dinner, it's women in the kitchen, men in the parlor. No excuses. If any one of 'em was a no show, Lewis'd take a chunk out of the next week's paycheck. And he offered Maired and Linda a bonus if either one of them got pregnant. Man, I could go on and on. You told me about his whacking Ron at that talk of Austin's, Maddy. That's just the half of it."

"Why didn't the boys just move on?" Madeline asked.

"Oh, they tried." Lila widened her eyes and shook her head. "A few years ago, Jensen got a job offer from a big dairy farm in Illinois. Near Champaign-Urbana, which was sophisticated enough for Miss Maired, I guess, because both of them really wanted to go. Lewis got wind of it, and put the kibosh on it. No one knows how, for sure, but Cordy thinks his father told the dairy people Jensen was on psychiatric drugs."

"Good god." I began to have some sympathy for Cordy's behavior.

"Well, that just sucks," Ally said. "It's just mean."

Lila lowered her voice, although there was no one else around to overhead but the horses. "I hear that Ron and Linda just decided to leave. Right in the middle of the night. Lewis found out—my guess is that awful Angela ratted on her own son—and put Ron in the hospital for a week. Whacked him with a tire iron."

"Indeed," I said thoughtfully. "A tire iron, you say."

"On his own son. Not that it's any worse than hitting a perfect stranger with a tire iron. I mean, the whole idea's revolting." Lila shuddered. "Anyhow, if you see anybody dancing at the funeral, you'll know why."

"Whoa," Ally said. "And I thought my fa . . ." She bit her lip.

Madeline patted her shoulder. "It's a hard old world, Ally."

"Anyway," Lila concluded, "There's a whole pile of motives there. Money's the least of it."

"Except for the timing," I said. "Lewis's behavior should have driven any one of the three to homicide years ago. So the question is: why now? What's changed? And the answer is. Cordy knows about the money. And if Cordy knows, perhaps the other brothers do, as well."

"So you're thinking money's the motive for the murder?" Lila asked.

I pondered the alliteration, and then said, "Perhaps. This case is proving to be quite challenging."

"Three million dollars," Madeline said. "I can't imagine."

Lila, whose several husbands had left her much more than that in the aggregate, said, "Well, I can. And you'd be surprised how little that is, these days."

"If that's so, I'm sure you'll be quite comfortable with the size of my bill." I withdrew my case from the rear trunk of the Bronco. "We seem to have forgotten the reason I dropped by. What's the problem with the horse?"

"Violet's colicky again. I tried a couple of ccs of Banamine, but it didn't seem to help." Lila was sometimes indiscriminate in her attitude toward men, but she cared deeply for her horses. She bit her lip. "I've got her in the back, in the big stall. She's not in pain at the moment, the Banamine took care of that. But she hasn't passed manure for more than twelve hours."

Constipation in a horse is not to be treated lightly. The equine digestive system is simple to the point of ineffectiveness. Food is processed only one way through a horse. There is no gag reflex. And the digestive enzymes in the equine system are not equipped to handle complex feed. If the intestines are blocked, the horse can rupture. If that occurs, there is little than can be done to save the animal.

I turned toward the barn, and they fell in step behind me. Colic is a portmanteau word, a vague diagnostic term that covers a multitude of possible gastrointestinal diseases. I wasn't quite sure was going on with Violet. But after noting her respiration—too fast at fifty beats a minute—and her temperature—too low at 96°F—I suggested that we take her to the Equine Hospital at Cornell.

"We'll do a CT scan. And a full run of lab tests." I snapped my case closed with a regretful sigh. "If a fifth of the money poured into the research of common human diseases were put into equine research, we would be a lot farther ahead in the treatment of horses. A gastroenterologist would be able to target the cause of Violet's bellyache within hours."

"It'd help if she could talk," Allegra said. She patted the mare's sweaty neck. "What do you want me to do, Lila? I can stay here and take care of things or I can truck her to the hospital and stay with her while they do their thing."

"I'll take her in. You keep an eye on the barn help." Lila ran her hair through her dark curls and sighed heavily. "I'll tell you what, Maddy. You want to make this a permanent arrangemen, Ally living here with me, I'd jump at the chance."

I glanced at Madeline in alarm. And—thank goodness—Allegra glanced at Lila in alarm. "Thanks, Lila. I really appreciate it. And you're giving me just amazing help with Harker. But I'm so homesick I could just spit."

Lila looked wistful, which made me regret the jab of happiness that Allegra's words had given me. Not enough, however, to suggest that Ally take Lila up on her offer.

"Let's get poor Violet loaded up," Madeline said briskly. "And then it's time you and I went home, Austin."


I withheld discussion of the results of my investigation until after dinner, when Fulbright retired to the junk room with Lee Child's latest thriller. Fulbright was, come to think of it, living an existence like Child's hero Jack Reacher: alone, friendless, without a place to call home. The difference was, of course, that Reacher liked it that way.

"I think," Joe said after I had summarized the day's events. "That somebody ought to bring Gil's lawyer up to date on all of this. I know Krippendorf. He's a jerk. And if he's trying to score off the school, he's a criminal jerk. But it seems to me that there's enough of a motive there to interest the police in an alternative theory of the murder, and Gil's lawyer should know about that right away. As for that three million bucks!" Joe shook his head. "Man, what I could do with three million bucks. Either of those two motives is a lot better than the one the cops have for Finnegan. I mean, the poor schmuck can always get another job."

"Not if he were fired under the threat of prosecution for theft. Which is what O'Leary was alleging." I took a welcome sip of Scotch.

"Yeah, but everyone around here knows O'Leary pulls that crap all the time," Joe said. "A good defense attorney could pull a lot of people who've had that kind of trouble with O'Leary before. I think we should give Finnegan's lawyer a head's up."

"You're right," I said.

"Good." Joe sprang to his feet. "Anything else she should know?"

"Yes. Please stop by Finnegan's home and get copies of the e-mail relevant to the research scam. Finnegan's wife is named Bea. Call her first, to let her know you're coming. And give copies of the e-mails to Ms. Beaufort."

Madeline looked up from the button she was sewing onto an old denim shirt of mine. "You're going over to the lawyer's now?" she said in mild surprise. "Does she keep late office hours? I know some of them do."

"I'll offer to buy her a drink to make up for it," Joe said. He tipped his hand in a mock salute. "Don't wait up for me."

Madeline watched him go with a smile. "I wondered why he was wearing his polo shirt."

"His polo shirt?"

"Yes, Austin. He only has the one nice shirt, Haven't you noticed?"

"No." I said frankly, "and I can't think why I should."

"Is she pretty? Gil's lawyer?"

I stopped to consider. "She's beautiful. Joe was quite struck."

"And you, darlin'? Were you quite struck?"

I set my Scotch down. I haven't been happily married for twenty-two years without learning something. "This is a trick question," I said. "And I refuse to answer it. She is quite lovely. And a southerner, as you are. I think you would like her a great deal."

"I bet I would." Madeline rethreaded the needle. "I talked to Thelma today."

"I thought she and her mother were headed to Atlanta."

"They're partway there. She called to see if maybe Victor had called you. Did he?"

"No. But I was all over the county today." I got up and poured another finger of Scotch. "I'll leave word of my cell phone number at his office. He's bound to drop in there at some point."

"I feel so bad for Thelma, Austin. I've been thinking that maybe you should talk to Victor after all."

"I know I have to speak to Victor."

"So you'll set aside the investigation for a little bit? Try and track him down tomorrow?"

"I will. And it is related to the investigation, you know. After I alert John Wu to the attempted defalcations of his student, I have to let Victor know. He's chair of the department. He'll be the one who decides how far the school wants to take the matter."

"Do you know where to find him?"

I sighed. Lucinda Whitby's home address was undoubtedly at the university offices. Yes, I knew where to find him. But I wasn't at all sure that he wanted to be found.

# Seventeen

JOHN Wu's face shuttered shut. Then he said, "Shit."

John's office had a window facing my old stomping grounds, the cow barns, and a comfortable armchair. I sat and watched two Belted Galloways sharing the feed trough. Cows have something in common with humankind. Most herd members share the trough peaceably enough. But there are others that grab as much as they can for themselves.

John slammed the article he'd been editing into the desk drawer and leaned back in his office chair. "So what now, do you think? Jeez. I should have known something funny was up when he kept putting off presenting the data. The guy's a sleaze, and he may actually have committed an indictable offense, which makes him a crook, too. But by gosh, Austin, he's a smart son of a gun. That additive's worth a bundle to the school if it works. It was brilliant work, brilliant."

We both sat there, saddened and repelled. "Nothing is worse than a scholar gone bad," I said.

"Oh, I don't know. Islamic terrorists disgust me a lot more.

But it's bad enough. And thank god you discovered this before it blew up into a scandal. What do you think we should do now?"

"There's e-mail evidence of attempt to sell the research. I've made copies. Joe Turnblad picked up Finnegan's laptop from his wife last night. And he very wisely asked her to lock the computer up, in case we need to defend the authenticity of the messages. And Finnegan, of course, will testify, if need be. And there's what Gil keeps referring to as corporate, of course."

"But they're in Illinois. The department doesn't have the funds to get them here."

"I doubt it will come to that." A thought struck me. Karen Crown had left several phone calls for me, presumably regarding the parameters of my job as the Green Seal consultant. I hadn't had time to return them. "But they have a representative here in Tompkins County. She may be able to help."

"Good. The less expense associated with this thing the better. Well. I'll get on it, myself. How's Joe doing?"

I smiled. "I should ask you that, shouldn't I? What's his reputation here?"

"His work last year was terrific. Now, there's a student who could have a future in research. Give him a nudge for me, will you?"

"It's a little staid for him at the moment. But I'm glad to hear he's doing well." At the end of a discussion about the possibility of increasing the amount of scholarship money for Joe, John said, "Of course, if this thing with Krip blows up, we can kiss any future grants good-bye."

"Nonsense."

"You held the chair for fifteen years, Austin. What do you think we should do?"

"I'm not the chair now." I got to my feet. "We need to talk to Victor. It's his call."

"Oh god, Victor." John rolled his eyes.

"Do you know where I might find him?"

"This time of day? He's probably in the cow barn. He's fiddling around with some new endocrine studies. Eight hours from now?" He chuckled. "I hear he's shacked up with that little nitwit Lucinda . . ."

I didn't want to hear any gossip about my old friend. "I'll be in touch," I said firmly.

I said my farewells, closed John's office door behind me, and wound my way through the quiet halls to the exit facing the cow barns.

The school has been fortunate in its endowments. The cow barns are spacious and beautifully laid out. Well-equipped labs are at hand, and there is no shortage of interesting research. If Victor was working on a study involving endocrines, he was likely at the east end of the sprawling building, where the gravid heifers were located.

And I did find him there, poring over an electron microscope in a small lab space directly opposite the stalls.

I stopped in the doorway, my hand poised to rap the door frame to gain his attention. He did not look well. The substantial pouches beneath his eyes were baggier than ever. His hair stuck up in the back of his head. His hands trembled as he removed a slide from beneath the scope and replaced it with another.

I struck the frame with my knuckles and said, "Well, Bergland. Loafing as usual, I see." A small stool was tucked in the corner of the lab; I pulled it out and sat down on it.

"McKenzie!" Victor said, in parody of his former self. "Dropped in to see how it's supposed to be done?"

I repressed my response to this irrelevant twaddle. How what's supposed to be done? Make a total ass of myself? "So what's on with that?" I nodded toward the microscope.

"Nothing terribly new. Artificial estrogen. There's some evidence we can modify bovine endocrine more efficiently than equine. It's a small project, but it will save somebody some money somewhere." He packed the slides neatly away in a case, and then placed the case in the refrigerator underneath the countertop. "Can I buy you a cup of coffee?"

This, I had learned some time ago, is a colloquialism. Victor did not care for coffee and we jousted to see who was stuck with the bill. "Surely. What about your office?"

"Cafeteria's closer."

We stopped in the aisle and looked at the pregnant cow who was the source of the hormones Victor used in his experiment. I like cows. I've always liked cows. In general, they are peaceful creature with mild, contented expressions. Looking at them makes me feel quite serene. This cow was a Guernsey, an exceptionally pretty breed of dairy cow, valued for the high butterfat content of their milk. I particularly liked looking at cows in the university barns. There is a superfluity of student labor available, and the stalls are always filled with clean shavings and the aisles swept free of debris.

Victor patted the cow on the head. "Thanks for the donation, old girl." He turned to me. "Have you noticed that the eyelashes on a Guernsey are longer than other breeds?"

"I can't say as I have, Victor."

"Lucinda's eyelashes are like that. Long and curling."

It is a curious fact that a man in the throes of an affair will let no opportunity pass to mention the name of the beloved. I corralled my impatience and said nothing.

"Her eyes are brown, too. More of a leafy brown, if you know what I mean."

"The cow's?"

"Lucinda's." Victor's tone was reproving.

As we began to walk out of the building, I began, "You're aware I've been looking into the O'Leary matter."

"The O'Leary matter. Yes. Lucinda's made that quite a cause celebre."

"Good heavens. Why?"

"I may have mentioned the Organized Outrage Over Factory Farming."

"OOOFF. But what does that . . . ? Oh! No. Lewis O'Leary was murdered three days ago. That's the matter I'm looking into." I scratched my head. "What does OOOFF have to do with O'Leary?"

"The welfare of the turkeys has everything to do with the O'Learys. Lucinda has hopes that the death of the old man would make a difference. She has hopes of bringing the younger generation to their senses."

"Anything's possible. But I was at the grower facility not two days ago and the birds seemed quite happy to me."

"It'd be difficult to convince Lucinda of that," Victor said with a wry little laugh.

We had left the building for the sunshine of this mild July day. I stopped on the sidewalk. "Victor. Do you realize how often you mention . . ." I bit off the rest of my sentence. "Never mind."

"How often I mention what? Lucinda says . . ."

"I said never *mind*." We walked on in silence for a bit. "What you should have asked me is why I was in the grower shed." We had reached the student cafeteria. I opened the door to let Victor precede me. It was quiet inside, almost empty of students and faculty, and smelled faintly of canned vegetables and floor wax. "You aren't going to like what I discovered there."

He didn't like the answer at all. His response to the news that Alan Krippendorf had attempted to steal valuable university property was not as vehement as his disgust over the tainted data. A whole five minutes went by without one mention of the annoying Lucinda. (Of course, I hadn't met the girl. For all I knew, she was genuinely in love with my banana-nosed old friend.)

"I'll have to call a department meeting." Victor took a sip of the cafeteria's horrible stewed tea. We had seated ourselves at a table by the windows, as far away as possible from the servers and cashiers. "Who else knows about this? You went to John first, I take it."

"I've just come from him. He had no idea."

"He should have been on top of the study, however." Victor's tone was dispassionate. "His supervision was lackadaisical, if not downright sloppy. The carcass pattern should have alerted him, if nothing else. If you've got one dead turkey, you should have several more dead turkeys. Coccidiosis may not wipe out a whole flock, but it doesn't limit itself to one animal at a time. Any freshman biology student knows that. It's interesting though. You could make a case that this proves the vaccine works. The only way the birds died was if injected with a live bacterium. Hm. Well. Thank you, Austin. If we can keep this to ourselves you've prevented a scandal in the department. I'm grateful."

But I was caught up in Victor's offhand comment about the putative freshman biology student. "John said Krippendorf is bright enough."

"Very bright," Victor grunted. "Damn shame. Have you noticed, though, that the really genius ones always have a kind of a kink?"

"I hadn't noticed that, no. But it does occur to me that he must have realized this one carcass at a time stuff is atypical. And you're right. It would have been a red flag to John had John insisted on seeing the data. Krippendorf was taking quite a risk. I'll tell you something." I paused, thought it over, and concluded I must be right. "Someone else injected those turkeys. Krippendorf's not that stupid."

"So?"

"So he must have had an accomplice." I sipped at my own, equally terrible coffee. "Hm. Interesting. I must say this detective work is as fascinating as any study of viral infections or back fat striations. Something's always popping up and leading me a new direction. Madeline says that one should totally shake up one's patterns every so often. Keeps you on your toes."

And wasn't that a mistake. Victor certainly agreed that one should shake up life patterns every now and again. I listened to paeans to Lucinda for quite half an hour before I had had enough and left him.

I returned to the Bronco with my mind made up. Heretofore, I had avoided a collegial discussion of the progress of the case with Simon Provost. I could delay no longer. The evidence I'd turned up surrounding the victim was too relevant to the police investigation to be ignored. I withdrew my cell phone from my pocket and punched in the number of the Summersville Police Department. Simon was in. He would spare me half an hour.

He was also eating a large, sloppy submarine sandwich.

"Hey, Doc."

"Hey, yourself." I gestured at the wooden captain's chair in front of his desk.

"Go ahead and take a load off."

I sat and surveyed my surroundings. The Summersville Police Department is not as small as one might think. It provides police services for six of the small towns surrounding Ithaca and is a large enough to have a policeman in charge of crimes against persons. It is not large enough to have more than one. Simon's office was nondescript: indoor-outdoor carpeting on the floor, metal desk in fairly good condition, a credenza constructed of pressboard in the corner. Photographs of his wife and children stood on his desk. A bowling trophy held pride of place on the credenza.

Simon leaned forward to get the maximum amount of sandwich in his mouth with the least amount of spillage. He had been unsuccessful in the first few attempts. Marinara sauce spattered his tie.

"New sub shop opened off of Taughonnick Parkway," he mumbled. "Sauce is almost as good as Becky's."

Rebecca Provost smiled at me from a large-framed photo on Simon's desk. She was a large, genial-looking woman with a happy smile.

"So what's up with you?"

"I have information relevant to the O'Leary case."

Simon put the sandwich down. "Austin. For Pete's sake. The evidence against Finnegan is pretty damn foolproof. What the heck have you stirred up now?"

"You aren't bothered by the discrepancies? You should be." I began to list them. "First: the river water on the seat of the corpse's trousers."

"What's to say O'Leary didn't take a stroll down by the river while he was waiting for Finnegan to come and crack him over the head and then fall in?"

"Was there river water on his shoes?"

Simon's eyes narrowed. "No," he said slowly. "I missed that."

"Second: The egg albumen on the victim's overalls and the *lack* of egg albumen on Finnegan. If the turkey feathers and turkey blood were transferred to Finnegan's clothes as he struggled with O'Leary, why wasn't all of it transferred?"

"Now, that did bother me," Simon admitted, "but with the weight of the other evidence, I just figured it was one of those loose ends that crop up in cases once in a while. Real murder's not like your mystery stories, McKenzie. Sometimes stuff doesn't mean anything at all."

I conceded that this might be true. "What I have next to offer is opinion. It is opinion based on a presumption of innocence. That is the foundation of the judiciary in this country."

Simon burped. "McKenzie, sometimes you're a real pain in the patoot."

"So my wife informs me. I'll try to be less sententious."

"If I knew what that meant, I'd ask you to try and be that, too."

"If we assume Gil's telling the truth, the physical evidence forms a clearer, more ominous pattern."

"Yeah?"

"A frame-up."

"A frame-up." Simon stuck a toothpick in his mouth and rolled it from one side to the other. He contemplated the ceiling. Finally he said, with an air of great restraint: "You've been reading too many mysteries, Doc. And I'm going to call the cable company and get them to take the PBS station off your receiver."

"Ha ha." I said composedly. "Very funny."

Simon held up a marinara spotted hand and ticked off the points one by one. "The victim's blood in the back of the pickup. The blood and brains on the tire iron. Finnegan's fingerprints on the tire iron. Seems pretty darn obvious to me that it all points to Finnegan. How does that particular evidence add up to a frame?"

I evaded a direct response. It would only inspire Simon to further gibes. "I've a suggestion. Is Finnegan's pickup still impounded?"

"Probably. We're kind of slow on getting that sort of stuff back to the family. Why?"

"Would it be possible to check his tires? He had two tire failures within half an hour of one another. At a time when it would be most desirable to have him out of commission. That seems quite a coincidence to me."

Simon bit down on the toothpick so that it stood out at an angle. He sighed heavily. But he made a note. "Anything else?"

"Someone else did this, Simon. There are several alternatives. Some possible motives have come to light. I believe you'll find them compelling."

I told him about Krippendorf. Then I told him about O'Leary's checking account.

"Three million bucks?" Simon looked younger when he was astonished. Perhaps it was because the wrinkles in his face smoothed out when his mouth was open.

"Quite a sum." I tried to avoid sounding complacent.

"The old bastard." Simon shook his head wonderingly and

dumped the toothpick in his wastepaper basket. His eyes went to the pictures of his family. "You know I've never known any of that crew to get any time off to speak of. No vacations. No help to spell them on chores, either. He kept 'em hunched over and plowing hard."

"It's rare that somebody likeable's murdered, isn't it?"

"I suppose so. Well. First thing is to question Cordy. That's clear. And Jensen, too. And this Krippendorf? Sounds like I can nail him for false representation, at least."

I had my Honorary Deputy badge at the ready. I flourished it.

"Yeah. Fine. I give up. You can come along with me." He stuck another toothpick in his mouth. "Good work, McKenzie. Now let's go see if we can catch us a murderer."

# Eighteen

~~~

RIDING in a police cruiser put me forcibly in mind of my early days as a student at Cornell. I'd owned a 1955 Ford LTD sedan that rode as low and as squashy as the department's Chevy. Simon drove in quite a relaxed manner, although I noticed that he kept an alert eye on everything going on around us.

He hadn't precisely *sprung* into action at the police station, but he managed to get quite a bit accomplished before we left. He called Victor to see if the college wanted to press charges. Victor did. He alerted the Syracuse district attorney's office to Alan Krippendorf's activities and dispatched a patrolman to get an order to acquire Finnegan's computer.

Finally, in an action that I thoroughly approved, he ordered Krippendorf brought in for questioning. We then headed out to the turkey-growing facility, where the main farm office was located.

The place had the same rigidly dispiriting air that had so unsettled my wife. With one notable difference. I waited until Simon had come to a halt near the sign reading OFFICE O'LEARY'S POULTRY FARMS and tapped him on the forearm.

"The pickup truck." A brand-new Chevy three-quarter-ton pickup was parked at the back steps of the house.

"Yep. Already heard about that." Simon rubbed his nose. "To tell you the truth, Doc, I was a little uneasy about the case myself."

"Who purchased it?"

"Cordy. Cute little gal at the Chevy place let him drive it out of the lot on credit." He eyed me. "Thing is, he seems to have got it *before* the old man kicked the bucket."

"Perhaps he was anticipating profits from Krippendorf's scam."

"Maybe. Maybe not."

Simon pushed open the office door without knocking and eased himself into the office. Cordy sat at the desk, intent on the computer screen.

"Cordy?"

He jerked to awareness. Then he got up out of the chair and extended his hand in greeting. "Lieutenant. Dr. McKenzie. It's good to see you both."

I was beginning to understand Madeline's "sexy pirate" comment. I was even sympathetic to Lila's escapade. The man was quite good-looking. More than that, away from what must have the oppressive presence of his father, he had an easy, relaxed charm.

"So what can I do for you two gentlemen?"

"Just a couple of questions, O'Leary. But before I get to them, how's your ma?"

"Ma?" He looked blank. "Oh. Of course. She's doing as well as can be expected."

"And how well is that?"

Cordy shrugged. Then he grinned, very man-to-man. "You know how it is, Lieutenant. What with Pa gone, I've practically been chained to the desk here. This is a pretty big operation, and Pa was an important part of it, rest his soul. I've got some big shoes to fill."

Rest his soul, indeed. Hypocrite. I revised my notion about Cordy's charm. "That a fact," Simon said with mild interest. He glanced at me out of the corner of his eye. It was clear that our two minds were running along the same channel. Cordy's assumed piety didn't sit well with either one of us.

"You want to check up on Ma, it's a good idea to ask Ron." A peculiar expression crossed his face. I couldn't read it. I wished Madeline were with me. She would have identified it right away. Envy? Dislike? Even hatred? Whatever it was, it wasn't pleasant.

"I'll get around to that. And did you get around to talkin' to the family lawyer about the will? Seems I recall your family uses Howie Murchison, over in Hemlock Falls."

"As a matter of fact, I did. What with Ma in the hospital and not able to sign the checks, we had to get a grip on what's going to happen here."

"And?"

Cordy did his best to suppress a smile. "Looks like he left it all to me."

The silence was pregnant with the unspoken.

"That a fact," Simon repeated. He appeared to rely on this locution when his brain was busy elsewhere. "Disappoints your brothers some, I expect."

"Well." Cordy cleared his throat. "You can say what you like about Pa, but he set up a pretty solid business model here." The response was evasive, to say the least.

"Right." Simon fumbled vaguely in his shirt pocket and brought out his notepad. "Got a few questions I'd like to ask you about the night your father was murdered."

"Just clearing up a few loose ends, Lieutenant? Or am I under suspicion?"

Simon opened his very wide and looked directly at him. "Oh, you're under suspicion, Cordy. Yes, indeed."

Cordy's alibi for the night of the murder was interesting. He claimed he had left the Embassy soon after the fight with his father and gone home to the farmhouse where he lived with his parents. His mother, he claimed, would back him up. But his mother was in the ICU at Tompkins County Hospital, unable to speak. And an unsettling idea troubled me. A son able to kill his father wouldn't stick at knocking his mother off, too. I made a mental note to inquire about the etiology of the poor woman's stroke. In short, Cordy's alibi was not airtight—but it was suspect.

"Simon, you're a very good policeman," I said as we made our way back to the police station.

His cheeks turned red. "Why, thank you, Doc."

"But do you find yourself gloomy about the capacity of human beings for each of the Seven Deadly Sins? I am not a religious man, Provost, but I am struck over and over again with the perspicacity of the earliest theologians."

"I'd say I'm no gloomier than the next fella," Provost offered. "You've got your good guys and you've got your bad guys. A lot of police work is trying to figure out which is which."

"And you're not worried that Cordy's going to take a powder?"

He glanced at me and laughed. "Where does stuff like 'take a powder' come from? I swear, Doc, you haven't noticed we're living in the twenty-first century, here. And no, I'm not worried Cordy's going to skip town. He's got three million reasons to stick around. If nothing else, that'll buy him one heck of a good defense. The rich get away with a lot more than the poor do." He caught the look of dismay on my face. "Hey," he said comfortably, "it is what it is. You're going to make yourself crazy if you expect things to be different. Ah." He slowed down to make the turn into the police department parking lot. "Kiddermeister's back. I hope that means he's collared our crooked graduate student."

Kiddermeister had indeed brought Krippendorf in for questioning. The Summersville Police Department has a small interview room set between its two jail cells, or to be precise, the holding pens, and the dispatcher told us Krippendorf awaited us there.

All three areas were carpeted with indoor-outdoor carpeting, "Which," Provost said as we approached the interview area, "has turned out to be as big a mistake as I told the town council it would." The dispatcher had given him a folder as we had entered the station, and he waved it rather absentmindedly under his chin. It was hot. And the air-conditioning appeared to be struggling. "Nope. We're going to have to get rid of it one of these days."

I raised an eyebrow.

"Drunk college kids don't care where they pee," he said as he opened the door to the interview room, then, "Well, well, well, if it isn't Mr. Krippendorf."

Krippendorf had thrown himself into one of the two chairs

in the room. He turned with a snarl and said, "It's Dr. Krippendorf, you fool, and you'd better have some damn good insurance against false arrest."

"You haven't been arrested," Simon said mildly. "Officer Kiddermeister brought you in for questioning. Did he tell you you've been arrested?"

"No." Krippendorf said sulkily.

"Now, if you'd like to confess to a crime I'd be happy to arrest you. But at the moment, I'd just like the answers to a couple of questions."

"Questioning about what, for god's sake? I haven't done anything."

Provost is about four inches taller than I, and broader by some eighty pounds. I had of, course, deferred to his authority and allowed him to precede me through the door. As a result, Krippendorf failed to see me immediately. When he did, he turned white. His jaw dropped. He shrank back into his chair. Then he turned red.

"You know Dr. McKenzie," Simon said.

He recovered himself quickly, I'll give him that. "Everybody at the school knows McKenzie. So what?"

The second chair in the room was situated on one side of a small, linoleum topped table. Simon dropped into it with a sigh. "So, he has an interesting story."

I folded my arms across my chest and leaned against the wall. Krippendorf worried his lower lip with his teeth and looked everywhere but directly at me.

"That's a story he's going to take to the folks at the school," Simon continued. "But I got to say it's not something I'm especially interested in. At the moment, that is."

"Fine. I don't give a rat's ass, either. Is that it? I can go?"

"Come on, now, Dr. Krippendorf. You have to be smarter than you look. I'm not real taken with the thought you might have tried to steal a million-dollar idea from your school, but we'll save that problem for another time. I'm much more interested in something else. The murder of Lewis O'Leary."

"What!?" The sound came out in a turkeylike screech. "What are you talking about? I don't have a thing to do with the O'Learys. They happen to own the place where I do my research. So frickin' what?"

Simon laid the folder on the table and flipped it open. "What I have here is your arrest record."

Arrest record? How interesting. How very interesting.

"Mm," Simon said as he read through the file. "My, my. I've got you down here for malicious mischief. You and a . . . Lucinda Whitby? Yep. Lucinda Whitby. Says here she's a second-year vet student at the school. It also says here that you and her . . ."

"She," I said. "You and she." I scarcely noticed my own interruption. My brain was reeling. Lucinda Whitby!

Simon looked over his shoulder at me in a very deliberate way. He turned back to Krippendorf and resumed, "It says here that you and Lucinda Whitby threw yourselves in front of the Green Seal Feeds truck while it was making a delivery this May."

"Oh. That." He flushed an unattractive red. "You know how it is, Lieutenant."

"Can't say as I do."

"Well. I'm the TA in one of her classes. She came to me for some tutoring help." He shot a look at me, and then looked away. "Anyhow. You ever met Lucinda? No? Well, she's . . . um . . . hot. And one thing led to another and she's very committed to this organization that she founded."

"OOOFF?"

"The Organized Outrage Over Factory Farming. That'd be it. So my being there for her was sort of a quid pro quo, you might say."

"Pah," I said in disgust.

Simon leveled that look at me again. Then he flipped a page in the folder. "Says here you're married? With a couple of kids?"

"Well, yes, and when Robin found me out, there was hell to pay, I can tell you." He made a weak attempt at a gobbling sort of chuckle, which increased his resemblance to a Narragansett Bronze. "Anyhow. Ellen threw me out. And Lucinda threw me out, too, for the fat old geek that chairs my department, as a matter of fact."

"Ah huh." Simon read on. "Says here further Miss Whitby was arrested for trespassing on O'Leary land the day Lewis O'Leary was murdered. She refused to leave the premises.

There was a scuffle of some kind. Lewis O'Leary ended up knocking her to the ground and threatening to run the manure spreader over her. He called us. She was arrested. She said she was going to blow the place up if she had to." Simon looked up. His eyes were cold. "She gave us the member names. You're at the top of the list. And you say you didn't have anything against Lewis O'Leary?"

The remainder of the interview was frustrating in the extreme. Krippendorf's account of his movements on the night of the murder was vague and unconvincing. He'd left the high school and driven to Lucinda's apartment. She wasn't in. He'd knocked. Maybe one of the neighbors had heard him, maybe they hadn't. If the police did their job, they'd find someone who'd heard him. He'd returned home around 10:15, and gotten into a brief altercation with his downstairs neighbor over the neighbor's failure to recycle garbage. The argument had grown heated. He went to bed—alone—and got up around nine. In addition to being a crook and bad scientist, the man was a sloth.

It also occurred to me that the murderer had been extremely clever, selecting a time when the best alibi other suspects could come up with was that they were asleep.

An argument that Lucinda Whitby offered up when we interviewed her as soon as Provost let Krippendorf go home.

# Nineteen

❧❧❧

IT was by now well after three o'clock. I had not seen my wife or my dog since early that morning. They are so much part of my day that I felt oddly isolated without them. I sat down in the interview room to think about this.

"You feeling okay, Doc?" Simon was reviewing the comments he'd scribbled into his notebook. "Can I get you anything? Glass of water? Jeez, sorry. I just kind of forgot how old . . . I mean I forgot that you aren't part of the team. Most cops are used to standing for hours on end. We have to be. Let me get you a glass of water."

"I'm fine," I said shortly. "And seventy-two is no age at all, Provost. I merely sat down to reflect on the perfidy of humankind. Krippendorf is not exactly a sterling example to his students or the rest of us. Not to mention," I added, having just recalled this, "I managed to skip lunch."

"Why don't you go on home and get some," Provost suggested. "I'm going out to track down this Lucinda Whitby, president and founder of . . ." He squinted at his notes.

". . . the Organized Outrage Over Factory Farming. Phooey! I'll let you know how it goes."

"Thank you, Lieutenant. But I might mention that Lucinda's 'fat old fart'—to whom Krippendorf referred to in his jeremiad—is my oldest friend, Victor Bergland."

"You're kidding me. Victor? Nah. You're nuts!"

"I wish I were. He has left his wife and joined Miss Whitby."

Provost gave his wife's photograph an affectionate pat. "Well, no offense meant, Austin, but I've met Mrs. Bergland and . . ." He stopped in midsentence.

"True," I said, acknowledging the unsaid. "Not to mention the fact that she looks like an artichoke."

"Might help things along if you come with me, then."

"I'd appreciate that."

"Tell you what. We'll stop on the way and pick you up one of those submarines."

The submarine sandwich was delicious. Provost recommended the Italian Stallion, which was even drippier than the Submarine ala Milano that still adorned parts of Simon's shirt. I enjoyed it immensely. And the food invigorated me. Here I was, tooling along this beautiful countryside, with a delicious sandwich, on the trail of a cold-blooded killer. Life couldn't get any better than this.

"Ms. Whitby lives off the Octopus." Victor negotiated the tricky curves into Ithaca proper with aplomb. He was referring to the notorious intersection of three main highways at the entrance to town. Built on the shores of Cayuga Lake, between the folds of glacial moraines, the town has nowhere to sprawl; hence the Octopus. Lucinda's apartment was located just off this annoying piece of traffic engineering in a shabby row of town houses that face the little marina and the lake.

It was summertime, the parking was easy, and we soon found ourselves rapping on the door of apartment four.

Victor had mentioned his plan to work at the cow barn for most of the rest of the day; I hoped he was still there communing with the long-lashed Guernsey. And I admitted to a rabid curiosity about Lucinda.

The door opened a crack and a voice demanded, "What do you want!"

For one stupefying moment, I thought that Thelma had returned from her trip to Atlanta, coshed Lucinda over the head, and taken up residence in her home. The voice was exactly the same as Thelma's—more of a caw, really, with an undertone of fingernails screeching down a blackboard.

The door opened wider and I found myself looking at a much younger—and to be honest, extraordinarily sexy—version of Thelma Galloway Bergland. She was even shaped like an artichoke. "Oh! It's you, Lieutenant. What is it this time? Come to drag me off to jail again?" She batted her eyes at me. They were brown, long lashed, and a whole lot sultrier than any cow I'd ever seen. "I know who you are. You're Vic's friend Austin. You can come in. You," she addressed Simon viciously, "can show me a warrant."

"I don't need a warrant to talk to you," Simon said in his I'm-just-an-ordinary-fellow tone of voice. "That's all I'm here for. Just a couple of questions."

This collegial approach to the public serves Simon well. Mild, nonthreatening, and genial, he manages to break down hostility every time. I made a mental note to myself to remember to tell him that.

Lucinda backed away and opened the door to allow us to enter. I followed Simon inside.

In one sense, the apartment was no surprise to me—except in the variety and extent of the clutter. All students have bookshelves made of block and board. All students have futons for living-room couches, an expensive stereo system in the corner, and inexpensive prints on the walls. I lived that way myself more than fifty years ago. What was different about Lucinda's apartment was the nature of the posters on the wall, and the incredible mess. The posters featured dead baby sea lions, foxes flattened by semi tractor-trailers, and woeful-eyed veal calves peering out of tiny crates—the latter a practice that has been abolished in American farming for some years.

The mess, as Madeline would have said, was something else. Crusted foil containers of macaroni and cheese were perched on the bookcase. Heaps of T-shirts, socks, patterned skirts, and jeans were piled on the floor. There was a litter of books, empty bags of potato chips, and crumpled candy wrappers on the large wire spool in use as a coffee table.

Victor had lost his mind.

Lucinda planted herself in the middle of the living room and crossed her arms defiantly. "Well?! I'm telling you right off that I've Googled all I need to know about my right to protest. And I have been exactly within the law, every time. So I don't know why you're here, or what you think you're up to, but go ahead. Assault me." She threw her head back. She had a swanlike neck with exceptionally creamy skin.

Simon and I exchanged glances of alarm.

There was a shabby wooden table with four chairs in the kitchen alcove. The remains of breakfast—several days of breakfasts—were on it. Simon looked at it with distaste. "Why don't we all sit down over there?"

Lucinda frowned heavily, then swayed over to the head of the table and sat down. She wore a longish, shift-like kind of sundress that exposed the tops of her bountiful breasts. Her feet and ankles were dirty, but shapely.

I sighed to myself. Poor Victor.

"Well," she said in that Thelma-like caw. "Sit if you're going to sit."

I sat at the opposite of the table. Simon took a chair and sat as close to me as he could without actually settling in my lap. I knew how he felt. We were men. She was a shrill-voiced siren. We were besieged.

"The Summersville Police Department is investigating a homicide," Simon began.

"Lewis O'Leary," Lucinda said. "Couldn't have happened to a nicer guy."

"Where were you on the night of July seventh?"

Her long-lashed, heavily lidded eyes were nothing like the Guernsey's in intent. She looked at us from lowered lids. "I don't know. That was what, a couple of days ago?"

"Monday," I said. "The day you were arrested for trespassing. The day Lewis O'Leary shoved you into the manure spreader, or tried to."

"Oh. That day. Let's see. You mean what did I do that night?" She slung one knee over the other. The dress fell away and exposed a long length of satiny thigh. "I went down to the newspaper office to tell off that Rita Santelli character. She's totally ignored OOOFF activities." She pronounced it with a shortened diphthong, so that it sounded like *off*. "And it's news, isn't it? People have the right to know what happens in those dungeons that jerk O'Leary . . ."

"Prisons," I said. "If you are going to use a confinement metaphor, the proper one is prison. Or jail. A dungeon is below ground."

"Whatever." She shifted in her chair and smiled at us. "I've never been inside one of the turkey barns. That would be breaking and entering. I know my rights as a protester. But you can just see from the outside what it's like. Torture, that's what they do in there."

I rose from the chair and walked over to the pile of dirty clothes. "You've never been in the growing barns?"

"Of course not." I can tell when people lie to me, Simon had said. They look me straight in the eye. She looked me straight in the eye. "That would be break . . ."

I nudged my toe through the pile. "So if I examined that plastic shoe cover there, the one with the turkey feathers on it, you would tell me that the last time you wore those was at Thanksgiving?"

She gasped. And clamped her mouth shut. "I want a lawyer."

"Don't be more of an idiot than you already are, young lady. You aren't under arrest. Although, like your compatriot Krippendorf, you might be. You were the one who injected the turkeys with the coccidiosis virus, weren't you?"

"Is that true?" Victor demanded. "Lucy? *You* did that?"

I jumped. Unnoticed by either Simon or me, Victor had arrived. A key to the apartment hung from his hand. He took three strides across the room and grabbed Lucinda by the upper arms. "You helped that little rat Krippendorf fake his data?"

"Absolutely not."

I cleared my throat. Done at the proper volume, it gets people's attention. "Before you answer, Lucinda, I would do well to warn you that the syringes at the grower barn are disposed of once a month. A thorough search of the biohazard barrel will undoubtedly turn up fingerprints."

Her lower lip jutted out like the prow of a battleship's. "Sometimes you have to sacrifice the few for the good of the many. Krip said that if we could create enough stink about the bird deaths, we could maybe shut the whole place down." She glared at Victor. "And you let me *go*." Victor let her go.

"I wouldn't have to do any of this if you people just woke up and smelled the coffee," Lucinda said.

"Just what is it that you want the O'Learys to do?" I asked out of sheer curiosity.

"Run free, of course," she said indignantly. "Free-range turkeys are happy turkeys."

"Free-range turkeys are prey for coyote, fox, even domestic dogs," I said. "Not to mention the parasites they'll pick up."

"That's natural," she said indignantly.

"And by free range, do you mean free to run around Summersville? And Ithaca?"

"That's how they do it in Mexico." She shot another lazy-lidded glance at Victor. "I'm planning a field trip there, as a matter of fact. Like, maybe next week. I've been meaning to tell you, Vic, that Keith Gonzales? The first year in my bovine anatomy class? He's thinking of maybe taking me along with him when he goes home after this summer class is over."

I was still bemused by the thought of free-range turkeys running free through Summersville. It would be chaos. It would be noisy. It would be a mess.

"I think there may be an ordinance against fowl on public roads," I said. "Do you have any idea about that?"

"If there isn't one," Simon said grimly, "there's gonna be one goddamn soon. Turkeys!"

"That is stupid beyond belief," Victor said. "You are stupid beyond belief." He stuffed his car keys in his pocket and headed for the front door.

"If people like Rita Santelli would pay some attention, places like O'Leary's wouldn't exist, Victor!" Lucinda's voice at full volume had nothing on cell yell.

Her only response was a slam as Victor banged the front door shut.

I exhaled softly. If there were any justice in this world, my friend was headed straight for home.

"Can we get back to the task at hand, here?" Simon said. "Miss Whitby, where were you at about nine o'clock on the evening in question?"

"I came home," she said sulkily. "After all that time in that swamp and all that hassle from that old goat O'Leary. . .

". . . and I fell asleep." She shot one last volt of that astonishing sex appeal at the two of us. "And I was alone. Alas."

# Twenty

"POOR Victor," Madeline said. "So he went back home with his tail between his legs."

"Lucky Victor," I said. "The woman is a lunatic! And at least poor Thelma isn't sex-mad." I reconsidered this as I admired my wife's bosom. "On the other hand, perhaps that was part of the problem."

It was just after ten o'clock in the morning at the McKenzie clinic. I had gotten home late from a long day of accompanying Simon on his interviews the day before, and gotten to bed even later. We had been wakened by an early morning call for veterinary assistance. One of the neighboring farmers dropped off a calf that'd been run over by a tractor. "Little guy just wiggled through the fence and I didn't even see him," Petey McWhirter had said as he left the calf to return to his morning chores. "What do you think? Is his back broke?"

"Something is," I'd said. "We will call you with a diagnosis."

While I went through the diagnostic procedures, I filled Madeline in on the prior day's events. I had been too pooped to summarize them the night before. Hence the comment: poor Victor.

The bell on the X-ray machine dinged and I pulled out the X-ray I'd taken of the calf's left leg. His back wasn't broken, but a hind fetlock was crushed. I looked at the X-ray again. "Well, I can put a walking cast on the little fellow and this should heal in about six weeks. The bruises and the cuts will heal a little faster than that. The calf will have to be kept in a stall for the duration, which means bottle feeding." I set the X-ray down. We'd anesthetized the small creature and it lay sprawled out on the stainless steel operating table. Madeline smoothed its ears. It was a young Black Angus. "Do you want to call Petey, or shall I?"

"It won't be worth it to him to pay our bill, will it?"

"Probably not."

She went into the office proper, and I heard her on the phone. All commercial farming comes down to one thing: the balance sheet. The calf stirred drowsily. I checked the flow of saline in the IV tube and I increased it slightly.

Madeline returned. She shook her head.

"Oh, dear."

"Austin, we can't just . . ."

"You told Petey we'd take the calf in return for the bill, didn't you."

She looked abashed. "Well, darlin', we've always got room for one more. I'll get the liquid bandage, shall I? And let's call him . . . Roger."

Before the arrival of our two assistants. Madeline had been my right hand in the practice. She'd lost none of her old skill. We cast Roger's leg and stitched up the cuts left by the blade of the harrow in nothing flat.

"So Cordy inherits and that young fool Krippendorf had a different motive than we thought," Madeline mused. She handed me the surgical scissors and I snipped off a length of suture. "And you say Simon put Lucinda on the official list of suspects?"

I nodded. Then I turned off the IV and began to clean up the detritus any such procedure leaves. The calf would wake in ten minutes or so, and we would remove it to one of the recovery stalls.

"Poor Victor." Madeline said again. She glanced at the clock on the wall, and said, "My goodness! It's almost time to take Sam to Green Seal."

"You've been carting him back and forth to his job? My dear, isn't this encouraging him to hang around? I thought we agreed—tacitly, to be sure—that he was to leave as soon as practicable.

"Just once in a while," she said a little guiltily. "He's in sore need of someone to listen to him, Austin."

"I'll bet," I grunted. "The Byco investors listened to them, and a good many of the older ones had to take jobs at Wal-Mart."

Roger coughed and opened his eyes. He began to move his legs in a swimming motion. "All right. Let's get him into the stall before he gets too frisky."

Madeline rapidly cleared off the instrument trolley and rolled it to the side of the operating table. I grasped the head and withers. Madeline grasped the hindquarters and said, "On the count of one, two, three," and we hoisted Roger onto the makeshift gurney. I strapped him on with a roll of wide gauze. We wheeled the cart out of the clinic and into the barn and none too soon. By the time we reached the recovery stall, Roger was bawling for his mother and making valiant attempts to get off the cart and away from us. I snipped the gauze free, and we wrestled him to the floor. He thrashed a bit, and then struggled upright. He made a couple of attempts to shake the cast free of his hind leg. Then hopped to the farthest end of the stall and stuck his nose in the corner.

"If he can't see us, then we aren't there," Madeline said in amusement. "Do you mind fetching the bottle, sweetie? I'll just go along and get Sam over to Green Seal."

"You're sure we're doing the right thing—getting involved with this as we are?"

Madeline tucked a stray strand of auburn hair behind one ear. "I'm not sure, no. But there are fathers and fathers. I mean, look at O'Leary. That man was a toxic father if there ever was one. And all three of those boys should have high-tailed it out of there years ago, if you want my opinion."

"I always want your opinion."

"But Ally and her dad? I don't know, Austin. It's a hard

thing, losing your dad, whether it's to death or dysfunction."
Sometimes when Madeline smiles, her dimples are more pronounced than others. This was one of those times. "*I* don't
know. We'll see. But if there's a halfway decent dad beneath
that jailbird's exterior, Ally should know about it."

"I suppose you're right." I put my hand in the small of my
back and straightened up. "But all I want to know at the moment is what's for breakfast."


IT was that rarity in my diet, eggs and bacon for breakfast although the cholesterol was offset by grilled salmon for dinner.
Madeline prepares both to perfection. I spent most of the day
catching up on the clinic records, in a sad state due to Allegra's absence and a necessity I got out of the way as quickly
as possible. I then fell to more absorbing work: creating a time
line for the murder. It was a hot day, the hottest of the summer
so far. The inside work became stuffy, and we decided to eat
the salmon outside and put in on the grill by the pond.

The small pond at the foot of our lawn provides a welcome
respite on long, hot afternoons. Joe swam vigorously. I inflated
our air mattress. Madeline doesn't swim, but she plunked herself down in the center of the mattress and paddled decorously
around the periphery (and managing to keep her hair dry, which
had been her first concern). The ends of the air mattress rose
about her like blue plastic wings.

Our charcoal grill is set at the edge of the water closest to
the house. Many years ago, Madeline rescued a wooden picnic table from the side of the road, replaced two of the splintered boards, repainted it, and it has served us well ever since.
It is set near the pond, too. While Joe, Madeline, and the ever-
silent Sam fiddled about with dinner, I sat under one of the
willow trees that surrounded the water, and went over the
timetable I'd created to chart the activities of the suspects in
O'Leary's murder. Our interviews yesterday had cleared
Jensen, Maired, Linda, and Ron. Jensen had slammed out of
the Embassy at 8:30 and driven straight to Maired's parents'
home on the outskirts of Covert, where Maired had retired after their fight in the bar. Her parents verified that he'd arrived
around 9:15. Too drunk to drive, he'd fallen asleep on the

living-room couch and kept them all awake with his snoring. After a prolonged and weepy talk with her mother, Maired retired to her girlhood room to sleep. Linda and Ron had gone to Syracuse for a late movie with another couple. That left Krippendorf, Lucinda, and Cordy as suspects. And our client, of course.

I regarded the charts I had made with satisfaction.

## CASE NO.: CC004
### Murder Night: Finnegan's activities

8:00 p.m.: follows V to parking lot. Sees V drive off. Sits in truck and "thinks about things."

8:15 p.m.: cell phone call from V who demands his presence at the Embassy by 8:45.

8:22 p.m.: tire blows on F's pickup truck. F pulls over in a cul-de-sac by Winston St. Changes tire. Sees no one.

9:10 p.m. (approx.): races into parking lot. V not there. Races out of parking lot. (Verified by A and M McK.)

9:20 p.m. (approx.): second tire blows on F's pickup truck. Back in the Winston St. cul-de-sac. Sits and "thinks about things." Falls asleep.

2:45 a.m. (approx.): drives home via Rte 332 and Rte 15. (Verified by witness for the prosecution at 7–Eleven.)

3:00 a.m. (approx.): arrives home to angry wife. (Prob. not a likely witness for the defense.) Falls asleep on couch.

7:00 a.m.: arrives at work at Green Seal.

I had similar time lines for each of my three suspects: Lucinda, Cordy, and Krippendorf. I had sketched a map with the distances drawn between the high school, Ithaca, the O'Leary Farms, and the Embassy, with close approximations of the distances among the three penciled in.

And I had four questions:

1. *How and when did river water get on the seat of Lewis's trousers?*

2. *How and when did Gil's clothing get stained with Lewis's blood?*

3. *Why were there albumen, feathers, and blood on Lewis's coveralls, and only feathers and blood on Gil's clothing?*

4. *Where was the body between the time of death and its appearance in the Dumpster after two o'clock in the morning?*

After some contemplation, I added a fifth.

5. *How and why did the tires on Finnegan's pickup blow at exactly the right time?*

As Simon had admitted, without resentment, I had been right. The tires on Gil's pickup had been trifled with. A nail had been driven into the right rear radial. The forensics lab had theorized that the nail had been fired from a nail gun. Similar mischief was applied to the left rear tire. Up to this point, I had a mental image of our murderer, faceless, to be sure, but a person of strong, decided character with an appetite for detail. The tire sabotage didn't quite fit the profile. How could the murderer be sure that tire would go flat before Gil reached the Embassy? The intent was to delay him so much that he would assume O'Leary had left the parking lot in disgust when Gil finally got there. And how could the murderer be assured that the second tire would blow on the isolated Winston Street cul-de-sac, thus assuring that Gil would be out of action—and out of an alibi—at the time when the murderer moved the into the Dumpster? Did the perp lurk under the truck chassis and pull the trigger on the nail gun at the right time?

And did knowing how this was accomplished really matter?

I thought about this carefully. I came to the conclusion that this was what I would come to call in future cases, a secondary lead. At the moment, I was concerned with the cause-and-effects data that would point directly to who and where. Finnegan's flats were purposeful. The mechanics of the sabotage could wait.

The most critical time in the whole affair was the hour during which Lewis died. A witness placed Lucinda at Java Joes coffee shop at about quarter to nine and on Treadway Avenue at about ten o'clock. There was no way she could have gotten to the Embassy to murder Lewis and back in that period of time. From midnight until about 2:30, she was with Victor. Despite the depth of his infatuation, I could not believe that my old friend would like to cover up a murder. This was a man with of sternest ethics and the highest probity. He would not lie to me.

Krippendorf claimed he went from the high school directly to Lucinda's apartment and from there to the altercation with his neighbor at 10:15. He could have made it to the Embassy and back between 8:45 and 9:15, but no one had seen him during that period of time. Madeline and I were in the parking lot at that time; Deirdre was looking at the parking lot at that time. And no one had seen Lewis after 9:15, although Lewis's truck was still there. After 10:15, Krippendorf claimed to be asleep—and there was nothing to prove his whereabouts after than time.

Cordy's alibi was his mother, who was, according to the latest word from the clinic, out of critical care, "resting comfortably." I would see her in the morning.

I laid my pencil on the table and rubbed my eyes. Madeline let out a whoop, waded into the pond, and sat down on the air mattress. I stared at her. I stared at the air mattress. And I looked again at the map and the distances between the relevant locations.

What if someone had hit Lewis with the tire iron, then strapped him to an air mattress and stored him in the river? All three of my suspects had access to Gil's tire iron days before the murder. Easy enough to swipe it, replace it with a temporary tool, and replace with the murder weapon after the deed was done.

I imagined the murderer striking Lewis over the head. The crime has been committed in an area where patrons of the restaurant are likely to drive in and park at any minute. The murderer slings the corpse over his shoulder, hides in the brush until the coast is clear, and then settles the body onto an air mattress seat first. The air mattress would sink briefly into the water. The water would pool in the center of the mattress, dampening the seat of his trousers.

Once the body is floating and concealed from discovery by the thick brush that edges the water behind the Embassy parking lot, the murderer could return at his leisure to move the body. Lewis's pickup truck was at hand. The murderer took the keys, jumped in the truck, and returned later to dump the corpse in the Dumpster.

Question: Why the Dumpster? Why not shove the body into the river and sink it?

I could think of three reasons.

Because the murderer had a solid alibi between midnight—when the first load of the Embassy's garbage was placed in the Dumpster—and two o'clock—when the second load was dumped on top of him.

Because the murderer had gone to great pains to make sure that Gil Finnegan would be at the scene of the crime at the *time* of the crime.

And because it had to be in the Dumpster to establish the parking lot as the scene of the crime. But the scene of the crime was elsewhere. The murderer had floated the body downriver. Downriver from where?

I grabbed at my map.

I sat up straight in my deck chair and uttered, "Aha!"

The O'Leary hatchery was three miles upriver from the parking lot of the Monrovian Embassy.

Angela's statement may not have been the maunderings of a stroke victim, but simple fact. If Lewis had been murdered at the hatchery—it would explain the albumen on his clothes. Albumen is found in the whites of poultry eggs. And the O'Leary hatchery was full of them.

I took a deep breath. A great deal would depend on what poor Angela O'Leary would be able to tell me. I needed to see her as soon as possible.

I bent over the map in great excitement, mitigated somewhat by the fact that this theory of the crime did not necessarily exonerate my client. The timetable still held, although the location was different.

Now, as to the alibis for those midnight to early morning hours—

I reviewed my notes.

Lucinda was with Victor.

Cordy was with his mother.

Krippendorf had no alibi to speak of. But he was the smartest of the three suspects and the least likely to plan the disposal so carefully, and neglect to give himself a clever alibi.

So somebody was lying. Cordy's mother? Or my old friend Victor?

The scent of grilled salmon floated through the air. Joe placed a large bowl of fruit salad to my left. Sam Fulbright set Madeline's dilled potato salad to my right. I put away my case notes and suspended my speculations. Sometimes it was better to take several steps back from a problem and let the subconscious do its work. I would feed it further information when we visited Angela O'Leary at the hospital after dinner.

Madeline and I drove back to Ithaca a short time later and arrived at the Tompkins County Hospital just as evening visiting hours began. Angela occupied a double room on the cardiac floor. She was sitting up and eating red gelatin when Madeline and I walked into the room. Linda O'Leary was reading a magazine in a chair next to the hospital bed. She greeted us with a relieved smile as we walked in. Angela looked our way, set her spoon on the bed tray, and said, "Lewis went to the hatchery. He hit him over the head and dumped him like a bag of garbage."

Linda shook her head worriedly, but greeted Madeline with a shy embrace and me with a friendly nod. Madeline had cut a large bunch of miniature Dutch iris from our garden. Linda took them with a soft "oh" of pleasure and arranged them in vase on the night side table. Madeline walked up to the bed and said, "Hello, Angela. Are you feelin' a little better today?"

Angela repeated her statement about Lewis, the hatchery, and the garbage. Madeline took her hand and patted it. I fairly danced with the desire to question the poor woman. Madeline looked at me and shook her head slightly. We had discussed the manner in which we could safely question Angela on our way to the hospital. The first step would be to talk to other sources. The second would be to talk to Angela, if her condition made it possible.

Linda turned from her flower arranging. "She's been saying that over and over since the stroke. The doctors think she's going to get a lot better soon, but right now it's scary to hear it." Linda stood by her mother-in-law and looked down at her worriedly. The old lady stared straight ahead, her fingers working at the hem of the sheet covering her. "But they say it's just a matter of time before she gets back to her old vigorous self, don't they, Ma?" Linda reached over and drew the sheet up higher on her mother-in-law's chest. "The what d'call'em, CT scans shows that she has some kind of clot on the left side of her brain. Which is weird, because it's her right side she's having trouble with. But I guess it's all part of this stroke business."

I opened my mouth to explain the basics of brain neurology, but closed it at Madeline's look. "Yes. Well. Perhaps I could speak to you outside for a moment, Linda?"

"I'll sit with her," Madeline said. "You go on out in the hall with Austin."

"You look tired, my dear," I said, as we stepped out into the hall.

"It's been a strain," she admitted. She swept her bangs out of her eyes with one hand. Her hair was drawn back in a careless ponytail. She had on an old pair of cotton trousers and rumpled cotton blouse. "Not because of this," she waved vaguely in the direction of the hospital room. "But all the rest of it. You heard about Cordy and the will?"

I nodded. "The farm has been left to Cordy?"

"All of it." She bit her lip. "I'm not one to complain, Dr. McKenzie. But it's so unfair! I mean, the farm was Lewis's to do what he wanted with. God knows he reminded us often enough of that. But don't you think he could have left us something?"

"It does seem odd that Angela wasn't named as partial beneficiary."

"Right," Linda said in disgust. "As if Lewis thought he owed her anything for the years she put in on the farm. She wasn't the best mother in the world, Dr. McKenzie, but she wasn't the worst. She did what she could for the boys."

I recalled the story that Lila had told me, that Angela was the one who'd tipped Lewis to the midnight flight planned by Linda and Ron. Linda must have seen something of this in my skeptical expression. "Oh, she had her faults. I won't lie to you. And she made some pretty dumb mistakes. I mean, what'd'ya expect, married to a man like Lewis?" She blinked back tears and dashed at her eyes with the back of her hand. "Sorry. It's been a weird couple of days. I'm babbling. Anyhow, I'm assuming even Cordy won't throw his own mother out in the road to fend for herself."

I raised my eyebrows. "Surely it wouldn't come to that?"

Linda laughed, a hard sarcastic sound at odds with her gentle demeanor. "He's already let Ron and Jensen know that he's putting the farm up for sale. He's going to take what he can get and run." She rummaged for a tissue in her pants pocket and blew her nose. "Anyhow. We'll manage, Ron and me. He's got a lot to offer. What he doesn't know about poultry isn't worth knowing. There are a lot of places we can go."

I was silent, both out of sympathy and because there was nothing to say. Lewis O'Leary had been a bad husband and a worse father. None of this was fair.

"You'll forgive me, but I do have a question I'd like to ask you."

"Fire away."

"Angela's statement about Lewis going to the hatchery the night he was killed . . ."

"Oh, that," Linda said dismissively. "The doctors think that's some part of this whole stroke thing. And the whole stroke thing is part of the whole shock over the murder."

"When was the last time you saw your father-in-law alive?"

"Gosh." Linda blinked. "At your speech, I guess."

"You were all seated together in front of the steam tables."

"That's right."

I cleared my throat. "I couldn't help noticing that there was a disagreement of some kind. Between Ron and his father."

She sighed in a resigned way. "You mean because Pa clipped Ron over the ear."

"Yes. I'd be interested in knowing what that was all about."

"Why?" Her shoulders went up in a defensive posture. "I don't see what it has to do . . . wait a minute.' She flushed bright red. "Somebody told me that you've set yourself up as a kind of a detective. You can't think that *Ron* had anything to do with this!"

It is always prudent to move quietly around stock that is easily frightened. "I'm sure he didn't," I said calmly.

"Because we left the high school right after that dinner and went to Syracuse with Al and Denise Williamson. We were there . . ."

I patted her shoulder. "Easy, now, Linda. I am convinced neither you nor Ron had anything to do with Lewis's death."

She drew a great, shuddering breath.

"But I am not so sure that Cordy is in the clear."

It took a moment for her to take this in. Then she said, "You're kidding." Then she said. "They're all bastards, you know. All except my Ron."

"Every bit of information should be taken into account in a murder investigation. And I would like to know why Lewis hit your husband."

"It was this business of Gil Finnegan and the feed delivery. He'd tried it with feed salesmen before, this bullshit about the delivery being short, and then getting a ton of money knocked off the bill. Ron and I always thought he did it because the operation had such a tough time making a profit, and of course," she continued bitterly, "it turns out all along that the old bastard was socking away a ton of cash in that bank account of his. Anyway. Lewis got this call on the cell phone while we were eating. And then he got this smug look on his face and he said something like, 'Well, now I've got Finnegan right where I want him. We're going to hit him up for a clear thousand, this time.' And Ron just sort of lost it. He said we couldn't go on operating like this, it was making him physically sick and . . ." She raised both hands in the air and let them drop, helplessly. "It just sort of got out of hand and Pa ended up hitting Ron."

"Was the call from Finnegan?" I said.

"Well, sure it was."

"It couldn't have been. We were with him the whole of the dinner. He made no phone calls."

"Well, that's what the hassle was all about. And when we were leaving, Pa told us to take Ma home because he was taking the truck. I assumed he was meeting poor Gil." She frowned. "Who else would have called him?"

Who, indeed? If I discovered that, I would have discovered our murderer.

Madeline came into the hall and smiled at Linda. "She's fallen asleep. I noticed that she finished most of the dinner the hospital sent up. I didn't see that you got anything to eat, though. Would you like to go with me down to the cafeteria? Some hot soup will do you good. Austin can sit with Angela for a while. You will, darlin', won't you?"

"Certainly."

Madeline drew Linda down the hall in the direction of the cafeteria, and I went to take up my post by Angela's bedside. Animals recover from trauma much better in familiar surroundings. I am certain the same is true of people. The hospital was no place for Angela to have a deep, healing sleep. And in fact, she woke soon after Madeline and Linda had left. She turned her head and stared steadily at me.

There is almost nothing of consequence to say to an acquaintance in a hospital bed. If the person were feeling well, they wouldn't be there. If the person was feeling poorly, there is nothing one can do to alleviate it, other than call a medical professional. So I said, "Would you like to me call a nurse?"

She shook her head. "Lewis went to the hatchery."

"I believe he did. I believe he was killed there."

The lines of worry in her face smoothed out. She gave a great sigh. Was it relief that she had been finally understood? She nodded. "He was hit over the head and dumped like a bag of garbage."

"Yes, he was." I leaned closer. "Mrs. O'Leary, you recall the night of the murder. You and your family were at the high school for my talk."

She nodded again.

"And Lewis received a phone call while you were eating dinner."

"Turkey," she said.

"Yes. We were all eating O'Leary turkey."

"Good."

I nodded. "It was excellent turkey."

She sighed and closed her eyes. I touched her hand, lightly. "Mrs. O'Leary. Angela. Do you know who called your husband while you were at dinner?"

She was asleep again. I sat back in the chair, frustrated. It was more than possible that the clue to unraveling this entire affair was in the poor woman's addled brain.

There was a busyness at the door to the room, and a nurse with a clipboard swept in, a client, as a matter of fact, whose Quarterhorse I treat for intermittent navicular disease.

"Well, Phoebe."

She stopped in midbustle. "Why, if it isn't Dr. McKenzie!"

"And how is Rocket?"

Phoebe is short, round, and cheerful. If she took as excellent care of her human patients as she did her horses, Angela was in good hands. "Same-old, same-old. But you know how you said I should get a different pair of shoes on the poor old guy? I talked to our farrier about it, and we're working on it, and Rocket's sound enough to enjoy a trail ride or two. No offense, but I hope I don't have to see you professionally for a long time."

"None taken."

"So how is our patient, here?"

I got up and withdrew to the side of the room. Phoebe checked her pulse, took her temperature, and cast an eye over the IV drip. Angela slept through it all.

"And how is Mrs. O'Leary doing, Phoebe?"

Her cheerful expression dimmed, but she said, "She's doing great. And I'm sorry, Dr. McKenzie, but visiting hours are over."

"I hadn't realized it was so late." I said farewell to the patient and followed Phoebe into the hall.

"I didn't want to say anything in there, of course, since you never know what a patient can hear even in a coma, much less a good sleep, but Dr. Faraday isn't real happy about her progress, that's for sure."

"I'm sorry to hear that."

Phoebe sighed. "She's had a couple of bad knocks, that's for sure." She glanced over my shoulder and her face brightened. "Oh! Madeline! How've you been? It's so good to see you!"

There is something about my wife that inspires affection. Phoebe embraced her heartily. "And Mrs. O'Leary. I'll just bet Madeline got you down to the cafeteria and got some food into you. You look a whole lot better."

"I feel a whole lot better," Linda admitted. She looked at the door to Angela's room, which Phoebe had closed against the noise in the hall. "Any better?"

"About the same," Phoebe said with professional brightness. "Dr. Faraday will be doing grand rounds tomorrow about eight, if you and your husband want to talk to him directly."

"He thought we should be making arrangements for some permanent care," Linda said. She looked at Madeline a little hopelessly. "I'm not sure how much coverage there is for that. Maybe I should be making arrangements to take care of her at home."

". . . which is," Madeline said fiercely, as we drove our way home a short while later, "a crying shame, that's what it is. That poor Linda's a saint. And that mother-in-law of hers is a terror. She was tellin' me a little bit about it in the cafeteria. If there's any justice in this world, that Cordy will fork over a part of that pile of money that terrible old man left him, and they'll find a nice comfortable place for the old lady to spend the rest of her days." She fanned her face vigorously with my notepad. "Honest to the good lord almighty, Austin. Life can be a mean and messy business."

I agreed with her—Madeline is always fierce when faced with injustices large and small. It is one of her most attractive qualities. But I have to admit that the solution to this murder was uppermost in my mind. My adversary was more elusive than ever. Gil Finnegan had been set up with a cunning hand. The tire iron taken from his vehicle well in advance of the crime. The scene of the crime that turned out to be not the scene of the crime at all. The forensic evidence on his clothes and in his truck. How did it get there? Who put it there?

And suddenly, I saw it.

I put my foot on the brake.

"Austin?" Madeline said in alarm. "You all right?"

"Finer than a frog hair," I said. "Madeline. The answer has

been staring me in the face all along. At least, I'm fairly certain of it." I swung the car in a U-turn, to the parent consternation of the automobiles behind me.

"You mean you know who did it?"

"I believe I do, my dear."

"And where are we going?"

'I should have thought of this days ago, my dear. We are going to see Mrs. Finnegan. We are going to see Bea."


"WHY, yes, he did!" Bea Finnegan said. She was a pretty woman, with tightly permed hair in blonde curls all over her head, and a round rosy face. She wore wire-rimmed spectacles. Behind them, her blue eyes were tired. There were dark circles under her eyes. She had been watching television with her three children when Madeline and I knocked on her door, and she'd fluttered to open it with a "what is it *now*" expression of panic that struck me to the heart.

"I was just furious with him for being late," she confessed. "And I was so darn mad. He usually calls me, you know, if he's going to be late. And he didn't this time. And he's been so worried about work. I feel so bad. I was so mean to him. When he came in I made him sleep on the couch in his clothes, and he did. He wore those same clothes right to the store and changed into his Green Seal coveralls right there." Her eyes filled with tears. "I never got chance to wash them, you know. The police went to the store and bagged them up and took them away for all those darn tests." The tears fell down her cheeks. "And then the police took him away, too."

So we had our murderer. And there was one more step to get the proof we needed to arrest and, god willing, convict.

I had to get Sam Fulbright in the same room with Cordy O'Leary.

# Twenty-one

❧

KAREN Crown sat behind Gil Finnegan's desk at the Green Seal Feeds Store and smiled thinly at me. "I'm so glad you decided to answer my phone calls at last, Dr. McKenzie. The folks at corporate were beginning to wonder if you intended to honor our consulting agreement with you." Her smile widened to reveal abnormally sharp eyeteeth. "Accounting tells me that you've cashed our check."

"I do apologize for not responding to you earlier than this," I said. "May I?" I sat down across from her without waiting for an invitation. "Things have been busy lately."

"So I understand. And how are your efforts to acquit Mr. Finnegan of murder coming along?"

"It's been a challenge," I admitted. "But we appear to be at the end of the case."

"Oh? That's great." Her eyes shifted to the right and to the left again. "So has your local policeman put the cuffs on the guilty party?"

"My goodness," I said mildly. "You're perfectly aware of why I am here."

Her lips stretched back in a smile. Her teeth were so tightly clenched that her jaw muscles stood out like small fists. "I have no idea what you're talking about."

"You most certainly do. You and Lewis O'Leary had been bilking Green Seal for several thousand dollars a month in phony supplies and phony feed bills. I'm not sure how long ago it started, but that's because we don't have access to last year's ledgers. Not yet."

"This is ridiculous. You can't prove a thing."

"On the contrary," I corrected her. "According to information received . . ."

"To what?"

"We have the facts," I said succinctly. "We had an inside man. Someone highly experienced in relieving corporations of available cash. It took him no time at all to match the phony bills you sent to Lewis O'Leary with the actual feed and equipment received. Your own inventory will further buttress the truth."

"I don't know what you're talking about. This is crazy. This is insane. Who do you think you are, anyway?" She half rose from her chair, both hands knuckled on to the glass-topped surface. Her face looked like the demon masks in a Japanese Noh play.

"I think what led me to ignore the obvious is that the fraud is so obvious. The thievery so simple. And the murder itself was both clever and adroit. The tenor of the crimes didn't match, so to speak."

I rose from my chair and faced her. Simon would be here in a moment—and undoubtedly furious that I had gone ahead and confronted Karen Crown without him. But I had spent an intense, exhausting week in pursuit of enough facts to indict the woman, and I hoped that Simon would forgive me the need I felt to confront her.

"Your biggest mistake was Gil's clothing. Who else would have an opportunity to dab them with damaging evidence but you? You had no way of knowing that he wore the same clothes to work that he'd worn the night before. I believed him, you see. I believed in his innocence. And when he told me that the only person he came in contact with that night after he left the parking lot at the Embassy was his wife, I had to look for a time when the evidence could be planted. And the evidence in the truck, the tarp, on Gil's clothes—that all came from you. Right here at the Green Seal office. I don't know when you stole the tire iron from his truck, but you certainly had access to it well before the murder itself."

"It doesn't prove a damn thing," she said. Her voice was a hoarse whisper. Behind me, I heard the clatter of the front door to the store opening and then closing, and Simon's distinctive voice.

"I'll tell you what does prove a damn thing. The call from your cell phone to Lewis, setting him up for a visit to the hatchery. A call from your cell phone to Gil, setting him up for a visit to the Embassy. And you set up the flats on Gil's pickup so that he would be out of the way and have no reliable alibi. You met Lewis at the hatchery, hit him over the head with Gil's tire iron, and floated his body down the river to the Embassy on one of the air mattress that's on special right now in front of your store."

"That's stupid."

"Not so stupid. You couldn't take the risk of *any* forensic evidence appearing anywhere. A trip by water was the safest option. I'll wager anything you like that you committed the entire crime suited up in the biohazard gear at the farm."

"You don't have any proof!" she screamed.

"Our inside man did a quick inventory check, and you are, in fact, missing an air mattress from stock. Not to mention a battery-powered nail gun, several rolls of duct tape, and a remote control from your automotive section. Forensics has been over Gil's pickup one more time, and they found a great little spot where you taped the nail gun in the wheel well." I shook my head. "You should have taken the time to *buy* the items, Miss Crown, rather than steal them."

Simon pulled open the door to Karen Crown's office. At least three uniformed patrolmen ganged up behind him. He shook his head and said, "Dammit, McKenzie. Why in heck don't you just go home?"

So I did.

"I can't believe my father helped you solve the murder," Allegra said. The picnic table at the foot of our pond seated the four of us—six when you counted Lincoln and Juno. Madeline had chicken barbequing on the grill. It was a fine July evening, although a bit warmer than we all wanted it to be.

"So he's taken off for good?" Joe said. "Your father, I mean."

Allegra stared up at the willow branches waving gently over our heads. "Well, he's gone back to Connecticut. I don't know how it's going to work out. But I had a long talk with my mother . . ." She sighed. "I don't know. It was so weird, seeing him like this. He was so . . . I don't know. So much smaller than in my imagination."

"Well, maybe he'll grow bigger again, in the right way," Madeline said comfortingly. "We'll just have to see. Families can be a pile of misery. But not all the time. And they surely are important. Amazing things can happen. Look how Cordy's given his two brothers a part of the business. Who would have thought that could happen?"

Cordy's change of heart was indeed the talk of Summersville. Had he come to see how far down the road greed has taken his father? Had he discovered a latent affection for his older brothers? I took a sip of Scotch. God only knew.

Madeline expertly flipped the chicken breasts over on the grill. "Now, Joe. I thought you'd invited that nice Miss Beaufort to come and have barbeque with us?"

Joe rubbed the back of his neck and stared into the willow trees, too. "She's gone back to North Carolina, I'm afraid."

"Well, that's all right then," Madeline said. "The six of us are having a fine old time right here." And with the smile that always gladdens my heart, she passed me a plate of chicken.

# GET CLUED IN

Ever wonder how to find out about all the latest Berkley Prime Crime and Signet mysteries?

## berkleysignetmysteries.com

- See what's new
- Find author appearances
- Win fantastic prizes
- Get reading recommendations
- Sign up for the mystery newsletter
- Chat with authors and other fans
- Read interviews with authors you love

# MYSTERY SOLVED.

berkleysignetmysteries.com

# Cozy up with
# Berkley Prime Crime

## SUSAN WITTIG ALBERT
*Don't miss the nationally bestselling
series featuring herbalist China Bayles.*

## LAURA CHILDS
*The Tea Shop Mysteries are the
toast of Charleston, South Carolina.*

## KATE KINGSBURY
*The Pennyfoot Hotel Mystery
series is a tea-time delight.*

**For the armchair
detective in you.**

penguin.com